Officially
withdrawn by
Xavier U. Library

D0153673

AFRICAN WRITERS SERIES

Editorial Adviser · Chinua Achebe

44

The Great Ponds

AFRICAN WRITERS SERIES

The Great Ponds

ELECHI AMADI

Xavier University Library
New Orleans, LA 70125

HEINEMANN EDUCATIONAL BOOKS

NAIROBI LONDON IBADAN

Heinemann Educational Books Ltd.

48 Charles Street, London WIX 8AH

PMB 5205 Ibadan . POB 25080 Nairobi

EDINBURGH TORONTO AUCKLAND MELBOURNE

HONG KONG SINGAPORE NEW DELHI

ISBN 0 435 90044 7

© Elechi Amadi 1969

First published 1969

First Published in *African Writers Series* 1970

Xavier University Library
New Orleans, LA 70125

Printed in Malta by St Paul's Press Ltd

1 OLUMBA was in his reception hall mending some fish-traps. He sat with his back towards the main village road and seemed engrossed in what he was doing. Ikechi came into the compound unannounced and tiptoed towards him until he was close. Then he stood still and watched him.

'Why don't you sit down, Ikechi?' Olumba said without turning round.

'Hei!'

'What is it?'

'How did you observe me?'

'I know your steps don't I?'

'But I made no noise.'

'Ha-ha! No noise indeed! You made as much noise as a herd of elephants.'

'Really?'

'Your father has a lot to teach you about stalking. You young-sters are so clumsy.' Ikechi smiled. He knew only too well Olumba's opinion of boys in his age group. As far as Olumba was concerned they were just a bunch of girls.

Ikechi unhooked a three-legged chair from a railing attached to the reception hall and sat down.

'When is the meeting?' he asked.

'After the midday meal.'

'Which means right now?'

'Yes, but have you eaten?'

'No.'

'Why not?'

'I didn't feel like it.'

'Are you excited?'

'Not really.'

'You are, my boy. One of the first things a fighter must learn is to eat properly when he should. With a yawning stomach you would be as much use to us as old Ochomma.'

Ochomma was the oldest woman in the village. Ikechi thought of how she trembled at every step and laughed outright.

I

'Come and eat with me or you will not go with us,' Olumba said. At this invitation Ikechi suddenly realized how hungry he was and readily shared Olumba's meal with him.

After the meal Olumba removed a small black amulet from his neck and substituted a bigger one. The former was for general protection at home, the latter for protection and luck while travelling. Ready at last he picked up his matchet and headed for the chief's house with Ikechi behind him.

Olumba walked ahead looking upwards as usual. Just what he was searching for in the sky Ikechi couldn't tell. Perhaps his shortness accounted for this habit since he often had to look up into the faces of his taller companions. What he lacked in height he made up in solid muscle and he looked strong. His wrestling pseudonym was Agadaga, a name which meant nothing but which somehow conveyed an impression of strength.

Eze Diali, the chief, sat at one end of his reception hall ringed by the village elders. The rest of the hall was filled with much younger men.

'People of Chiolu,' the chief began, 'I have learnt that poachers from Aliakoro will be at the Great Ponds tonight. There is no doubt that they will try to steal from the Pond of Wagaba which as you know is rich in fish. Our plan tonight is to bring one or more of these thieves home alive and ask for heavy ransoms. This line of action will have two effects. Firstly it will prove our charges of poaching against the people of Aliakoro, secondly the heavy ransoms they will be obliged to pay will be a deterrent. We need seven men for this venture. I call for volunteers.'

Immediately eager hands went up. Olumba's hands were folded across his broad chest and a faint smile played on his face. The chief looked at him.

'Olumba what about you?' he asked.

'We have enough volunteers already, my lord,' Olumba said, his smile broadening.

'Who will head this party?' the chief asked looking round. Chituru, one of the elders, said: 'Eze Diali, let us not waste time. Olumba is the man for the job. We all know that he has led many exploits like this one.'

Many elders echoed the suggestion.

'We still need six men,' Eze Diali said. Again eager youths came surging forward. Their well-formed muscles rippled as they elbowed one another. It was difficult to choose.

'I suggest Olumba should choose his men. He knows the boys very well and his judgement should be reliable.' It was Wezume, another village elder, who spoke.

'Choose your men then Olumba,' the chief said, 'and make whatever arrangements you want. By tomorrow morning we want a couple of prisoners here.'

Olumba said: 'You will have them unless they don't turn up.' He chose six men, among them Ikechi whom he rather liked. He took them outside to a corner of Diali's large compound and discussed plans with them. Later the men dispersed and Olumba went back to his compound with Ikechi.

'I am glad you chose me,' the young man said.

'You may not be quite so glad after the fight tonight,' Olumba said chuckling.

'Will the fight be tough?'

'Of course. Do you suppose our enemies will hand themselves over to us without a struggle? We may even be taken prisoners.'

'Are you afraid?'

'I fear no man. Rather I fear the gods on whom depend the results of any fight. But I have never failed to offer sacrifices to them. I am sure they will always be by me.'

'Gods or no, I can't imagine anyone taking you prisoner,' Ikechi said studying Olumba's formidable physique.

'Never play with the gods, my son. They are powerful and should be respected. I would rather face a whole village in battle than have the weakest of the gods after me. At times I wish I were a dibia, for then I would be able to see the spirits myself, know their desires and minister to them promptly.'

Back in his compound, Olumba continued work on his fish-traps.

'Leave your traps and prepare for the task ahead,' Ikechi suggested.

'There is nothing to prepare. My matchet is sharp and I am not ill.'

3

'Do you really think we will need to cut down anyone with matchets?'

'We shall not if we can help it. But a fight is a fight and we might as well prepare for the worst.'

The shadows were lengthening but the sun was shining brilliantly in spite of the efforts of deep grey clouds to cover it. A rainbow monopolized the eastern sky beating the chief's costly peacock feathers for colour. It arched just over an iroko tree far behind Olumba's compound, and its arms dipped gracefully into the forests hard by.

'Where are the ends of the rainbow?' Ikechi asked, his youthful face perplexed.

'At your age you ought to know simple things like that,' Olumba said. 'You will soon get married and your children will ask questions. What are you going to tell them?'

For answer Ikechi looked down grinning boyishly.

'Listen,' Olumba said authoritatively, 'one end of it is in the land of the Wakanchis, an ancient race of dwarfs. The other end is in Eluanyim where a group of very old dibias offer sacrifices to it. In return the dibias acquire a deep knowledge of herbs and roots and the ways of the spirits. These dibias diseminate their knowledge to their pupils who come from all over the world. Any medicine-man who has not been to Eluanyim is not worth a cowrie.'

'Has Achichi our dibia been to Eluanyim?'

'I am sure he has. I shouldn't rely on him otherwise.'

'But how do you know for sure?'

'Well think of his work in the village. This talisman round my neck is his handiwork. It is for protection and luck while travelling. In times of danger I simply vanish. The first day I wore it to the forests a leopard passed by me within two paces. I went on my way unharmed.'

It was time to move. Olumba went into his room and strapped an amulet above the biceps muscles of his right arm. This charm was for fighting and it had cost him a lot of money.

As they moved through the village the other five men joined them. One look at Olumba, and the men realized they had a tough

4

assignment. When Olumba wore that amulet round his upper arm, things were going to happen.

'Looks as if vultures will visit the scene of our fight tonight,' Eziho said smiling at Olumba.

'Not necessarily,' the leader replied.

'But I see signs.'

'Oh, this,' Olumba said glancing at the amulet on his arm. 'Well I just want to make sure we accomplish our task tonight.'

The rainbow disappeared, the sun, now beclouded, sank rapidly. Distant thunder growled persistently as if unwilling to give way to the dry season now overdue by some people's reckoning. The men walked on, chatting and making fun, but beneath their gaiety lay tension and alertness.

Great forests loomed ahead. The dying rays of the sun failed to pierce the smoky haze enveloping them. These primeval forests formed one long vast belt passing by many villages. Deep inside them were the Great Ponds, very rich in fish. Once a year these ponds were flooded and after the flood villages reaped great harvests.

Many villages shared the Great Ponds but some villages like Chiolu had remarkably rich ponds which their neighbours coveted and ravaged when they could. Year after year men from Aliakoro poached freely from the ponds of Chiolu. Eze Diali had complained bitterly but to no effect. Now the poaching was getting out of hand and the men of Aliakoro were actually beginning to claim some of Chiolu's ponds, particularly the very productive pond known as the Pond of Wagaba.

The forests thickened until the path became a tunnel in the woods. The soil changed from loose dark loam to slippery white clay. So despite the approaching darkness the track remained visible like a long grey worm. Not that visibility mattered much since the men knew every turning in the path. Indeed they needed the cover of darkness for a successful operation.

Now the edge of the Great Ponds was as far as a man could shoot an arrow. Olumba who was leading the company raised his hand and immediately the men disappeared without a sound. The rapidity with which they took perfect cover impressed Ikechi who immitated them only after an awkward pause. But there was no immediate danger. Olumba merely wanted them to stop for a short conference. He beckoned and the men reappeared, some of them from unexpected hideouts.

'We shall watch the Pond of Wagaba', Olumba said. 'We shall travel there by rafts and lie in ambush by the bank. How many rafts have we?'

'Three,' Eziho said.

Quickly Olumba divided the men into three groups to man the three rafts. He knew who would work well with whom and he did not hesitate.

Silently the men approached the Great Ponds. The smell of fresh water and decaying vegetation filled their nostrils. It was a pleasant smell reminiscent of many highly rewarding fishing sessions. They brought out long bamboo poles from where they had been secreted and with them shoved off on the rafts. It was impossible to avoid the liquid sound of the poles as they pushed along, but fortunately the sound was indistinguishable from that made by the many fish drinking and surfacing playfully in the ponds.

During the rainy season the Great Ponds formed one mysterious stagnant sea of reddish-brown water ranging in depth from the waist to four or more times the height of a man. Fishing was not done then. Only the palm-wine tappers disturbed the chilly placidity of the dark waters with their rafts heavily loaded with calabashes of white effervescent palm wine begging to be drunk. Then wine-tapping was easy since a man standing on his raft needed no ladder to reach the top of the palm wine tree.

During the dry season the floods subsided. What water was left collected in individual ponds restless with fish. At this stage the ponds were not completely isolated, but linked to one another by narrow necks of water barely navigable with rafts.

Villagers did not wait until the middle of the dry season. Fishing usually started towards the end of the rainy season when thundery showers often bathed the sweating bodies of eager fishermen.

Olumba and his gang floated as silently as they could from one pond to the other. Their eyes were now accustomed to the darkness.

They crossed the Pond of Walele and inched their rafts towards the Pond of Wagaba. Olumba placed his men along the neck of water by which they thought the poachers would come. He repeated his instructions to his men and took up his own position.

The Pond of Wagaba was large. No trees grew in it and the branches of surrounding trees tried in vain to form a closely knit roof of foliage above it. There were gaps here and there, and through these the moonlight struck the surface of the pond giving it a leopard-skin effect. Now and then a wild fruit splashed into the pond and a second splash was heard as some fish made for it.

For a long time the night life of the great forest went on undisturbed. The men's eyelids grew heavy and sticky as they tried to blink themselves into alertness. Then suddenly the look-out man came back.

'Men are coming,' he whispered excitedly to Olumba. The latter gave a low whistle much like that of a common jungle bird. He did it three times and heard with satisfaction the gentle rustling of men preparing for action. The poachers came in two rafts. They talked in low tones not because they suspected ambush but because of the overwhelming effect of the ancient forest.

'I feel cold tonight,' one said.

'You'll feel warm when you see your trap full of fish,' another replied. Two other men chuckled at the joke.

Olumba guessed he had four men to deal with.

'The Pond of Wagaba can never be impoverished,' one man said. 'I have never seen a pond so full of fish.'

'A pity it doesn't belong to Aliakoro,' another said.

'It may one day.'

'How?'

'Eze Okehi, our chief, intends to claim it. He says that Chiolu's claim to it is dubious and that from what his grandfather told him, the pond rightly belongs to us.'

'That will mean a lot of fighting.'

'The pond is worth fighting for isn't it?'

'It certainly is. It will be a great day when we will fish here in daylight without any fears of challenge.'

'It should . . .' The man's voice was drowned by a mighty war-cry from Olumba's cavernous chest. Amidst splashes the men of Chiolu closed in. The rafts swayed precariously for a moment and were abandoned as dark masses tumbled into the water. There were groans and sighs and the thump thump of heavy blows. Eziho found himself carried shoulder high and dashed into the turbulent water. He got up quickly and grabbed the nearest man. The man's body was slippery and Eziho knew he was holding a comrade. He let go, and looked around. Everyone seemed engaged. Then someone broke loose and ran. He intercepted him and kicked his legs together. The man fell headlong and Eziho fell on him. As he was struggling with his opponent a man ran past closely followed by another. Presently the last man turned back.

'Who is here?' The roaring voice was Olumba's; Eziho could recognize it a mile off.

'Eziho,' came the reply.

'Have you secured your man?'

'I am about to. He is still struggling but I . . .' Eziho did not finish. His opponent pushed him off with a savage thrust and got up. The two men came to grips again. Olumba decided to help. He was just in time to prevent Eziho from being dashed violently to the ground. He grabbed the enemy by the waist from behind and pulled him down. Eziho came crashing on them both. Olumba thought that the job was done but the poacher managed to get up and faced them again. Now Olumba was really angry. Who was this that defied his strength?

'Eziho, keep clear,' he shouted as he grabbed the man again. They twisted and turned and pulled until Olumba's anger turned to surprise. His adversary was strong, without a doubt. But he had told Eziho to keep off. He could not call him to help now for shame. He knew he needed more of wits than anger. He let his body go limp and swayed backwards. His opponent followed through. Half-way through his fall he twisted suddenly and had his man on the ground. He pounded the man's head brutally with his fists until he felt him weakening. He loosened a cord round his waist and secured the man's hands.

8

'I have got him,' Olumba announced.

'Well done,' Eziho said.

'He is a very stubborn fellow.'

'As all thieves are.'

'I am not a thief,' the prisoner panted.

'Shut up,' Olumba roared. 'You are caught stealing, and you say you are not a thief. You must be the most stupid liar that ever ate fish.'

'I am not a liar,' the captive said.

'People don't trifle with me,' Olumba said and handed out a vicious slap. He raised the man to his feet and pushed him along to join the other prisoners.

'How many prisoners have you?'

'One,' Ikechi said.

'I have two; that makes three. Anyone seriously hurt?'

One man said: 'My left eye is aching, otherwise I am all right.'

'All right, let's move. Put the prisoners on the rafts.' Captors and captives boarded the rafts and began to cross the Pond of Wagaba. Olumba was personally in charge of the last man he had fought with.

'By the way, who was the fourth man who escaped?' he asked his prisoner. The man ignored him.

'I say, who was the other fellow?' There was still no answer. He slapped the man hard first on the right cheek then on the left.

'It just shows how hardened these thieves are.'

'I repeat we are no thieves,' the prisoner said calmly.

Olumba was beside himself with rage. His hand shot out again but Eziho who was sharing the same raft held his hand.

'Let's wait till daybreak.'

'I have no time to waste. Look, why don't we kill these men right away and declare war on Aliakoro? I have never seen such impudence in my life.'

The men knew that if Olumba got any angrier he would carry out this threat. They did not want this. It was enough to take the prisoners home and ask for large ransoms. Ikechi said, 'You fellows know you are absolutely in our power. Why can't you shut your mouths and think of your troubles?'

'They are all quiet except this stupid fellow here,' Olumba said.

'I am not stupid,' the prisoner said calmly. Olumba was at a loss for words.

'Who is this loud-mouthed idiot?' Eziho said.

'I am Wago, the leopard-killer, if you want to know,' the prisoner replied. For a moment a hush fell on the company. Wago the leopard-killer was well known and was a man to be reckoned with. He had three magnificent leopard skins to his credit, a feat unequalled by any man they knew of. His skill in hunting was uncanny. He had on several occasions brought home live antelopes whose bodies bore no traces of any violence or struggles whatsoever. How he caught them no one knew. Tall and sinewy, he was an able wrestler.

Olumba admired brave men. When Wago revealed his identity his anger went down appreciably. Brave men had every right to talk anywhere, he thought.

'But Wago, why did you get yourself involved in this disgraceful affair?' Olumba asked.

'What makes it disgraceful?'

'Is it not disgraceful to steal?'

'How can we steal that which is ours?'

'Is this pond yours?'

'Certainly,' Wago said, unperturbed.

'What?' several men shouted simultaneously. The men of Chiolu were surprised and angry.

'And why do you come to fish in the night?' Olumba asked.

'To avoid open conflict until our claim has been established beyond doubt.'

'Who gave you this idea?'

'Never mind who did.'

'And you believe we'll give up the pond?'

'Yes, we'll force you to.'

Olumba was too full to continue the dialogue. He ordered his men to push on faster. There was no point in arguing with a prisoner who had such ideas.

They floated past the Pond of Wagaba. When they got to the

Pond of Walele, Wago pushed Olumba violently to the left and he fell awkwardly into the cold water. Wago himself dived to the right. By the time Olumba had recovered sufficiently to give orders Wago had disappeared. There was nothing to be done. It was too dark to track him.

'Was he not tied?' Ikechi wondered.

'Of course he was,' Olumba said between clenched teeth. 'I don't know how he got loose.'

Olumba would gladly have exchanged the two remaining prisoners for Wago. All he could do now was blame himself again and again for not tying him fast enough. He ground his teeth in deep regret.

The two remaining prisoners were more securely tied. One of them screamed in pain during the process.

'You don't need to break my hands,' he said. 'I am not running away. I can't trace my way from here.'

'Thieves can always trace their way from anywhere,' Olumba said. 'Tie him very fast.'

When the men disembarked finally, they washed off the slimy stuff they had rubbed on their bodies. This lotion had made them slippery to the touch during the struggle. It had also helped them distinguish friend from foe in the darkness.

2 FOR the two prisoners it was a long night. They sat miserably in Eze Diali's reception hall nursing their bruised bodies by the fire which was kept going for them. They turned their fronts and then their backs to the glowing ends of the big logs.

A distant cock from a far village crew. As if they had been waiting for this signal the cocks in Chiolu took up the cry and broke the stillness of the dewy morning.

'I thought all the cocks in this hopeless village were dead,' Chileru one of the prisoners said.

'Shut up!' a guard snapped.

'Don't you want the day to break?'

'The day will break whether the cocks crow or not.'

'I prefer a normal day announced in the usual way.'

The guard offered no reply. The prisoner smiled and then laughed. His companion joined in the laughter, made hoarse by the morning staleness in their mouths.

'You fellows are hardened thieves,' another guard said. 'Why don't you hide your faces in shame?'

'What is it after all?' Chileru replied. 'Poaching is universal. I bet you have poached at one time or another.'

'If stealing is commonplace at Aliakoro, it isn't here.'

'You must differentiate between stealing and poaching. If you remove a few palm-nuts from a huge collection of palm fruits by the wayside, that is not stealing, is it?'

'If you make it a habit, it becomes stealing.'

A door opened and Eze Diali came out yawning. He went into his reception hall and looked the prisoners over.

'What is your name, my son?'

'Chileru.'

'And yours?'

'Ejimole.'

'Who are your fathers?'

The captives named their fathers. They were well known to the chief. He had wrestled with them in his youth. Ejimole's father had been notorious for poking his fingers into his opponents' eyes and throwing them in the ensuing confusion. It was against the rules, of course, but wrestlers were often so close and moved so fast that referees could not always detect such foul play. Eze Diali smiled at the recollection and turned to go.

Three men entered the compound at a brisk pace. They greeted the chief. As they spoke the moisture in their breaths condensed into white smoke in the cold morning air. The chief ushered them into the reception hall and ordered one of his sons to fetch kola.

'Now what do you want?' the chief opened up formally.

'We have come for them,' a spokesman of the party said pointing at the two prisoners.

'It is not as easy as that,' Diali replied, with a piece of kola poised between his lips. 'Eze Okehi ought to have sent older men in an affair of this nature. You are too young to know what to do.'

'At least we can relay the message from Eze Okehi,' the spokesman said.

'What is it?'

'Eze Okehi says you should release the men. Negotiations over their ransom can be arranged afterwards.'

'Ha-ha! Who ever heard of such a proposal? Let me come to the point and save words. Tell Okehi to come down with his elders for a full discussion not only on the release of these boys here but also on the vexing problem of poaching.'

There was a ring of finality in Diali's last statement and the messengers rose to go.

Chituru and Wezume, the two elders next in rank to Eze Diali, walked into the compound. Diali sent for more kola. The three old men crunched their kola and studied the two prisoners.

'Let's get in and talk,' Chituru suggested.

Inside, the men held a long discussion which ended with the sounding of the Ikoro.

While women and children were busy sweeping out the compounds, the men gathered at the wrestling arena in response to the call of the Ikoro. The Ikoro was employed only in very serious situations like the loss of a man in the forests, invasion, and murder; and men turned up fully armed and ready for any emergency. On this occasion everyone knew beforehand what the emergency call was all about. All through the night before, the ambush had formed the main topic of conversation among the men. The women had no idea of what was happening. They could not be entrusted with such top secrets.

Within a short time the arena was filled with men. They stood around the two captives whose embarrassment was mounting every moment. They had not expected this. Diali came forward and cleared his throat.

'Chiolu, meka!'

'Hei!'

'Meka!'

'Hei!'

The arena resounded with the echo and the ground shook as over two hundred men stamped their legs in unison.

'Our plan has worked well,' the chief began, 'and your thanks are due to Olumba and his gang. We have here two young men from Aliakoro who were captured last night while trying to fish in the Pond of Wagaba. There were four of them but two escaped in the darkness.

'Early this morning three men came from Aliakoro to beg for the release of the prisoners. Through them I sent word to their elders to come here for negotiations. We expect them after the midday meal. We do not intend to fight but nevertheless I want you all to come fully armed. As you know, it is always wise to allow for danger even when there is none.'

Diali walked home flanked by other elders. Like many others he wore a smile of satisfaction. His plan had worked out perfectly. No one praised him. The villagers expected him to do his duty and to take the right decisions at all times. When he failed no one blamed him either. It was assumed that anyone else would have failed under those circumstances. Diali had little personality in terms of bulk. He was short. He was neither frail nor stout. He was simply small. When he was much younger people said he was very nimble. He was a brave fighter relying more on tactics and speed than on sheer strength. In his old age his wrinkled skin made one think of those unripe shrivelled apples that fell off prematurely from trees during the harmattan and defied decay under the cold dry wind. To the younger generation Daili had always been the same – small, old, wise, hardly ever sick, respected and welcome in every compound. To the children, Diali was 'Lali the ikoro-man' who for no real reason at all would on a misty morning disturb the whole village with his ikoro. Their fathers would run out with ridiculous haste and their mothers would suddenly lose interest in the preparation of a promising breakfast. But the children liked Lali because he never spoke harshly to them and had lots of climbable trees and unbelievable nooks ideal for hide-and-seek in his large compound. Besides, his many children were indispensable in games and adventures in the surrounding bushes.

To a casual visitor Diali seemed a nonentity, but what a wrong impression that was. Eze Diali's influence permeated the whole village like the cult of Amadioha. Men stopped fighting and women ceased verbal exchanges at his intercession. Yet in a way Diali was a nonentity, just the man in the next compound. He did not interfere in his neighbour's affairs; he did not order anyone around. He worked as hard as anyone else and the few privileges he had were not enviable, like being present at every important burial. But Diali's subtle leadership was indispensable to Chiolu. It was a leadership that defied immitation, an inborn leadership whose incredible strength lay in its gentleness.

It was evident that the morale of the captured poachers was sinking. Gone were the devil-may-care smiles and insolent remarks. They were stupified and ashamed. As the guards dragged them away, Ejimole the younger of the two wept.

'This treatment is worse than death,' he sobbed.

'Keep calm, our people will soon be here,' Chileru said, trying to maintain a brave front.

'Now you see why it does not pay to take other people's things,' said a guard. 'Last night you wouldn't let us put in a word, now you are crying like a woman. Reserve your tears for this is only the beginning.'

'At any rate you can't kill us,' Chileru said.

'Don't be too sure; in any case death is not always the worst thing that can happen to a man.'

When the prisoners were brought back to Diali's they were offered a breakfast of yam-and-pepper soup. Ejimole refused to eat.

'You have let them convince you that you are a thief,' Chileru said disdainfully.

Ejimole looked round to make sure no one was listening and then asked:

'But are we not?'

'Certainly not.'

'And why have we not tried to put forward our claims all this time.'

'Ask Eze Okehi that. Before we were born though there was a big fight over the Pond of Wagaba. Chiolu won and has held the pond ever since.'

'Then it belongs to them.'

'Winning a fight does not prove ownership.'

'How do we hope to reclaim it?'

'We shall probably have to fight for it.'

'But you say victory does not establish ownership.'

'Well we happen to be the real owners.'

Ejimole thought that over.

'One other thing bothers me.'

'What?' Chileru asked hauling a piece of yam into his mouth.

'My mother warned me not to step out last night. She must be frantic now.'

'Well the best thing you can do for your mother right now is to eat and keep up your strength.'

Ejimole admired Chileru's practical sense. He was a jolly young man, not too scrupulous but likeable. Ejimole needed no persuasion for the midday meal. He was very hungry and ate with a huge appetite. Soon after the meal they were whisked off to the arena. Diali and some elders were already seated in the cool shade of a large oil bean tree in the arena. Chileru saw Olumba among the group of younger men who were talking animatedly about the events of the past night. They wore their sheathed matchets by their sides with careless grace.

To the right of the elders a set of three-legged chairs had been arranged, evidently for the men from Aliakoro. It did not take long before they arrived clad in war dress. Eze Okehi their chief walked in front, staff in hand. He was a white-haired old man but he looked strong and well-preserved. The journey from Aliakoro to Chiolu took half the morning but he did it without undue strain.

Eze Diali rose to greet the visitors. He walked to Eze Okehi and raised his right hand high above his head in greeting. His guest responded and their right hands met in a cold handshake above their heads.

Kola was served. Okehi took it and murmured platitudes. He passed it to his immediate junior. It passed from one elder to another until it came back to Okehi who then handed it back to Diali. The arena was hushed as the kola did the rounds. It was a ceremony requiring a good knowledge of tradition and even history.

Diali broke the kola, took one piece and offered the rest to Okehi. Again the kola did the rounds. The wooden bowl was almost empty by the time it got back to Diali. The chief took one piece, broke it into smaller fragments and scattered them on the ground, thereby offering them to Amadioha, the god of thunder and of the skies, Ali the earth-god, Ojukwu the Fair and Ogbunabali, the god who kills by night. The important gods were mentioned by name in public functions, the lesser gods received their due in the more intimate rituals in family shrines.

The elders crunched their kola with deliberation, studying one another in the silence which was broken only by the hissing sound made by men drawing in air to lessen the effect of the pepper in their mouths.

Okehi cleared his throat and got up to speak.

'Men of Aliakoro, Growers of Big Yams, Leopard-killers, Eyes of the Night, Eight-headed Warriors, I greet you!'

The men of Aliakoro answered with a mighty roar.

'Men of Chiolu who use fish for firewood, Terrors of the forests, Hunters with Invisible Footprints, Greater Sons of Great Fathers, I greet you!'

There was another deafening shout as the men of Chiolu acknowledged the greetings.

'Eze Diali,' Okehi went on, 'we have come to ask you to release our two sons whom you captured last night and whom you still hold as prisoners. We come as friends and we hope to go back with our two sons but without any humps on our backs.'

'Eze Okehi,' Diali replied, 'the circumstances under which your men were captured were such that we shall demand a ransom for their release. When you have paid this you may go back with them. As for your safety, that is assured. It is weakness to attack a guest.'

'Before we talk about ransoms I would like to know from your prisoners the circumstances under which they were captured,' Okehi said.

Chileru and Ejimole were brought forward and asked to describe the incidents of the past night. Chileru gave a vivid description and ended by saying: 'The amazing thing about all this is that we were doing no fishing when we were attacked.'

'Where were you when you were attacked?' Diali asked.

'In one of our ponds.'

'That is a lie,' Olumba cut in. 'You were about to float into the Pond of Wagaba.'

'In any case,' Chileru said, 'we were not fishing when you attacked us.'

'What were you doing there at that time of the night?' Diali queried.

'We went to lay traps for wild hogs.'

'Another lie,' Olumba said furiously. 'He went behind a bush and brought out some fish-traps. Are these not yours?' he said raising them high in the air for everyone to see.

'They are.'

'And what were they for?' Olumba asked.

'We were to do some fishing later in our own ponds.'

'Why don't you lay traps for wild hogs near your own ponds?'

'Sit down young men,' Okehi said rising. 'This matter is more complicated than is apparent at the moment. Diali your men have not acted right. Firstly my men were not fishing when they were attacked. Secondly, if they were fishing in the Pond of Wagaba, they had a right to; they have done so for years. The younger generation may not know the truth about the pond, but we old men know, don't we? We in Aliakoro have not pressed our claims because there have been no molestations until yesterday when you kidnapped my boys. Of course when you hit a goat you get to know the owner.'

Okehi's last words were drowned by angry protests from the Chiolu camp. Many men started pacing around in anger. Diali called them to order.

'Okehi my friend,' Diali said, 'so far you and your men have been arguing backwards and forwards. When a man is chewing his food awkwardly you can be sure there is sand in it. Now I am glad you have come to the root of the matter. You say the Pond of Wagaba belongs to Aliakoro?'

'Yes, Eze Diali.'

'Very well. I want to tell you that we are not prepared to discuss the ownership of this pond. It is indisputable. You will either pay the ransom we shall suggest or get back without your two men. Make up your mind so that this dangerous meeting may come to an end. We are like men about to disturb a nest of wasps.'

Okehi weighed the situation for a while. He looked at his men, at the men of Chiolu and lastly at the two prisoners with their hands tied behind them.

'Diali,' he said slowly, 'even if we agree to pay something, we haven't got the money to do so here and now. Your terms are as unexpected as they are unfriendly. You are creating a precedence whose repercussions may be quite unpleasant for all. We are not the only people who walk the forests. Your men do stray into our lands now and then and reprisals are easy. So release the young men. It is unwise to sieze the leopard's cubs.'

'If my men wander into your lands to steal, capture them by all means. If however you find them passing by without any evil intentions I do not advise you to touch them. He who pursues an innocent chicken often stumbles.'

'Diali, do you expect us to go back to Aliakoro and fetch some money before you release these boys?'

'If you have come without money it is your fault. I made it quite clear to your envoys this morning that the prisoners will have to be ransomed.'

Okehi ground his teeth in deliberation. He turned round and whispered to the elders sitting behind him. They rose and walked off to hold a conference. It seemed long and involved judging from the violent shaking of heads and the waving of walking-sticks. Eventually the younger men from Aliakoro joined their elders to help them come to a decision. When they had done they came back and Okehi said curtly:

'Diali, name the ransom.'

Diali was about to say something when Olumba half shouted: 'Let's hold a conference, Eze Diali.' It seemed to be the popular feeling and they rose and moved apart for a while. 'You will pay eight hundred manillas,' the chief announced shortly.

'Did the boys commit murder?' Okehi asked in genuine surprise.

'You have me to thank that it is as low as that,' Diali said. 'Some of the things you said embittered my people. I wish you hadn't said them. Even now I wish you could withdraw your so-called claim and say it was all a bluff. For generations the Great Ponds have been the cause of wars and heavy loss of lives. Some years ago our two villages fought a bitter battle over the Pond of Wagaba. My father was killed in it. My senior brother was taken prisoner and sold to the Rikwos across the rivers and we never heard of him again. However, we won this battle and this pond became ours. Might is not right but who can tell now who was right and who wrong? Time obscures many things, but time also establishes many things. That you have not challenged us for thirty years is proof enough that the Pond of Wagaba belongs to us.'

'We are not here to recount history,' Okehi said. 'The great talker often has much to hide. I don't believe in much talking; that is an occupation for women. We shall pay two hundred manillas.'

'No, we are not prepared to haggle.'

'Three hundred.'

'No.'

'Four hundred.'

'I think you are wasting your time Eze Okehi. The ransom is stuck at eight hundred manillas. It will go neither up nor down. If you have money only for one prisoner, pay up and we shall release one of them. You can claim the other later.'

'It is good to eat and be satisfied,' Okehi said, 'but it is foolish to

20

eat until one's stomach bursts. The ransom is too high. Take five hundred.'

Eze Diali hesitated, opened his mouth and closed it again without saying anything. At this point Olumba sprang forward and said:

'If they are ready to withdraw their false claims I think we can consider lowering the ransom.'

'We will not withdraw our claims,' a voice shouted from the other camp. People looked round to spot the speaker. He saved them the trouble by coming forward. 'From what our fathers told us, the Pond of Wagaba belongs to us, though you won the last battle. We shall stick to our claim. If you like, you can make the ransom twenty times eight hundred manillas.' It was Wago the leopard-killer who was speaking. His sinewy body swayed in the light afternoon breeze. As his words rushed out in rapid gusts, the veins in his neck bulged out.

Olumba moved nearer Wago shaking with suppressed anger.

'My lord Eze Diali I swear by Amadioha the god of thunder and of the skies to cut to pieces anyone who suggests that we lower the ransom. I led the gang that captured these wretched prisoners last night. This man here was among the poachers. With my hands I caught him and tied him, but he escaped by employing a coward's trick. However, I gathered from him before he fled that Eze Okehi has been telling them for quite a long time that the Pond of Wagaba belongs to them. Even if they recant here we can't take their word for it until they stop poaching. But they won't. Their minds are made up my lord. Let them pay the ransom.'

'And I swear by Ogbunabali the god that kills by night to cut off clean the head of anyone who comes forward to pay this ransom,' Wago the leopard-killer fumed.

There was silence as the two men glowered at each other. A few men who had come to the arena without matchets left unobtrusively to fetch them. No one said anything. An ominous silence prevailed. It was as if the whole crowd had been struck by Amadioha's thunderbolt. Slowly Wago's right hand sought the sheath of his matchet. Olumba noticed this and began to do the same retreating a short step as he did so. Wago retreated too, his deep set eyes riveted on his opponent. Many held their breaths, their hearts beating wildly. Diali watched grimly the men of Aliakoro fingering the handles of their matchets. He glanced at his men with the corner of his eyes. They too were doing the same. Many were sweating. Diali had to do something. He decided to plead with the two angry men, but he realized that by merely raising his voice he might trigger off a bloody fight. The two camps were poised like snakes ready to strike. They had done all their reasoning and had come to one conclusion, to fight. Now their minds were no longer working but their tensed muscles were ready to go into action at the least stimulation. A sound, a slight movement or even a deep breath from anybody could provide this stimulation. Diali spoke in a very low voice.

'Listen everybody – and please leave your matchets alone. There is nothing to be gained by fighting. We are here for a peaceful settlement. If we don't agree today, we can always arrange another meeting.

'Eze Okehi, you and I are old. We have nothing to lose if we die now but these young people have their lives to live. Let's give them a chance. I am sure your men are absolutely in your control, speak to them. I shall do the same to my people.

'Wago and Olumba, you are both men of valour. But valour that is not tempered with wisdom is useless and even dangerous. In a situation like this, fighting does not solve anything. Pepper can never be one of the ingredients of a soothing balm.'

This speech, delivered slowly and quietly had a soothing effect. Tensed muscles relaxed somewhat. Faces lost their grim expressions. Diali had a talk with his men.

'It appears that Aliakoro has not got eight hundred manillas here,' Diali went on. 'I think we should . . .'

'Before you go on, remember I am under an oath,' Olumba said, his eyes flashing.

'We shall take care of that my son,' the chief said. 'I understand your position.'

An egg, some kola and two leaves from a special tree were procured and placed in a wooden bowl. The bowl was waved round Olumba's head three times while Diali muttered some incantations.

This short ceremony released Olumba from his oath. The bowl was passed on to Okehi who subjected Wago the leopard-killer to the same treatment.

Negotiations were resumed and in the end Aliakoro paid six hundred manillas. The two prisoners were released and handed over to their people.

'Now that this is over,' Okehi said, 'I want to make it quite clear that we intend to stick to our claims. It is necessary that we arrive at a compromise over the Pond of Wagaba.'

'What compromise?' Diali asked.

'That is for us to work out. For instance our two villages might share the pond.'

'Never! Not in my lifetime!' Diali exclaimed.

'Well, my men will fish there as of right in *my* lifetime,' Okehi declared. 'In fact they will fish there tomorrow.'

'This is what comes of compromise my lord,' Olumba said addressing Diali angrily.

'Okehi, you dare not fish in the Pond of Wagaba openly,' Diali said.

'Shall we bet?' Okehi asked, his teeth flashing a smile of confidence.

'Yes,' Diali answered stretching his right hand and opening his palm. Okehi came forward and the right palms of the two men clashed as a sign of mutual defiance. It was a fearful bet.

Aliakoro's representative's left, half-dragging the ransomed men with them. They walked through the village swiftly, almost noiselessly. They bade no one good-bye.

Diali gathered his men round him and said solemnly: 'You all heard what Okehi said. You know the meaning of it. I want all the elders to meet me in my reception hall immediately we leave here. If we arrive at any decisions requiring your attention the ikoro will sound.'

The men dispersed quickly. Olumba ran all the way to his house, his square chest muscles vibrating. Ikechi followed closely behind him keeping up easily with the grace and light-footedness of youth.

'What will happen now?' Ikechi asked when they got to Olumba's compound.

'We shall fight – and hard too.'

'When?'

'Tomorrow.'

'Where?'

'Probably at the Pond of Wagaba.'

'But the men from Aliakoro may not turn up.'

'They will. I know Wago and the leopard-killer very well. He will persuade the men to go to the pond even if Okehi changes his mind.'

'This is more serious than I thought.'

'It is.'

'Will you lead our men?'

'Go home and prepare.'

'I shall stay and watch you. I have no preparations to make; my knife is sharp.'

'And your arrows?'

'My quiver is almost full.'

'Go and fill it. You will need all the arrows in your quiver and more.'

Ikechi left rather reluctantly. He was much attached to Olumba. He admired him very much and was learning many useful things from him. Olumba liked the young man too. He looked very much like his first son who had fallen into a well some five years before and died. Achichi said the boy died because of offences which Olumba had committed in his previous incarnation. It was a curious story. Olumba in his previous incarnation was passing by a pond after a heavy rain. He saw a drowning lamb in a pond and refused to save it. The lamb was drowned. The mother sheep cursed him and prayed Amadioha to deny him children in his next incarnation.

After this divination Olumba made frantic efforts to get an heir. He consulted any dibias he heard of. He married a second wife who had two daughters and a son who also died. After the death of this boy his two wives had two more daughters and he decided it was time to get a third wife. It was a wise decision. The third wife gave him a son a year after she arrived.

The baby, now over two years old, was so much like his father that people feared that Olumba had had a second incarnation. If this was true, then Olumba's death was imminent. Achichi the dibia was consulted and he showed clearly that Olumba's son was an incarnation of Olumba's grandfather, not of Olumba himself. To be quite sure Olumba consulted Anwuanwu, a dibia at Abii, a village near Chiolu. Anwuanwu's divination confirmed Achichi's, and Olumba's peace of mind was restored.

Olumba worshipped the gods of his fathers with a zeal that shamed even the priests themselves. No sacrifices were too great to placate the most insignificant of his household gods. It was a favourite saying of his that he would rather fight a whole village single-handed than defy the weakest god. So he was Achichi's favourite customer. His whole compound was full of charms. There was a mud bust of Ali, the earth-god, in his reception hall which was the wonder of the village. An old knife blade was stuck to one side of the bust and an arrow to the other. The effect was awe-inspiring. It was Achichi's masterpiece, beating by far the twin river gods in Chief Diali's reception hall.

Olumba's wives and children were bedecked with charms and amulets, his little son enjoying the greatest share. There were amulets for travelling, against poisoning, for social gatherings, against evil spirits by night, against mischievous imps by day, for growing big yams, for wrestling, for fishing and so on. These precautions proved useful because Olumba prospered under their influence. His misfortunes were few and far between, the greatest so far being the loss of his first son.

The villagers feared Olumba not only because of his undisputed physical strength but also for his many and reputedly powerful charms. Actually he never concocted charms to kill anyone, but charms for protection could be on the offensive when the wearer's person was threatened. Since a threat could be anything from a good-natured curse to a knife duel, the wearer of a really powerful charm was best avoided.

3

THE ikoro sounded, its deep hollow notes more insistent, more ominous than before. The meeting was short and to the point. The Pond of Wagaba was to be guarded all through the next day against marauders. Olumba and a few other braves were to work out details of strategy.

Men spent the rest of the evening preparing for the encounter. Knives were sharpened, and resharpened, salt being sprinkled on the whetstone for additional effect. Women and children gave these knives a wide berth knowing that careless handling could mean a gash deep enough to reveal the bone. Palm trees were invaded and their fronds quickly converted into arrows. Here children proved helpful; they fashioned the arrows and their fathers put the finishing touches to them. Bows were restrung and spare strings were put in the quiver.

It was time to perform small but hitherto neglected sacrifices. Charms for fighting were brought out, dusted and strengthened by the appropriate rituals. Achichi the dibia had the busiest day in his life. He ran from one compound to another, mending broken amulets, concocting new ones, prescribing quick and effective sacrifices, warding off evil influences, invoking the help of powerful gods. At one stage, the whole village ran out of akaneme, the gin distilled from palm wine. Achichi was forced to use ordinary palm wine.

Olumba had a small room adjoining his reception hall. This room was specially constructed to house costly images of gods and very powerful charms. Olumba had been in this room since he returned from the arena. He had been sorting out his various charms. His brow grew dark when he could not find an amulet that when worn could deflect arrows aimed at the wearer. He searched everywhere pushing down an image of Ojukwu in the process. He sacrificed a cock later to placate the god. As the sun sank and the shadows of surrounding trees darkened the compound he lit an oil lamp. What could have happened to this important amulet? Despair and anger siezed him in turns. His anger was worsened by the fact that he could not turn it loose on anyone. His wives were forbidden to enter his medicine-house and so he could not blame them, nor could they help him in his search. At last he gave up and decided to see

Achichi; may be he had amulets with similar properties. He picked up the small three-legged chair on which he was sitting and was about to hang it by the bamboo framework of the roof when the end of a thread caressed his nose. He pulled at it and it came off, the missing amulet at its end. He had stowed it away between the thatches. Greatly relieved he wiped his sweating brow and went outside for fresh air.

His charms had taken up so much time that Olumba had little time left to get other things ready. But he was not much worried because his quivers were always full of arrows and his knife sharp. However, as the next day promised hazards, he felt he ought to use the family fighting knife. This knife was many generations old and had beautiful designs on it. There were no signs of rust on it in spite of its great age. There were only two knives of this type in the whole village, Eze Diali had the other. Olumba sharpened the knife carefully and nodded with satisfaction as he shaved off hairs from his left arm with it.

Everything was ready. He had done all he could to deal with the dangers of the next day. He had one regret, that he had not been able to get that famous amulet that could make knives bounce off his body as off a rock. If he had it, he would be invincible. But it was forbiddingly costly. When Achichi had enumerated the necessary items, Olumba just had to give up the idea. However, he had one consolation – no one in Aliakoro had this charm. At one time there were rumours that Wago the leopard-killer had it. These rumours were proved to be unfounded when Wago accidentally cut his hand while trying to cut open a coconut. Only one man had this charm for certain – Anwuanwu the dibia at Abii. Achichi was too poor to own one.

Olumba slept well in the security of the gods. He woke up strong and confident and proceeded to fortify himself. The charm against arrows came first.

Before he left, his wives went into his room one by one to wish him luck. They came in cheerfully, knelt before him, said one or two encouraging things and went back. Women were not expected to cry when their husbands were going off to battle because tears would weaken them. However, Olumba's third and youngest wife, Oda, could not fight back her tears when, carrying her little son in her arms, she came to greet her husband. Olumba rebuked her as sternly as his own feelings would let him, patted his son on the head and strode out of his compound.

It was still dark but the misty outlines of many armed men could be made out on the arena. As soon as Olumba arrived they set out at a fast pace. It was important they should occupy the pond before their adversaries.

'Has any of the scouts sent in a report yet?' Olumba asked.

'None,' Eziho replied.

'Looks as if our friends from Aliakoro are not early risers.'

'I guess not.'

'They must be feeling guilty too.'

'Undoubtedly. Eze Okehi and Wago pushed their village on to this, otherwise the men would have been quite content with mere poaching.'

'Even that can be annoying, when it gets out of hand,' Olumba said.

Half-way to the Great Ponds Ikechi met Olumba and his men.

'Seen anybody?' Olumba asked.

'No,' the young man said, his face flushed with running.

'Where are the other four men?'

'At the ponds.'

'Why did you leave them behind?'

'I thought you would like to know the present situation.'

'You are right,' Olumba said, his eyes narrowing to slits as he thought rapidly.

'You have done well. Go home for some food, and join us when you have rested.' Ikechi had been hoping for this and he was relieved when Olumba said it. He was tired and sleepy. All night long he and four others had been at the ponds trying to spy on the enemy.

'He is a dependable young fellow,' Olumba said when Ikechi had sped homewards.

'No doubt of it,' Eziho said. 'He might lead this village in battle before he is thirty.'

'His father, Njola, has the right attitude too,' Olumba said. 'He does not pamper him as one would expect a man with an only son to do. He keeps pushing him on to danger. Last night when I requested that his son be among the spies, do you know what he said?'

'No.'

'He said, "Why do you ask me? He is at your disposal." I looked at him and he read the admiration in my eyes and said, "Olumba it is far better to have no son at all than to have one who is of no use to his village, particularly at a time like this. My father fought in the Great Ponds. He etched eight notches on his bow. When slave dealers swooped on Chiolu early one morning twenty years ago, I fought and etched four notches on my bow. Let Ikechi make his marks too".'

'Well,' Eziho said smiling, 'he has every chance of etching a notch or two today. It is bound to be a bloody fight.'

At the bank of the ponds a man was waiting for them.

'So far we have seen no signs of our opponents,' the man told Olumba.

'Where are your companions?'

'Near the Pond of Wagaba.'

At the pond, the men of Chiolu laid an ambush. The huge trees provided very good cover. The plan was simple but effective. If the men of Aliakoro moved in to fish they would be greeted with a volley of arrows, and killed or captured in the ensuing confusion.

They lay in position until the fierce rays of the sun began to pierce the almost perfect ceiling of leaves and branches. It looked as if Aliakoro had no intention of carrying out their threat.

Olumba heard a rustling behind him. Noiselessly he turned and looked back. It was Ikechi. Olumba signalled to him to crouch. Ikechi obeyed and crept near the leader.

'We have been spotted,' he whispered to Olumba.

'What do you mean?'

'As I was coming I saw one of our scouts chasing a spy from Aliakoro.'

'Was he caught?'

'No, he escaped.'

Olumba ordered his men to relax, but not to talk. Some sat while others stood to stretch their legs. Everyone gained some confidence. If their opponents had not arrived by now, they were evidently afraid, and if so the battle was half won. Olumba moved swiftly and silently among the men, exchanging views with them. They admired his square protuberant chest muscles and his marvellous fighting knife.

By midday Olumba ordered his men to eat what food they had brought. Parcels of cocoyam and plantain leaves were opened, revealing yams boiled in blood-red oil. One fat man had brought some foofoo.

'You really care for yourself,' Olumba said teasingly.

'Everyone knows his particular needs, Olumba,' the man said smiling.

'Will you use water for soup?'

'No need to,' the man said producing from a raffia bag a wooden bowl with a tight lid. The lid was kept in place by rounds of rope securely tied.

'Does the soup not pour away?' Olumba asked examining the bowl with interest.

'Not when the soup is thick with vegetables and what-not.' The man smacked his lips after the rapid up-and-down motion of his Adam's apple had announced that the first ball of foofoo was home.

'I like to fight with something solid inside me,' he commented as the second ball of foofoo journeyed through the air with an impressive load of vegetables, fish and a beheaded periwinkle. Olumba swallowed some saliva as he watched the man. He himself preferred fighting light. He had had a full meal the night before. He guessed that would see him through the fight. It was now midday and the men of Aliakoro were still not ready to fight. He felt a slight gnawing pain in his stomach and left his men for a moment. He wandered off a little way, uprooted a sapling, cleaned its taproot and thrust it into his mouth. As he swallowed the sour-tasting sap, the pangs in his stomach ceased and he felt strength suffusing his body.

Before he could get back to his men he saw the 'foofoo man' running swiftly towards him.

'They are here!' he whispered.

'In which direction?'

'That,' he said pointing.

Olumba ordered his men to lie low. There was just a chance that the enemy did not know exactly where they were. But the enemy knew well enough. They came to the other side of the Pond of Wagaba and halted well beyond the range of any arrows from the people of Chiolu. From his cover Olumba could see the invaders clearly. Wago the leopard-killer was obviously their leader. He moved among the men giving them instructions.

Wago now realized that fishing in the pond would have been easier if they had occupied the pond first. While some fished others could have protected them. As things stood, Okehi's promise that his men would fish this day seemed very difficult to fulfil. But Wago was not easily daunted. He had come to fish, and fish he would.

There were three men holding fish-traps. Wago tried to persuade them to wade into the pond and set their traps no matter how ineffectively. The men hesitated and then retreated farther into the mass of men like tortoises withdrawing into their shells on sensing danger. Wago grew angry.

'I am surprised at your behaviour,' he said. 'Are there no brave men here who can wade into this pond and fish?' There was no reply. He glowered at the men and they stared back at him sullenly. He read refusal in every face.

The men of Chiolu watched these proceedings with interest. The whole thing was resolving into a funny show. They smiled derisively but nevertheless brought their bows quietly into the shooting position.

In spite of his anger Wago realized he had mishandled the situation. A little discussion with his men before he started issuing orders would have placed him in a much happier position. But he had gone too far; it was too late to retreat. There was only one thing to do. Slowly but firmly he picked up one of the fish-traps and moved towards the pond. After a couple of steps he paused and surveyed the opposite bank. He saw the big trees with massive climbers encircling them in a life-and-death embrace. He saw brightly coloured butterflies floating about with oversized wings. He saw a kingfisher perched on a branch overhanging the pond, nodding its head in its characteristic way. He saw no man, but he knew what dangers lurked behind the trees. This knowledge transformed the trees into conscious beings. They seemed to be watching him intently, coldly, with four hundred eyes.

As Wago the leopard-killer got within a few steps of the pond a whistle like that of a familiar jungle bird was heard. In the next instant he was beclouded by a swarm of arrows. He caught six arrows on his ekpe ekpeke. He retreated and rejoined his men some of whom could not resist a chuckle. At the opposite bank the silence was ominous.

Slowly, quietly, Wago withdrew from his men and sat down a few paces away. He sat rigidly for some time and then proceeded to rub his head with an amulet he wore round his neck. He did this slowly at first then more rapidly. He stopped abruptly and his men who were watching noticed that his eyes were bloodshot and wet. Could he be crying? No, he was not. He was singing in a queer voice hardly recognizable as his.

He got up, capered about and slashed at branches with his matchet as he sang. Then in a loud voice he said: 'Men of Aliakoro, if you die today, you will not die tomorrow. The eagle has perched within shooting range! Eight-headed warriors, Eyes of the Night, Leopard-killers, follow me!'

With this he charged towards the enemy along the bank of the pond. Roused to action at last Aliakoro followed their leader chanting wildly. Wago was like one possessed. He raced across the swampy ground without sinking. Arrows sang past him, but he was not hit. One or two of his men fell behind him.

Now they were close enough to see their enemies hiding behind the trees.

'Shoot!' Wago howled. Arrows sped among the trees. Leaves

barely rustled as swift arrows pierced them and flew on to strike other targets. The trees were so thick that they stopped most of the arrows. Only a few men had fallen so far. They lay on the ground trying to pull out the barbed points. Those mortally wounded were calling on the gods to save them.

A man was running closely behind Wago. When some under growth lessened Wago's speed for a moment the man passed him and took the lead. He was a magnificent man with well-formed muscles. He seemed to be Wago's assistant judging from his enthusiasm. When he was a few paces from the warriors of Chiolu, Olumba suddenly sprang from behind a tree where he had been hiding. The man was completely taken unawares. He raised his ekpeke as Olumba's ancient knife flashed but he was too late. His head was chopped off completely the next instant. As the man's trunk sagged to the ground Olumba gave vent to a loud war hoot. A solid wall of men with bared knives rose behind him. The advancing enemies were stunned for a moment. Even Wago paused in his mad career. He recovered quickly and came on. Olumba was waiting to engage him and their knives clashed before the scattered columns of Aliakoro closed in on the defenders. The din was deafening.

The men of Chiolu held their ground as one solid block, cutting down their enemies with frightening ease as they advanced in disorder. When some ten men lay mutilated on the ground panic siezed the attackers. Those at the rear hesitated. Those in front began to retreat and Chiolu warriors advanced, slowly at first then rapidly as the invaders turned and scampered through the woods.

Ikechi was among a group of four chasing two men. The men ran with all the energy which the fear of death could conjure. They dodged trees and undergrowth with uncanny dexterity and quickly increased the distance between them and their pursuers. One man suggested they should give up the chase. The other two agreed and stopped, but not Ikechi. He jumped over a narrow neck of water, slashed down a barrier of shrubs, and raced on. Of the two fugitives, the one ahead was clearly a faster runner. The fellow behind was slowing down through fatigue. Ikechi observed this and made haste. Blindly the man ran into a quagmire and got stuck. By the time he extricated himself Ikechi was on him. The man was obliged to turn and face his pursuer. Sparks flew from their knives as they parried each other's blows. Ikechi did not seem to care much for his safety. The possibility of dying did not occur to him. He fought relentlessly with the singleness of purpose of a child. He exhibited the carelessness of inexperience too, now and then leaving openings which might have been fatal if his opponent had been strong enough' to exploit them. But he was not. He was a middle-aged man and he weakened under the remorseless attacks of his much younger assailant. His knees began to wobble, his eyes grew dim as he panted. Now there was a plea in his eyes, but he had no breath to translate this plea into words.

Ikechi, unseeing in his mad fury, did not heed this plea as his able hands worked his matchet this way and that. Parrying a particularly heavy blow the man sank to his knees. Before he could recover it was all over with him. Panting but elated Ikechi took the man's matchet and walked back to rejoin his comrades. On the way he etched a notch, the first ever, on his bow.

Ikechi could hear the noise of battle as he walked back. A few diehards were making a last stand. Chief among them was Wago the leopard-killer. Olumba did not underestimate him and so fought with all the calmness and cunning he could employ. Wago was an able fighter, there could be no doubt about it. He was as tough and resilient as akikara, a wild climbing plant. After foiling a particularly vicious attack from his opponent he would bare his teeth in a horrible grin, giving a quick counter-blow as his face resumed its sinister expression. Olumba's face was as rigid as that of a carved wooden god. He fought with the regularity and efficiency of a machine. The only sign of excitement he showed was the heaving of his massive chest. Neither of the two men was willing to retreat. They held their ground, moving back a step or two only when they had to dodge a blow, and springing back to the attack the next instant. Wago's knife began to show signs of strain. Its blade became twisted at several points as its wielder parried blow after blow.

Olumba's knife stood the test very well. The only signs of battle on it were the dark blood-stains of the man previously decapitated. Both men were getting tired, but they seemed to be weakening at the same rate. The blows were more feeble now, their movements duller, their nostrils smarted as they inhaled and exhaled large quick puffs of air with ebbing strength. Wago warded off a tricky blow but Olumba's knife slashed his right thumb and the gash bled. Wago realized what had happened when his grip slackened on his matchet. He quickly transferred the matchet to his left hand just in time to parry what Olumba meant to be a finishing blow. Olumba swerved sideways with the blow and recovered to find Wago racing away. He pursued him but Wago, a better sprinter, soon left him behind. He thought of throwing his matchet at him but realized that if he missed, he would be a dead man. He shot two arrows at the retreating figure. They went wide. He knew he was wasting his arrows since Wago evidently had the arrow-deflecting amulet. He stopped shooting and watched his enemy until the primeval woods swallowed him. He bit his lips and rejoined his men.

4 CHIOLU lost four men, Aliakoro thirteen. It was a clear victory for the fighters of Chiolu who went home singing and cheering in spite of their weariness. When they arrived they were greeted with mounds of foofoo in Eze Diali's reception hall. The women had not been idle. Achichi the dibia busied over wounded men. Some elders brought down ancient recipes from racks over their fireplaces and attended to the wounded themselves. The dead were buried with full rites.

But there was no time for formal celebrations. For all they knew this battle might only be the beginning. Their enemies might attack again. The warriors resharpened their knives, and made more arrows.

The next day found them at the Great Ponds. But they waited in vain. The poachers did not show up. As the shadows lengthened, the great forest began to darken rapidly, conjuring up as it did so the awe-inspiring orchestra of myriads of nocturnal birds and insects. The men went home. The next day Diali said to Olumba:

'I think the dispute over the pond of Wagaba has been settled once and for all.'

'You are probably right, but with Wago there I have a feeling Aliakoro may put up another fight.'

'How well did he fight yesterday?'

'Individually he fought well but he did not control his men very well.' Olumba did not want to discuss his last encounter with Wago the leopard-killer. He still felt bad over that narrow escape his enemy had.

The Pond of Wagaba was watched for eight days with no clashes. It looked as if Aliakoro had learnt their lesson. Chiolu relaxed and the elders began to think of staging a victory dance.

Ikechi was elated over that notch on his bow. It had made him a man. He looked forward to the victory dance in which only people who had notches on their bows could participate. His father was proud of him too, for he was the only lad in his age-group who could boast of a notch on his bow. Ikechi told his father in great details how he had killed his opponent at the Great Ponds. He exaggerated his opponent's strength and added embellishments not quite related to the fight.

Njola pointed out some of the mistakes his son had made during the fight and added:

'If your man had been smarter, it might have been a different story.'

'He was very smart, dede.'

'Not from the way you finished him off.'

'But I am smart too.'

'All right you are, Ike,' his father admitted laughing.

Ikechi enjoyed this chat very much. He was talking to his father as man to man. He could not help noticing that his father now had slightly more respect for him. Well, maybe not respect really, but still there was that in his father's eye which could only mean a new and better assessment of him. When his father tried to recount his experiences twenty years back when slave dealers had swooped on the village Ikechi would not let him get it out alone.

'I remember that morning when you left the house armed with your knife, bows and arrows,' Ikechi said.

'No you can't remember,' his father replied. 'You had barely started walking then.'

'I remember, dede. You went out and came back shortly afterwards and hid mother and I in a bush behind our house.'

'That is quite true,' Njola said baffled by his son's accuracy.

'When you came back from the fight with a cut on your shoulder, you asked mother to heat some water for you.'

'Do you remember all this?'

'I do. You killed four people in that fight.'

'How do you know? Surely you won't say you fought with us,' Njola said laughing.

'You told mother how many people you killed when you came back.'

'But you couldn't count then; you couldn't have remembered the figure.'

'However, there are four notches on your bow.'

'Yes, that's where you got the figure from.'

'Still, I can remember the other points.'

'Answer this question then: where did I hide you and your mother before I went off to the fight?'

Ikechi looked round and after some hesitation pointed to a clump of bushes behind his mother's house. His father laughed heartily and long.

'There you are,' he said still laughing, 'you are quite wrong. We were not even living in this compound at the time. Our home was on the other side of the village nearer the arena.'

Ikechi laughed in spite of his embarrassment. Indeed he was not to blame for claiming to remember these things. The raid of the slave dealers was recounted so often by fathers that their children had vivid impressions of them. These mental images were so

37

persistent that it was not unusual for a youngster to confuse incidents he actually saw and remembered with those narrated to him by his parents.

'Dede,' Ikechi said, 'tell me more about the victory dance coming up in four days' time. I am qualified to drink the wine with the eagle feather, am I not?'

'You are qualified, my son,' Njola replied and went on to explain to his son the intricacies of the victory dance.

A victory dance was unlike any other dance. The dancers wore their battle-dress. To qualify for the dance a dancer must have taken part in a real battle, but the highlights of the dance belonged to those who had actually slain enemies in battle.

The night before the dance Ikechi hardly slept. What sleep he had was troubled by dreams of frantic dancing in which he made embarrassing mistakes. The day broke at last and he jumped out of his sleeping-mound. He wondered how to occupy his time until the evening when the dance would be staged. Yams were all tied up in the barns now and there was no work to be done on the farm. He thought of going to inspect his traps in the bush and changed his mind. His traps were few and never seemed to catch anything. He could easily count the number of animals he had ever caught. He knew he was a poor trapper. What traps he had were set to show his mates that at least he knew how to set about the business. Tracing the spoors of animals bored him.

He had a late breakfast with his mother and his sister Ikigba. He liked the soup, and from the taste he knew it contained a large type of pepper with a delicious aromatic flavour.

'Where did you get this pepper?' he asked. 'I thought we had none left in the farm.'

'My friend Chisa gave me some. She says her mother still has a lot of it,' Ikigba replied.

'How is your friend Chisa?' Ikechi asked trying to appear indifferent.

'Instead of asking about her,' his mother said, 'why don't you go and greet her parents and see if there is anything you can do for them? It doesn't look as if you have much to do today.'

'The victory dance is set for today, have you forgotten?'

'I know but that is in the evening. Run along and greet Diali and his family.'

Chisa was one of Diali's daughters. Although no definite move had been made so far, Njola had hinted subtly that he would like to have Chisa for a daughter-in-law. Eze Diali had said neither yes nor no. He had merely smiled and changed the topic. Njola knew of course that marrying a chief's daughter was tough but he was determined that nothing less than a blunt refusal from Diali would thwart his schemes. Ikechi was pleased with the choice. Chisa was not particularly beautiful but she was a buxom cheerful girl whose warmth and ready smile were well known in the village. It was difficult to stay in her presence without feeling relaxed. She had a ready wit which had the desirable quality of rarely giving offence. When she did offend she was quick to apologize, often succeeding in making the offended person feel ashamed for having lost his temper.

Ikechi took his mother's suggestion. Instead of dropping in at Olumba's as he was planning he strolled to Eze Diali's compound. The big compound was bustling with life. Children playing hide-and-seek ran this way and that yelling. Two of them ran into each other as they emerged from adjacent sides of a building and their foreheads met in a painful collision. The lighter boy fell flat on his back and cried out, rubbing his head. The other boy merely winced, stroked his brow and disappeared into his mother's kitchen. The boy who was crying was one of Chisa's little brothers. Ikechi picked him up and walked to his mother's house somewhere behind Eze Diali's big house which monopolized the middle of the compound.

'Who is here?' he shouted. Chisa, who was in the kitchen behind the house, immediately recognized Ikechi's voice.

'Why don't you come in instead of standing there to ask?' she said pleasantly.

Ikechi went in with just a trace of shyness. Chisa soon put him at ease with her prattles.

'I hope you have recovered completely from the effects of the battle,' she said.

'Oh, I am strong and as tough as a drum,' he replied. 'Where are your parents?'

'My mother went to a farm near by to collect cocoyams. My father is in bed. He says he has pains in his joints.'

'Where are your younger sisters?'

'They went to the farm with Mother.'

'You are lazy. Why did you not accompany them?'

She laughed good-naturedly.

'I am not lazy. I am staying at home because father wants me to prepare a special dish to relieve his pains.'

'Can't your younger sisters prepare this wonderful dish?'

'Oh no, they are far too young to know how; it is a complicated business.'

'I didn't know you were such a good old dibia.'

'Indeed I am,' she said smiling in her peculiar way.

'I wish I had known this earlier. I should have come to you soon after the battle to have my wounds healed.'

'Wait till next time.'

'It is not too late. I still have a slight pain in my left knee.'

Ikechi moved nearer her and placed his left leg across her knees.

'Put down your leg: Father will be angry if he comes out and sees us like this.'

'Your father is too sick to come out.'

'I was lying when I said he was sick. He is as fit as ever and may be here any moment.'

Ikechi put down his leg quickly. Chisa burst out laughing.

'Now that I have got rid of you, I can prepare my father's dish.'

'So he is sick after all?'

'Who told you he wasn't?'

'You silly girl,' Ikechi said trying to smack her cheeks.

'Please don't, your palms are so tough.'

'They are supposed to be; I am a man.'

'You are a man of foofoo. I am stronger than you.'

'Are you? Let's see.' Ikechi gripped her right hand and twisted it until she was forced to turn right round to face him again. She moaned playfully.

'Look, if you break my hands, my father will not let you go free. You will have to provide him with another child as beautiful as myself.'

'I am sure you father would readily accept me in your place.'

'How can he accept an ugly thing like you?'

'Come now, you know I am handsome; why don't you confess? All the girls say so.'

'Which girls?'

'All the village girls.'

'You don't know what you are talking about. You are the ugliest and most troublesome man I ever saw.'

'Good, now you'll have it,' he said giving her hand another twist. She screamed. Ikechi let go her hand and strained her to his chest. She struggled but failed to break free even when Ikechi was holding her loosely.

'Let me whisper something into your ears.'

'Go on.'

Ikechi caressed her ears with his lips and whispered some jargon.

'What are you saying?'

'Are you deaf? Listen.' He mumbled some more jargon.

'You are guggling like a child,' she said giggling. 'Stop it, it tickles me.'

'You are deaf if you can't understand what I say even when I put my mouth right into your ears.'

'I agree I am deaf; now leave my ears alone please.'

'Let me play with your hair then.'

'Must you have a part of my body?'

'Yes.'

'Sorry I won't let you. My hair is mine, not yours.'

'Are you sure?'

'Certainly.'

'By this time next year you'll be saying something different.'

'Why?'

'You will be my wife by then.'

'I shall not marry you.'

'Are you too ugly to be my wife?'

'You are talking to me like that, are you?' she asked simulating anger, 'I'll show you.' She grabbed Ikechi in a wrestling tackle and began to struggle with him.

'What a wrestler you are!' Ikechi said, throwing her gently on to the sleeping-mound in the sitting-room.

'All right you've thrown me, now let me go.'

'No I won't.'

'Let me go, please.'

'I won't.'

'What do you want to do?'

'Nothing.'

'Let me go.'

'No.'

The next moment Ikechi cried out with pain as Chisa's strong white teeth closed on one of his fingers.

'Now will you let me go?'

'I will, but let go of my finger.'

'Not until I am free,' she said speaking awkwardly with Ikechi's finger still in her mouth. Ikechi let her go.

'Chineke, you are wild,' he said.

'You asked for it.'

'I must go before you eat me up.'

'I didn't invite you here.'

Ikechi rose to go. As he turned his back on her, she tickled his sides. He turned round and they resumed their wrestling. Ikechi threw her down on the sleeping-mound again and pinned her down.

'You have come again,' she said.

'This time I won't let you go until you call me dede.'

'Nonsense, I can't call a rat like you dede.'

'Shut up,' he said smacking her cheeks.

'Do let me go. Father may be out any moment.'

'I say call me dede.'

'No.'

'Stay on then.'

She struggled and fought to get up but Ikechi's strong hands easily held her down.

42

'All right, what do you want?'

'I say call me dede.'

'Dede.'

'Mmm. Call me Eze.'

'Eze.'

'Mmm. Call me Okorobia.'

'Okorobia.'

'Mmm. That's better,' he said and let her go. As soon as she was on her feet again she said:

'Fancy me calling you Eze; what humiliation for me!'

'You are all mouth.'

There was a noise in Eze Diali's house; a door was opening. Chisa sprinted into the kitchen to continue her cooking. Ikechi tried to look unruffled. He couldn't quite make it. Eze Diali ambled into the room and the young man greeted him.

'Dede.'

'Mmm. Ike, how is your father?'

'He is well, dede.'

'Are you preparing for the dance today?'

'Yes.'

'You have a notch on your bow?'

'Yes,' Ikechi answered proudly.

'Chisa, is that food ready?'

'Not quite, dede,' Chisa replied from the kitchen.

'Why not? You've been a long time at it.'

'Ikechi is to blame. He has been a nuisance.'

Ikechi was taken aback. He looked furtively at the old man. A good-natured smile suffused his face.

'I dare say you encouraged him to play with you.'

'No, dede.'

'All right, hurry up.' With that the old man went back to his house.

'Your father is an excellent man,' Ikechi said when Chisa re-entered the room later.

'He is the best father in this village,' she said.

'Many fathers would have made a fuss on seeing us here alone.'

'Not my father. He trusts me and I will never let him down. He is at times fussy over his other daughters but never over me. He calls me his little mother.' Chisa's face was serious for a while as she said this. Then suddenly the seriousness was gone and the usual irresponsible smile lit her face. Ikechi studied her face for a while.

'What are you staring at me for?'

'Nothing,' the young man replied.

'Are you looking at spirits?'

'Shut up,' he said and kept gazing at her. She turned round, embarrassed in spite of herself.

'Let me hold you before I go.'

'If you are waiting for that then you won't go.'

'Come on.'

She drew back and Ikechi chased her into the back yard. He embraced her and went away.

5

THE drums were beating. The elders were sitting round Eze Diali behind the drummers. The warriors were arriving one by one dressed as if for battle. The many tassels from their Ayoiri caps hung down to cover their faces almost completely, lending them a mysterious and wicked look which frightened the women very much.

First there was a general dance in which all the warriors took part. Then came the highlights – the moment when those who had notches on their bows were to drink the Wine with the Eagle Feather. Olumba came up first. He capered round the arena once and cut a heavy branch from a bush hard by. He dug a hole in the centre of the arena and planted the branch. Then he ran to a point near the drummers and from there stalked towards the branch he had planted. When he got to it, he crouched by it as if trying to hide.

44

There was an intense concentration on his face, his eyes flashed fire. His famous fighting knife was held in readiness. The drummers were now beating softly, their eyes fixed on the lone dancer. Spectators held their breath. Suddenly Olumba sprang up and his knife flashed in a swift cutting movement. The crowd roared in admiration. The drums rent the air as Olumba strode towards the elders. Eze Diali was waiting for him. The chief had in his hand a large drinking horn with two large eagle feathers tied to it. He offered the horn to Olumba and he drained it off in one quick gulp.

One by one others who had notches on their bows came forward to demonstrate how they had slain their enemies. Ikechi came last. First he ran round the arena half a dozen times jumping and making cutting movements. Then he occupied the centre of the arena and carried out a long demonstration which thrilled the audience. He was the youngest of those entitled to the Wine with the Eagle Feathers and as he took the horn, there was a resounding applause.

After the warriors, the elders also drank from the great horn. Only one or two of them were not entitled to it. Eze Diali drank last, shaking first his right fist then his left in the air. The villagers cheered him wildly. He was reputed to have killed some twenty people in various battles.

When the moon rose later in the evening there was an Oduma dance. The young women who had been onlookers during the victory dance now made up for their past inactivity. They danced with joy and enthusiasm. Those whose husbands had drunk from the great horn danced with a little more pride and abandon than the rest. Chisa was there. She was in an inner circle of women surrounded by an outer circle of men. The inner circle moved faster. Each time she came opposite Ikechi she flashed him a smile which he acknowledged by facing her and doing a special step or two. After the dance Ikechi escorted her up to the entrance to her father's compound. They lingered there for a while.

'Your demonstration was very good,' she said.

'Of course it was,' he replied smiling.

'Nonsense, it was one of the worst,' she said.

45

'Do you know why the lips are horizontal?'

'No,' she said.

'Because people talk to the right and then to the left, particularly women.'

'That is the most silly proverb I ever heard.'

'Shut up.'

'Yes, dede.'

'Aha, you have learnt to call me dede at last.'

'Can't you distinguish flattery from sincerity?'

'I don't care which so long as you call me dede.'

'Why do you enjoy it so much?'

'Why do you feel happy when I call you Adamma?' he countered.

'Who feels happy?'

'You.'

'You are crazy.'

'Let me demonstrate. I shall call you Adamma; if you laugh or smile then I am right.'

'Go ahead,' she said.

'Adamma!'

Chisa distorted her face in an attempt to restrain her mirth. Her cheeks bulged out and she exploded at last into laughter.

'Did I not tell you so?' Ikechi said triumphantly.

'You win'.

'May the day break.'

'May it break.'

Early the next day Ikechi went to the ponds to inspect his fish-traps. Many were full of fish that raised foam as they splashed about. By noon most people had gone home. Ikechi stayed on. He had gone to the pond with many new traps and would not go without putting them in position. He toiled on struggling with the gnats and leeches in the ponds. When a wasp stung him, he decided it was time to go home. He found a place to hide his unused traps till the next day. As he was emerging from a clump of bushes he heard some rustling and low voices from the other side of the pond by which he had been working. He peered between the trees and saw several men fully armed. He could not see all of them but he guessed

46

there were over twenty. Their eyes were darting left and right apparently trying to spot anyone who might be around. Ikechi felt they were coming in his direction. If they did they would certainly see him. He thought of hiding but there was no convenient place. Besides, they would see him as soon as he tried to move. Who were they? He looked closely and saw Wago the leopard-killer among the group. His heart gave a wild thump. If the poachers of Aliakoro had the guts to come back after such a heavy defeat they must be really desperate. Ikechi knew there would be no mercy in their stomachs now. Cautiously he began to edge backwards. He remembered Olumba's comment on his stalking and smiled in spite of his danger. As he progressed his left leg sank into green mud and he lost balance. As he tried to restore his foothold the invaders espied him and made for him. Ikechi extricated his leg and fled. He was not very worried. His pursuers had a handicap of about an arrow's range and he knew that unless the gods decreed otherwise he would escape. He jogged along at an easy pace until to his dismay he heard footsteps not too far behind him. He glanced back and saw someone who looked like Wago hurtling along with incredible speed. Now Ikechi really began to run. By the time he had developed a speed to match his opponent's the latter was quite close. Should he turn round and fight? No, the others would close in on him, he thought. He ran as he had never run before and began to gain on his enemy who was getting tired now. A matchet whizzed past his right shoulder. Should he pick it up? He quickly discarded the idea and took an obscure turning to the right known only to the villagers of Chiolu. His pursuer cut across diagonally without reaching the turning. He ran into an impossible bog and stopped abruptly. Ikechi guessed what had happened when he heard no more rustling behind him and smiled. He slowed down but kept up an even pace until he was fairly close to the village.

That evening the ikoro rang out again, and Diali's reception hall filled with men. Ikechi recounted his experiences in glowing details.

'What do you think of the situation?' Diali asked when Ikechi had done.

'Fight again, of course,' Olumba replied immediately. 'That fellow Wago must be taught a lesson.'

Everybody agreed that there was nothing else to it but to fight it out.

The next morning the men of Chiolu filed towards the Great Ponds. Half-way, Ikechi with another scout met them. 'Aliakoro villagers are already at the Ponds of Wagaba fishing,' he said. 'They were there before the cock crew.' This bit of information jolted them. Olumba called Eziho, Ikechi and two other men apart and held a serious discussion with them. At the end of it the men were ordered to march on. A long way from the Great Ponds they halted. Olumba divided the men into three groups – two large ones and a smaller group. The large groups were posted on either side of the path leading to the ponds, but the groups were not directly opposite each other. Olumba led the smallest group forward. As soon as they were inside the great forest they heard what were obviously footsteps running towards the Pond of Wagaba – enemy scouts no doubt. Olumba ordered two men to scour the flanks of his advancing column to guard against an ambush. Soon they got within view of the Pond of Wagaba. The invaders were there all right fishing, talking and feeling much at ease. Olumba studied the situation for some time and knit his brow in perplexity. He did not quite understand this show of confidence on the part of their enemies. Somewhere in the pit of his stomach something gave way as a wave of vague misgivings assailed him.

As before, Olumba could see Wago moving among his men. He seemed calmer this time. He ordered those fishing or pretending to fish to stop. His men massed round him. They were evidently preparing for battle. Olumba whispered final instructions to his own men.

For some time they stood watching the enemy, who did not seem to be much in a hurry. Some of them were even cracking jokes and laughing, though rather nervously. As the pause grew longer Olumba wondered if they were waiting for him to attack. That would mean altering his plans radically – an idea he did not like. He decided to wait as long as possible. He made his men sit down to relax somewhat. The next instant they stood up fast for Wago was advancing at last with his men. They came on boldly with their bows and arrows at the ready. Their number was surprisingly large.

As soon as they were within shooting range Olumba's gang sent a volley of arrows into the advancing mass. Two men fell but the others continued to advance apparently unworried. The men of Chiolu began to draw back slowly. The invaders quickened their pace. Another volley of arrows met them and disabled three men. They returned the volley but Olumba and his few men were well covered. Wago the leopard-killer who was in front broke into a run, and his men did the same. The men of Chiolu had just enough time to send in another volley before they turned and ran. They were men specially chosen for their ability to run and the invaders could not keep up with them. Only Wago and a few other men stood up to the challenge and slowly diminished the distance between them and their retreating foes. It was a race requiring not just the ability to run fast but also the ability to avoid quagmires and other obstacles at a moment's notice. For the warriors of Chiolu it was a beaten track, not so for the Aliakoro fighters, some of whom sank almost waist-deep in sludges. Outside the Great Forests desperate sprinting began. Wago flew like the wind and was soon almost within striking distance of the slowest of the Chiolu fugitives. He was flexing his long sinewy arm to strike when Olumba shouted in a loud voice. The next instant a cloud of arrows descended on the pursuers checking their speed for a moment as fallen men blocked the way of those behind. Wago was not hit. He ran on. His matchet curved through the air bringing down with it the right arm of the man in front of him, Olumba shouted again and another volley of arrows from the other side of the path visited the pursuers. This one shook them and they halted. At a third shout from Olumba, his men in hiding emerged from the bush while those running turned round and faced their enemies. Aliakoro was overwhelmed. They fell quickly under the fast matchets of their much fresher enemies. Then suddenly a fresh wave of invaders moved into the attack. Chiolu was taken aback but recovering from the surprise fought back gallantly. Olumba fought like a maniac, foaming at the mouth not out of fatigue but out of sheer anger and an inflexible determination.

Once more Chiolu held her own. Aliakoro was being driven back gradually. Olumba urged his men on, shouting, slashing, dodging. When he thought victory was theirs another wave of attackers swept in. Now it was clear that Aliakoro had invited allies. Olumba knew it was no longer a matched battle. He raised a peculiar hoop and his men turned round and ran. They were tired but had the advantage that they were running homewards and knew all the inconspicuous forest side-tracks. Running straight on would be suicidal and so one by one they turned into side-tracks as planned. The allies were running as a body and were unwilling to scatter in such unfamiliar territory. Besides, they thought it was not much use running after one or two fugitives. They would rather pursue the mass of men ahead. But in twos and threes the fleeing men disappeared into dark obscure trails and in a short time only a few men were running along the main path. One of them was caught and mowed down. The rest ran on. Ikechi was among them. They came to a junction with three tracks and split into three groups, each group running along one track. The pursuers reached the junction and hesitated. Their leader was behind and they waited for him to come up and decide which way they should go. This pause gave the exhausted fugitives just the break they needed and they vanished so quickly that the invaders were stunned. Their leader came up at last.

'Which way have they gone?' he asked panting heavily.

'All ways,' one man replied waving his arms in a semicircle.

Their leader studied the three narrow tracks in turn. There was nobody along any of them. There were not even bushes shaking to indicate men running or in hiding. The leader shook his head and called off the chase.

'It is no use,' he said, 'we don't know the lie of the land here.'

The men sat by the path panting. When they had regained their breath they turned back and joined Wago who was nursing a deep cut on his shoulder – Olumba had missed him again. Elendu the leader of the allies sat on a tree-stump and faced Wago the leopard-killer.

'What are we going to do now?' he asked.

'Go back,' Wago replied without looking up.

'And what will be our reward since we have neither prisoners nor booty?'

'That will be decided at Aliakoro.'

'And if we don't accept your offers?'

'A compromise can always be arrived at.'

'Look, Wago, you have messed up this battle with your bad planning. You are a good fighter all right but you have no idea of organization. With better handling we should have captured many prisoners whose ransom would have brought us much money.'

'Well it is not my fault if you killed all the enemies who came your way,' Wago retorted calmly.

'It is your fault. You are a real bungler. Think of Olumba's battle plans and you will realize you are nowhere. He planned this fight to the last detail taking into account every possibility. The result is that we have suffered more than thrice their casualties. Many of my best fighters are dead or seriously wounded.'

'And why didn't you help with the planning? It is easy to criticize you know.'

'But you wouldn't let me put in a word.'

'That is not true. You did not put forward any suggestion worth considering.'

'Do you think I was made the leader of Isiali warriors for nothing?'

'Well, when a man has no drum, he is obliged to beat on his chest,' Wago replied. Elendu bit his lips in suppressed anger.

'All right instead of bandying words like women let's test ourselves for stamina and staying power. Let us pursue those people right to their doors and continue the fighting. Many of their fighters are hiding in the bush now and we should be able to carry off many women and children from the village.'

'You had a chance of capturing prisoners when you chased those men up this path a short while ago. But you and your men ran like ducks and let the fellows escape. Now you are talking of capturing women and children.'

'I agree you ran like the wind but what good did it do you? You allowed yourself to be led by a handful of men into a deadly ambush and spoilt what could have been a splendid victory.'

'You could not have done better. After all you were behind waiting to come up only when the enemy were overpowered. You are angry because your cowardly plans did not work out exactly.'

'Who is a coward?' Elendu thundered.

'You,' Wago said still nursing the wound on his shoulder.

'How many men did you kill?'

'I don't count.'

'There were none to be counted.'

'I am Wago the leopard-killer!'

'You are a goat.'

'Shut up!' Wago said raising his voice for the first time.

'And if not?' Elendu rose and advanced a step. Wago leaped up, bared his matchet and faced him. The men who had been watching them moved in quickly to intervene. One of them said: 'Chiolu will feel happy if they see us quarrelling here. This is a disgrace. What is past is past. Let us come together and decide on what to do now.'

The two leaders sat down after much persuasion. Elendu said: 'I still suggest we go to Chiolu and finish off the fight. I am not satisfied with what has happened so far. I have lost many men and yet I haven't got a single prisoner. It is absurd. What will I tell the chief when I get back?'

There was no reply to this outburst. The warriors seemed to be considering this suggestion. At last someone said: 'It is not a bad idea but I think the raid should be carried out at night.'

Many supported this idea as they thought of the possibility of carrying off comely maidens under cover of darkness.

'I endorse your plan,' Wago said, 'but I cannot take part in it because of my wounds. My assistant and some other men from Aliakoro will go with you. They know the village very well and will direct you.' Having said this Wago limped homewards with some other injured men.

Elendu held a long discussion with the remaining men. One major problem was food. The shadows were long and they were very hungry.

'What shall we do for food?' someone asked.

'I have thought of that,' Elendu said. 'Yams have been harvested and stacked in barns in the farms. If there are farms along the path to Chiolu then we should be well provided.'

'What about fire?' someone asked. Elendu was baffled for a moment, then his face lit up. 'Let two men go to the bank of the Pond of Wagaba and see if there are any live faggots there. We had some orepe logs and they should be glowing still.'

Two men were dispatched and while they stumbled along the narrow track to the Great Ponds the rest of the men sprawled on the ground for the much needed rest.

Twilight found the men in a farm. There was no need to look for the barn. It stood out prominently in the middle of the farm. The men made several fires and fell on the yams, choosing the prize-winners among them. Some men roasted more than they could eat, leaving the remains scattered on the ground. Some went as far as cutting up raw yams out of spite. Elendu scolded them sternly.

'We are warriors,' he said, 'but we are also responsible men. Let us not destroy things merely for the love of doing so. The people of Chiolu are our clansmen and we must respect that link. Moreover, you know as well as I do that every farm has a god – Ajokuji. If we offend him we shall be fighting tonight not only against men but against angry gods, a situation I do not like to be in.'

The men understood and felt ashamed. A few picked up some discarded yams and put them back on the racks.

As soon as it grew dark the men began to march towards Chiolu. When they were close to the village they stopped and hid in a thick clump of trees. The moon rose but it merely emphasized the shadows of the trees under which the men were hiding.

'We must wait until the moon has set,' Elendu said. 'It is only a few days old and should not take too long to set.'

'Listen to the plan. We shall not attack the whole village; we are too few and too weak for that. We shall select a few compounds and carry off one or two women from each compound. If we capture seven women, it is a good job. Their men are tired and should be sleeping heavily. If you work fast and to plan you will not get into much trouble. With the help of men who know the village well, I have selected seven compounds, Olumba's and Diali's included.'

'Eze Diali has many daughters,' a man commented, chuckling.

'Keep quiet,' Elendu snapped and went on to give more details of the night attack.

Like many other men Olumba reached home by dusk. He was very tired. He would not have felt so tired if they had won. When he thought of his men scattered far and wide in the woods he felt very bitter. All the same it was the only thing he could have done. He hoped the plan had saved the men from complete extermination.

The fact that Olumba had sneaked in from the bush behind his compound told his wives that the village had lost the battle. Nevertheless they were relieved when he came back unhurt. The many scratches and bruises on his body were nothing compared to the loss of a limb or a deep knife-cut. His junior wife, Oda, prepared him a hot bath putting into it the roots and leaves Olumba had gathered before he set out to do battle. After his bath Oda massaged his body thoroughly with palm-kernel oil mixed with a certain balm Olumba had given her. At the end of the process the warrior went into his medicine-hut and closed the door.

When he emerged, the moon was shining outside. He had a quick meal and began a tour of the village. He visited Ikechi's compound first. The young man was back. An arrow had pierced his right ear lobe; otherwise he was unhurt.

'Do you know what to do now?' Olumba asked the young man.

'No,' Ikechi said.

54

'Make a hole in the other ear and wear ear-rings.' Ikechi and his parents laughed.

Olumba checked on Eziho; he was not back yet. He did his best to buoy up the hopes of his family. He assured them that he had seen him running with the rest during the retreat. He was a good runner and should make it. Olumba toured as many compounds as he could and went back to his compound. He would do the rest in the morning. He went straight to his bedroom, locked his door and slept.

After the birth of his son, Olumba had arranged for Oda and her baby to sleep in the spare bedroom in his house. Oda rarely slept in her own house. Tonight Olumba was so tired that without thinking he locked his door as soon as he entered his house, and went off to sleep. His wife seeing the door locked decided not to disturb him. She retired to her own house and locked the one-piece door. She laid her sleeping child on a low sleeping-mound in the room. She was a few months' pregnant and did not want to share the same bed with her son who was a restless sleeper. He would shoot his arms and legs this way and that at night causing her much discomfort.

Having made the child comfortable she went over to her sleeping-mound and lay down.

Presently she found herself awake. She did not know why she woke so suddenly but she had a feeling that a noise had roused her. Then Olumba's dog began to bark in the reception hall. But that was its habit. It had probably seen a cat or something. The woman fell again into a light sleep.

Soon a loud bang woke her and she sat upright on her bed to face a wide gap where the door had been. The next moment two figures entered her room and before she could shout a rag was stuffed into her mouth and her hands held behind her. The men carried her outside and off, making as little noise as possible. When they reached the main village path they set her down and ordered her to walk along. She tried to struggle but a smart smack on her buttocks soon convinced her that the men were not to be trifled with. What was worse she could not cry out. She walked along with the men until they passed the outskirts of the village. There she saw three other women in similar conditions. The men walked them off at a quick pace and soon the village was left behind.

Some time later Elendu heard the steps of people running towards them from behind. He ordered his men to take cover and they vanished into the bush – women and all. But there was no cause for alarm; they were the remnants of Elendu's gang. They had failed to make catches and had aroused suspicion by their clumsiness. After their arrival it did not take long before they heard the distant sound of the ikoro. They ran now, dragging the women with them.

When they arrived at the junction leading to Isiali, Elendu stopped and said:

'Men of Aliakoro, we shall part here for the night. Tomorrow we shall come down for further negotiations. Also we shall keep the four women we have.'

The warriors of Aliakoro protested but they were heavily out-numbered and had to give way.

'You are a double-faced dealer,' an Aliakoro leader said.

Elendu laughed and said: 'You don't expect us to go empty-handed after shedding our blood on behalf of poor fighters like you. Indeed we shall come to Aliakoro for further talks; these women are not enough compensation for our losses.'

The Isiali fighters plunged into the trail leading to their village and the darkness swallowed them. Wretchedly the Aliakoro men sought the path leading to their homes.

They had not gone far when they heard footsteps behind them. 'We are being pursued,' someone whispered. 'Hush, don't talk,' another admonished. The pursuers paused at the junction, listened and then plunged into the track leading to Aliakoro. The fugitives broke into a run as panic seized them. Someone was hit by an arrow and fell across the path. The rest raced on. 'Dash into the bush,' their leader shouted, and they scampered into the dark protective womb of the woods. It was dark and the pursuers could do nothing. They had come because they could not bear to wait till morning. They picked up the injured man who had an arrow gracing his neck. Luckily for him the arrow had not gone too deep. It was pulled out and he was dragged away. They all moved back a little way and entered the woods.

'Now tell us where the women are.' Olumba said. The prisoner murmured something incomprehensible and saw stars as Olumba's palm exploded on his left cheek.

'They are with the Isiali men,' the man managed to say when he had recovered somewhat from the effects of the blow.

'And where are the Isiali men?'

'They have gone to their village.'

Olumba ground his teeth. If only they had taken the other path, he thought. It was too late now. Moreoever, he was not familiar with the path to Isiali. He would get lost in the network of trails and tracks.

Olumba and his men decided to pass the night where they were. Two men were on guard at a time. One of them stood by the path; the other was deeper in the woods. At dawn Olumba's gang searched everywhere for the marauders. There was no trace of them except a few drops of blood on the grass by the wayside.

6 THE next day dawned on a miserable Chiolu. Several men had been killed in the last battle, many more injured. Four women, all of them with children to look after had been kidnapped. It was a gloomy situation.

When Olumba reached his compound that morning he stood by Oda's house and gazed for a long time at the gap that gaped at him where the door had been. He gnashed his teeth and moved over to his senior wife's house. His only son was there looking bewildered. When the child called on his mother Olumba strode out of the house in anguish. His two remaining wives knew how he felt. They went into his bedroom where he sat speechless and sat with him. They did not ask him questions. They knew he would explain the situation to them afterwards if he thought it necessary. At last Olumba looked up and addressed his senior wife:

'Nyoma you are now my son's mother. Look after him. You may all leave me now.' The women retired, Nyoma carrying the little boy. Olumba spent some time in his medicine-hut. As soon as he came out he walked over to Diali's. The chief was warming himself by a fire in his reception hall. Several of his wives and children sat round him. The women tried to comfort him, the children merely gazed at him as if he was a new father.

Olumba and the old man exchanged greetings.

'How was it last night?' Diali asked looking into the fire.

'We could not find the women. The man we captured revealed that the women had been carried off by Isiali warriors who were their allies in yesterday's battle.'

'Isiali is a long way from here.'

'It is, my lord,' Olumba replied studying the old man's face. 'Was anyone kidnapped from your compound?'

'Chisa is gone,' Diali said eyeing the prisoner in his reception hall. Immediately Olumba thought of Ikechi and wondered whether he was aware of this.

'I suppose we will sound the ikoro and decide on what to do,' Olumba said. The chief nodded without saying anything. Olumba left him and moved over to Njola's compound.

'Where is Ikechi?' Olumba asked.

'He is sleeping in his room,' Njola replied.

'Does he know that Chisa is among the kidnapped?'

'He does.'

'Then he can't be sleeping.'

'Maybe you're right,' Njola said.

Olumba burst into Ikechi's room and found him lying on his bed but wide awake. His eyes were red for lack of sleep. He greeted Olumba but did not move. He lay still studying the roof. The change in the boisterous rascally young man was dramatic. His face showed the temporary wrinkles of a youth in trouble. Olumba was touched, but he did not show his feelings.

'Get up young man and let's plan what to do. This is no time for brooding over sorrows. Oda, the mother of my only son, was kid-napped too. She is pregnant as well.'

Ikechi jumped out of his bed and stared at Olumba. 'Was she?' he asked in unbelief.

'She was,' Olumba said calmly.

'What shall we do?'

'I suppose we have to negotiate,' Olumba said.

'Where?'

'At Aliakoro.'

'Why not here? We have one of their men.'

'The fellow with the foofoo usually moves over to the man with the soup, never the other way round. Our women are not to be balanced against his half-dead prisoner we have here.'

Ikechi knit his brow as he tried to think. 'Are the women at Isiali or Aliakoro?' he asked.

'How many legs has a millipede?' Olumba retorted laughing.

Ikechi smiled for the first time that morning. 'I agree it is difficult to tell,' he said.

They were still chatting when the ikoro sounded. As many men as were able to move assembled in Diali's reception hall. After a brief discussion it was decided that envoys should be sent to Aliakoro to fix a date for negotiations.

Three days after, representatives of Chiolu were in Eze Okehi's reception hall trying to come to terms with their opponents. Some sheds had been put up by the hall to accommodate more people.

Eze Okehi sat at one end of his hall surrounded by his elders. It was a reversal of the situation in Chiolu's arena and Okehi felt elated. But his countenance was loaded with care – he could not help thinking of his many men killed in a struggle he had started and encouraged. But he could not alter circumstances now; he must pursue his plans to the end. No good thing was easy to get, he kept saying to himself.

Diali was not present at the talks. His joint pains would not let him come. Chituru the elder next to him in rank represented him. After kola with pepper had been presented, Chituru got up to speak.

'Men of Chiolu who use fish for firewood, Terrors of the Forests,

Hunters with Invisible Footprints, Greater sons of Great Fathers, I greet you!' Chiolu shouted lustily. 'Men of Aliakoro, Growers of Big Yams, Leopard-killers, Eyes of the Night, Eight-headed Warriors, I greet you!' The response shook the reception hall.

'Eze Okehi,' Chituru went on, 'we have come to take our women who were snatched away from us last night. Isn't it true that we don't do violence to women with children? This is a strange situation.'

Okehi cleared his throat and replied:

'Chituru, I shall not waste your time; you have a long way to travel. Your village has established a precedence for this type of thing. We are going to copy from you. What a man does not know he learns from neighbours. You will pay four times four hundred manillas for each woman.'

'Eze Okehi, I understand how you feel. He who does not know his next-door neighbour must be blind. However, I must remind you that one of your men is our prisoner; what applies to our women is bound to apply to him.'

'I am aware of this. Indeed I am anxious to have him back so that we can treat him. No amount of fish is worth a man's life.'

'If only you had reasoned this way before, you would not have urged your men on to this bloody battle over a pond that clearly does not belong to you. Unfortunately one is wise only after an event.'

'Stop!' Eze Okehi almost shouted, getting up. 'If you are here to argue that this pond belongs to Chiolu, you might as well get back. The gods will restore the pond to the rightful owners in due course. He who wrestles with a gorilla invariably finds his back dusty.'

'Let us stop wrangling, Eze Okehi. We shall pay you exactly what you paid for your two prisoners a few days ago. We know you will not accept anything less. On the other hand insisting on anything more will be like striking with an axe someone who has only scratched you with his nails.'

Eze Okehi sat down. 'I am happy you admit you have scratched us. But there is no need to waste your time. The ransom is fixed at four times four hundred per head.'

'Accept twice four hundred,' Chituru said. Wago the leopard-killer stepped forward. 'My lord,' he said to Okehi, 'if they are not prepared to pay let them get back. It would be sheer folly on our part to accept anything less. A few days ago they were swearing and foaming at the mouth in their arena, now they have the face to haggle.'

Olumba stood up. 'My lord,' he said addressing Chituru, 'I am beginning to think that we should be fools to pay anything at all. These women were not captured in any battle. They were stolen from us by night long after the battle was over. They were stolen by men who were unable to capture any prisoners in spite of numerous allies. Let us therefore demand our women back as of right. If they refuse we shall go home, retire into our shells like the tortoise and think of what to do.'

'Retire then and forfeit your women,' Wago thundered.

Everyone started talking and what was an orderly negotiation broke into chaos with several hot spots of bitter verbal wrangling. Okehi shouted to restore order but the din drowned his voice. He was forced to send for his igele at whose metallic sound order was restored. Chituru said:

'I shall confer with my men for a short while.'

'I shall do the same,' Okehi said.

The men of Chiolu moved apart and held a spirited conference. Aliakoro took their seats before them. Eventually Chiolu came back.

'Eze Okehi,' Chituru opened up, 'we have decided not to pay any ransom because these women were stolen and not captured in war. If you will hand them over to us we shall leave now. If you don't we shall leave all the same.'

The men of Aliakoro were taken aback. They had not expected this stand. Okehi conferred with his men in whispers, then he said:

'The mind is like a bag, only the owner knows its contents all the time. If you want to leave your women behind, that is your affair. Nobody attends the waking ceremony of a suicide. However, we want our man back and we are willing to exchange one woman for him.'

Chituru had no immediate reply. He conferred with his elders

C

outside for quite a long time. Although Olumba was not an elder he stood with them. From the way he was shaking his head and gesticulating it was clear that he was holding up the conference. At last they trooped in again. Olumba got up to speak.

'Chituru, my lord, please let me give them our views. Listen, men of Aliakoro. There is no place in the world where one man is equated to one woman. Our village maintains that one man is equal to four women or more. If you want your man, you must let us have our four women back in exchange.'

'Never!' Wago the leopard-killer shouted.

'Are you equal to your wife?' Olumba asked. Wago was stumped for a moment, then he said:

'Your women have children. The lives of those children depend largely on their mothers, so you can see why in this situation one woman is as important as one man.'

It was a strong argument and everyone saw the point. The Chiolu camp accepted the proposal.

'If you are ready,' Chituru said, 'we shall produce your man.'

'It will have to be tomorrow,' Wago replied, 'we are not ready for the exchange now.'

Olumba suddenly burst out laughing to everybody's surprise.

'Chituru, my lord, we have been wasting our time. I forgot that our women are at Isiali whose warriors did all the kidnapping. Aliakoro could not get even a woman for all their troubles.'

'That is a lie. The women are here,' Wago lied hotly.

'Produce them.'

'Produce our man.'

'Your man is somewhere up the road we have come. If you are ready we shall produce him in a moment.' Wago was about to speak when Okehi cut in. 'We have given you our answer. Come tomorrow for one of your women. When you are able to collect enough money we shall hand the rest over to you. We know why you have refused to pay. You are hoping to kidnap our women in revenge. I assure you we shall take all precautions to see that you don't. We are not as careless with our womenfolk as you are.'

'Any exchange should be carried out at the boundary between our two villages,' Chituru observed.

'That is the tradition,' Okehi agreed.

The conference broke up and Chituru led his men home. The next day some warriors led the prisoner to the boundary and waited till dusk, but Aliakoro did not turn up. They tried the next day with no results and gave up.

Diali discussed the situation with the elders. He said: 'Either the women are at Isiali, or our enemies have deliberately refused to fulfil their promise.'

'They are at Isiali,' Chituru said, 'and I shall not be surprised if Isiali warriors refuse to give them up. Everyone of those women is beautiful.'

Olumba and other warriors were called in. The possibility of kidnapping Aliakoro's women was discussed. They agreed it would be futile to make such an attempt as the women would be too well guarded.

Olumba said: 'Immediate reprisals will be neither effective nor wise. Let us go back home and think for a day or two and then meet again. I want whatever we do to be thoroughly planned so that Aliakoro will feel it to the bones.'

'How about the ponds?' Ikechi asked.

'Are we going to let them fish there unhindered?'

'Do you think they will try to do any fishing just now?' Chituru said.

'It is quite possible with Wago there,' Olumba said.

'They know that when once they can fish unhindered now it will be difficult for us to oppose them later. We must fight on until they give up.'

Diali turned to the young men, 'What do you say?' he asked them. 'You have fought very well so far and it is up to you to decide whether to carry on or give up. In our days we the elders fought to pass on the heritage of the Great Ponds to you. Now it is your turn to defend this heritage. What do you say?'

7 FOUR days after the last meeting with Chiolu, Eze Okehi sat in his reception hall resting. It was past midday and most of the women had gone to the farm under the heavy escort of their menfolk. Some men, posted at strategic points, guarded the village.

Groups of children played at shooting, hide-and-seek, and intricate games forged in the sand. They roamed from one compound to the other seeking new interests. Sometimes in the middle of a game someone would mention a tree with low, well-formed branches begging to be climbed. They would forget the game in hand and rush to the tree with mad enthusiasm as if seeing it for the first time. While there, someone might mention Azoka, Okehi's old dog. They would desert the tree and rush to Okehi's spacious compound to tease the old dog and coax it into pursuing them.

Okehi watched them trooping into his compound. His dog was not around so he guessed they were making for the fruit tree behind his compound. They greeted him one by one as they trooped past, some carrying their toddling brothers and sisters on their backs. Okehi's children were among them. One of them broke away from the rest and joined his father in the reception hall. It seemed he had had enough judging from the tear stains that lined his face. He sat down in one corner of the reception hall and proceeded to undo a small parcel of cocoyam leaves. Okehi wondered what was in it. It turned out to be a collection of green and yellow grasshoppers disabled in one way or the other so that they could not fly off. The youngster played with them intercepting them as they made a bid for freedom.

Tired at last the boy looked out of the reception hall for new adventures. He saw several birds, the kinds that usually herald the dry season, hopping about in the compound picking up insects and seeds. He picked some stones and threw them at the birds. Many flew off only to touch down again soon afterwards. He noticed however that two particular birds did not attempt to fly off. He hurled stones at them again and again. They did not budge. He became fascinated and tiptoed towards them. His father watched him absent-mindedly.

As he drew nearer and nearer he became more puzzled and excited as the birds did not fly off. They merely hopped about as if unaware of the boy's approach. When he was near enough he sprang forward and caught one of them. The other moved off a pace or two. The boy went after it and got it too. Then he ran to his father, shouting and waving the two birds in the air.

Eze Okehi was amazed.

'Did you hit them with stones?' he asked.

'No, dede.'

'Are they hurt in any way?'

'No, Father.'

'Bring them here.' Okehi examined the birds. They were strong and healthy. They chirped away as if holding an interesting conversation with each other. Okehi's brow grew dark with doubt and fear. This was a terrible omen.

'Let them go,' he told the boy. The little boy hesitated, puzzled over his father's attitude.

'Let them go,' the command came again. The boy threw them into the air. The birds flew off and disappeared behind the compound chirping plaintively. Greatly worried Okehi sought the seclusion of his bedroom. He pondered over the matter. Even the tamest of birds would never be caught by a little boy. If the birds had been injured, that would have been a different matter. But they were strong and healthy and had flown off on being released. The more he thought about the incident the more afraid he grew.

By evening Okehi sought the advice of Igwu the dibia and his drums. Unlike many other dibias Igwu had no divination cowries. Instead he had a pair of small quaint mystic drums by whose help he divined things which baffled many a dibia. Indeed in the field of divination and concomitant sacrifices Igwu was outstanding. But he was rather poor with herbs and roots. He confessed that he was too busy seeing spirits to focus much attention on the field work which the knowledge of roots and herbs entailed.

Okehi paid two manillas and the drums – male and female – rang out. The beating sounded random and senseless to anyone unused to them. Patient listening revealed a queer rhythm very much unlike what one heard in say an Oduma dance. Igwu belaboured his drums until perspiration studded his brow and his eyes shone.

'Two birds!' he blurted out at last as if someone was speaking through him.

Okehi's face was all surprise. He was used to Igwu's proverbial accuracy in divination yet every instance of it surprised and impressed him.

'You have come to see me about two birds,' Igwu said again giving the drums a rest for a moment.

'Yes, dibia.'

'Your child caught them while playing.'

'Quite right.'

'Without bows and arrows.'

'Yes.'

'Without a knife.'

'Yes.'

'Without even a stone.'

'Yes, dibia.'

Each pronouncement was preceded by frantic bangs on the drum.

'Ali is angry, very angry.'

'Why?'

'Those women you kidnapped from Chiolu must be returned. One of them is pregnant and the god of the earth as you know does not tolerate violence against any woman with child.'

'Isiali did the actual kidnapping,' Okehi said.

'Yes,' came the reply, 'but you invited them to do so.'

'What is to be done now?'

Drumming filled the air once again as Igwu communicated with the gods.

'There are two things to be done. Firstly you will have to perform a sacrifice to placate Ali the god of the earth. Secondly you will have to return the women.'

'All the women?'

'The pregnant one at least.'

'Without a ransom?'

'With or without, it doesn't matter provided the woman gets back to her people.'

The next day Okehi performed the sacrifice and dispatched men to Isiali to fetch the captured women. Isiali refused to give them up. They demanded heavy sums of money. Okehi was in a difficult situation. Igwu the dibia had warned him that the sacrifices were merely an interim measure to persuade Ali to stay action while the women were being restored. A long delay could spell disaster.

Eze Okehi called a meeting of the elders and gave them details of Igwu's divination. They saw the urgency of the situation and collected money quickly.

The next day Wago and six other men travelled to Isiali. The allies received the money but produced only two women. Worse still Oda, Olumba's pregnant wife, was one of the two missing ones. Chisa, Diali's daughter was the other. Wago was angry.

'Are you so untrustworthy?' he fumed. 'How can we pay the price of four women for two?'

'Do you know how many men we lost in that stupid fight?' Elendu asked with some bitterness. 'You are lucky we did not ask for more money.'

There was nothing to be gained by getting angry; that much was clear. There was no question of fighting; Isiali was one of the most thickly populated villages around, boasting of maybe twice the number of fighting men in Aliakoro.

'Where are the other two women, anyway?' Wago asked after cooling down somewhat.

'They have been sold off,' Elendu replied simply.

'To where?'

'How can I tell? Some men came and said they wanted female slaves. We sold off the two women. They were the most beautiful of the four and fetched much money.'

Wago slumped back in his chair with disappointment and a vague fear. What was to be done? He took the two available women home to Okehi who was stunned at the turn of events.

Igwu the dibia was consulted again. Another sacrifice was to be performed to plead with Ali to extend his patience while they set about finding the woman with child. Meanwhile the priests of Ali the god of the earth and of Amadioha the god of thunder and of the skies were sent as envoys to Chiolu to fix a date for the exchange of prisoners. Only priests could play the role of envoys in such circumstances since none would dare capture or kill them.

The two men sat in Eze Diali's reception hall gnawing at their bits of kola. They looked venerable, the mysterious and far-away look in their eyes making onlookers feel they were not quite of this world. They were completely surrounded by Chiolu men but they felt as much at home as in the protective shrines of their gods

When kola had gone round, palm wine was dispensed by a middle-aged man who knew the order of seniority perfectly well. When the priests were handed their cups of wine they poured them away as libations. They had to be offered a second round of drinks.

'Amadioha of the Skies will bless our talks,' one priest said.

'And Ali the earth-god will prevent further quarrels,' the second priest put it. Many people devoutly echoed their wishes.

'Aliakoro suggests four days hence for the exchange of prisoners,' the priest of Amadioha said.

'That should suit us,' Diali replied.

'No it won't,' a voice said in a drunken drawl. People looked round. It was Ikechi. He had a cup of wine in one hand and some kola in the other. He winked at the priests, drained off his cup in a rapid gulp and thrust it forward to be refilled. The priests eyed him with some amusement.

'Eze Diali, since our proposals suit you, there is nothing more to be said. He who does not stop speaking when he should may bite his tongue,' the priest of Amadioha concluded.

'Why should you bite your tongue? Ha-ha! your tongue must be too long for your mouth,' Ikechi drawled again. A few young men laughed but Diali and the elders were aghast.

'What frivolity is this?' Diali asked sternly.

'If you are drunk get away and sleep it off. Whoever heard of a young rat like you disrupting a conference of elders.'

'I am very sorry, my lord,' the young man said laughing stupidly. 'Maybe I am drunk but I speak the truth.' Other young men tried to

68

hush him but succeeded only partially. He still managed to punctuate the talks with silly remarks. The elders were very angry. His father, Njola, all but slapped him.

When the talks ended his father held him and tried to drag him home. Gently but firmly he disengaged himself and ran after the departing priests, drinking as he went.

'Do you want to go to Aliakoro with us young man?' the priest of Ali asked.

'I could,' he replied.

'It would not be wise.'

'Why not, I am strong enough to beat anybody.'

The priest of Ali fell silent wondering whether it was worth while speaking to the young drunk.

'You Aliakoro men will have a hard time,' Ikechi said.

'You are not finding things easy either, particularly now that you have to pay heavy ransoms,' the priest replied.

'Who will pay heavy ransoms?' Ikechi asked draining off the dregs in his cup.

'You.'

'Look here, if the ransom is too heavy we shall fight for it. Ha-ha, Chiolu is tough. We shall come to the talks fully armed.'

The two priests exchanged glances. Here was something interesting. They goaded him into saying more.

'You are merely drunk. I am sure Chiolu will not attempt to fight.'

'I tell you we have already decided to do so because we know you will quote impossible amounts as ransom.'

'I am sure your elders will not support any fighting. They are wise and can easily predict the result of such a fight.'

'I tell you, they themselves took the decision,' the drunkard said lurching forward in an attempt to keep up with the priests. But the latter felt they had heard enough and quickened their pace.

'Friends wait for me,' the young man shouted. He stumbled and fell flat on his face. The priests glanced back, and walked away. As soon as the priests had disappeared in a bend, Ikechi got up and ran to Eze Diali's compound. The chief was still very angry with him; Ikechi could see the scowl on his face. Olumba had requested the elders and a few young men to wait in Diali's reception hall. As soon as Ikechi came in they began a serious discussion in very low tones.

Four days later, representatives of the two villages met at their common boundary. All the Aliakoro warriors came fully armed. In striking contrast, representatives of Chiolu were few. Wago the leopard-killer was surprised when he observed that Olumba was not among them. He must be thinking very much of his lost wife, Wago thought. Or was he hiding somewhere with some men in ambush? Yes, that must be it. Wago's eyes lit up with excitement as this thought crossed his mind. He must do something now to ward off any surprise attacks; he had had enough of them. So while the elders were trying to negotiate he was busy giving his men instructions. He ordered scouts to scour the surrounding forests in an attempt to locate Olumba and his gang. He warned the remaining men to be on the alert and darted nervously from one group of men to the other.

The old men of Chiolu were taking things easy. They sat quietly on well-worn logs which had seen many such negotiations and waited for their opponents to settle down. Diali opened the talks after the usual greetings. As they were in a no-man's-land, there was no kola.

'We have stood here in vain many a time,' Diali said. 'It is good that you are here at last.'

Okehi said: 'Things cannot always go as planned. Even a drum can sound differently from what the maker intended.'

'I understand,' Diali replied smiling. 'There were too many factors beyond your control. No doubt you have done your best though we may not realize it. A goat may sweat but its fur always hides the fact.'

Eze Okehi was piqued but he bore it as best he could.

'We have brought two women along,' he said. 'The other two will be available in due course. If you can bring your prisoner forward we will proceed with the exchange.' Some warriors from both sides moved back along the path they had come to fetch their prisoners. As drums from both sides sounded the man and the woman were exchanged.

'There is one woman left,' Okehi said. 'Do you want to pay her ransom now or later?'

'What is the ransom?' Diali asked rather languidly.

'Four times four hundred manillas.'

'Take three hundred manillas.'

'It looks as if you are not prepared to pay. If you have no money we shall take her back.'

'And if we refuse?'

Eze Okehi glanced back at the many armed men behind him and smiled.

'No one attends the waking ceremony of a suicide,'

'You are right my friend Okehi,' Diali replied smiling good-naturedly. 'I was joking of course. It is a bad thing to fight during negotiations.'

Diali's evident good humour softened Okehi's aggressiveness. He relaxed somewhat.

'Take four hundred manillas.'

'There can be no haggling, you know that very well.'

'Take six hundred.'

'No,' Okehi said shaking his head in emphasis.

'If we pay too much your men may fall by the wayside under the weight of the money.'

Okehi smiled and replied: 'If you could bring the money down here, surely we can do the more satisfying job of carrying it away.'

'You know we had to bring the money here in several trips,' Diali said laughing heartily. The men by him joined in the laughter. Okehi and his elders could not resist either. They laughed loud and long at the joke. Indeed all tension seemed to have been broken. Okehi was pleasantly surprised at this show of warm friendliness. He was almost minded to reduce the ransom, but he knew Wago the leopard-killer would oppose any such concessions vehemently.

Wago who was in the background watched Diali's face and movements intently. He was not deceived by his easy-going approach to the talks. He was sure Chiolu had something up their sleeves. Where was Olumba? Where were the warriors of Chiolu? Only a fool would fail to sense a trap, but what was the trap? So while the elders

71

in front relaxed, Wago and the warriors behind grew more tense expecting Olumba and his gang any moment.

Wago was quite surprised when in the end Diali and his representatives paid four times four hundred manillas as ransom for the other woman. Drums sounded and both villages turned round to go.

Two scouts emerged from the bush to report their findings.

'Seen him yet?' Wago asked anxiously.

'No sign of anybody anywhere,' they said.

'Are you quite sure?'

'The others will confirm our statements when they are here.' A little later the other scouts came to report the same thing – Olumba and his men were not around. They were probably too ashamed to come to the talks. This was a reasonable assumption particularly as Olumba's wife was among the kidnapped.

'But Olumba ought to have come to see his wife ransomed, surely,' Okehi said as they walked home.

'Perhaps he knew his wife would not be brought,' Wago replied.

'Who told him?'

'I can't say, but it is not too difficult to find out a thing like that. He might have gone to Isiali to check on her. Chiolu is not at war with Isiali really.'

'Quite true. Still, Olumbu's non-appearance worries me. He is not only strong but also very crafty.'

Wago replied: 'It is clear that Olumba is mourning his wife's loss. I gather he loves her best of his three wives.' Okehi did not reply. He seemed lost in thought as they walked along the winding forest track. When they got to a small stream, Wago sent a few scouts ahead to check on possible ambushes. It was not necessary. The path was as safe as their bedrooms. They crossed the stream and Wago relaxed. They were now close to their village where no enemy would dare attack them.

Before the last bend to the village a warrior – one of the few left to defend the village came running towards them.

'Have you seen Okasi?' he asked panting.

'Seen whom?' Wago asked in return.

'Okasi.'

72

'Where is he?'

'We sent him to you.'

'What for?'

'To ask for help. Fighters from Chiolu invaded the village after you had left,' the man said.

By now he was surrounded by men staring at him incredulously. As soon as his halting speech explained the situation Wago and his men raced to the village. It was a deserted village. Women and children were nowhere to be seen. Some boys in their early teens and a few old men who still had some energy left stalked about the compounds carrying rusty blunt matchets obviously too heavy for them.

'Where are the women and children?' Wago almost howled.

'Locked up in their houses,' one old man explained. 'A few are hiding in the bush.'

Okehi came up. He was speechless with sorrow but not with surprise, for the possibility of this manoeuvre had occurred to him on the homeward journey. He had not mentioned it for fear of raising a false alarm. As Wago ran this way and that Okehi found his voice at last and said:

'Go to your compounds, find out how many people are missing and reassemble in my reception hall quickly.'

The men could hardly wait to hear him out. With thumping hearts they ran to their compounds calling on their wives and children. The whole village was in a terrible state of nerves, comparable to the confusion created when a herd of hungry elephants had tramped through the village some three years back.

Those whose families were intact were the first to reassemble. The less fortunate few hung around their houses calling on their missing wives and daughters. They turned over every stone, every log of wood. They looked behind doors. They looked into crevices too small even for rats to hide in. Okehi was among the first to make a nerve-racking discovery – his last but one wife was gone. His children told him vividly how a group of men had broken into the backyard where she was cooking, fed some rags into her mouth and carried her off before the other women could come round.

It was a miserable crowd that gathered in Okehi's reception hall. Eleven women were reported missing at first. Soon reports came in that some of the women had emerged from their hiding-places. Only three could not be traced. Okehi's wife and Wago's twelve-year-old daughter were among the three.

The man who gave them the first news of the disaster was called in.

'When did you say these men came?' Okehi asked him.

'When you were at the boundary or maybe a little before you got there,' the man said. Wago bit his first finger when he realized it was far too late to go after the invaders.

'No need, Wago,' Okehi said reading his thoughts. 'It is too late.'

'Why did you not come to tell us immediately they attacked?' Wago demanded fiercely.

'We sent Okasi to tell you. It is surprising you didn't see him.'

'You ought to have sent two men.'

'There were very few fighting men and we were busy trying to protect the women and children who were running helter-skelter screaming and crying. It was a terrible situation, difficult to imagine.'

'I am sure you did not send anyone to alert us,' Wago insisted.

'Let us not argue,' Okehi said quietly, 'this is not the moment for it. Tell us exactly what happened.' The unhappy man cleared his throat and began:

'When you left, I posted the men at look-out points and ordered them to sound the alarm if anything unusual occurred. I myself occupied a point at the extreme part of the village nearest the path to the Great Ponds. Suddenly I noticed that several goats that had been feeding quietly somewhere to my right were running as if pursued. I looked up and saw a young man running after them. With one sweep of his matchet he cut down one huge breeder. Then he grabbed a small he-goat with his left hand, tucked it under his arm and began to run away. I concluded he was a thief and sounded the alarm. The other men came to my aid and we chased him. He was a good runner and kept up the gap between him and us easily. Sometimes he slowed down but when we redoubled our efforts to catch him he sped on again. In the end we thought it wise to give up the chase. We rested for a short time and turned back. When we came to the village again the whole place was in confusion. We saw frightened women and children running for their lives. It took us some time to know what was happening because the women were so confused that they mistook us for the invaders and ran away from us when we tried to ask them questions. It was an elderly man who finally told me what was happening.

'We ran to the central part of the village only to be confronted with a shower of arrows. Two men dropped dead. We were heavily outnumbered. We took cover behind a house and fought as best as we could. When it seemed they had retreated I sent Okasi to you. When I saw no signs of any reinforcements I decided to go to the boundary myself. That was when I met you.'

'Who were these men?' Okehi asked breaking the silence that fell on the audience after the man's story.

'They were Chiolu men. I saw a man who closely resembled Olumba. Now that I think of it, the young man who was posing as a thief chased me during the first battle at the Great Ponds. He is a fast runner but I outstripped him when some undergrowths barred his way. He closed in on the man behind me and killed him.'

'I believe you did your best,' Okehi observed. 'We ought to have left more men behind as I suggested.'

'But the priests confirmed that Chiolu would turn up in great numbers to attack us during the negotiations,' Wago said anxious to avoid being blamed over the heavy catastrophe.

'Your decision to take all the available men was natural, Wago. No one can blame you,' Okehi said soothingly. 'But there is something we have to find out right away.'

'Okasi's whereabouts?' Wago guessed.

'Yes.'

A search-party was sent out. Late in the evening the body of Okasi was discovered a few paces from the path leading to Chiolu. A huge arrow had pierced his stomach.

8 OKASI and the other two men were buried with full rites the next day. The village looked gloomy. Warriors who strode about the village with careless ease only two days before now hardly left their compounds. Eze Okehi developed a painful backache and it was with difficulty that he went to his reception hall for the many meetings he held with the villagers.

At the first of these meetings Wago raved over the disappearance of his daughter. But he failed to rouse much enthusiasm in his fellow villagers. One of the elders said: 'Wago, this matter needs deep thought and planning. He who cannot recognize the power of his enemy is a fool. I am not saying that Chiolu is very powerful, but we have all realized now that she will not give up easily if ever. If we rush off with any childish plans we will come to greater harm and disgrace. What is more, three of our women are in their hands and we must proceed carefully.'

This observation was thought sensible by the majority of the assembly. Okehi dismissed the assembly and sought the privacy of his room. Apart from the general calamity the old man had personal reasons for uneasiness. That warning from Ali the earth-god over the kidnapped pregnant woman worried him. Okehi could not think of any way of getting the woman back. Who knew to what remote corner she had been taken? Okehi called his most senior wife and gave her two manillas, the fixed fee for a divination.

'Go to the dibia,' he said, 'and find out what I shall do about the woman with child whom Isiali sold off into slavery. I cannot find her as I promised Ali the earth-god and I was warned last night. I had a terrible dream which can only be a premonition. I was sitting in the reception hall when a huge snake came gliding towards me. I was so frightened that I ran off blindly and fell into a well. I was shouting in the dark well when I woke.'

Okehi's senior wife, a tall elderly woman ambled towards the dibia's house.

The dibia said between bursts of drumming: 'There can be no sacrifice to appease Ali for all time in this matter. The best we can do is to placate him each time he gets furious. No one sells a goat with young, much less a woman with child. It was a mistake for the warriors to have kidnapped her.'

Okehi's senior wife was in full agreement. She had never supported the idea of fighting for a fishpond and had on one or two occasions expressed this view as mildly as possible to her husband. Now that the war involved the kidnapping of women she was doubly resentful. She thought of her husband's young wife who was missing and tears welled from her eyes.

'Why can't men take advice?' she moaned. 'They think they are wise but they are as foolish as a baby in arms. Look at all the sufferings of the past month. What good will that pond do us? Who has ever grown rich from the proceeds of the cursed Pond of Wagaba?'

Igwu consoled the sobbing woman as best he could. Still he reeled off methodically the various items for the sacrifice and replaced his drums. He escorted Okehi's wife to the entrance of his compound, a thing he very rarely did. Like all powerful dibias Igwu was not married and avoided women as much as possible; not out of shyness but out of professional necessity. Quite a few of the rules he had to observe to maintain maximum efficiency were centred on women. At the entrance to his compound the dibia said: 'Don't worry much, your husband may not come to any harm. We think the gods are cruel when all they are doing is to keep us from killing ourselves. We often forget that the gods would rather have fun than run after us.'

Eze Okehi performed all the necessary sacrifices but he remained unhappy. The god could strike any day without giving him a chance to sue for mercy. And who could predict the vagaries of a god like Ali? Unlike Amadioha, god of thunder and the skies, Ali was popular and easy to placate, but difficult to shake off entirely when deeply offended. He had been known to punish families even after two generations. There was a case in which no living member of a family could remember a heinous offence committed by an ancestor and for which they were being punished. When Igwu divined the cause of their troubles, they thought that for once he was being fanciful. They only believed when a very old man, a one-time playmate of the long-dead offender confirmed Igwu's divination.

With a beating heart Okehi watched the skies, the earth, animals and trees for hidden omens. Even when one of his sons dropped a fragile keg of palm wine in his reception hall Okehi rushed to Igwu for interpretation. It did not take long before the strong hearty old man who could walk from Aliakoro to Chiolu with the best of the warriors became bedridden and humourless.

As Okehi became less active Wago the leopard-killer assumed more and more powers. He consulted the old chief less on security measures. He was extremely bitter over the loss of his daughter and would have carried out daylight raids on Chiolu if the elders had not opposed him. He harassed Okehi until the old man called a meeting of the elders and warriors. Wago spoke at length on how the dignity of the village was at stake, on the possibility of paying a ransom for the kidnapped women and on night raids. His head touched the roof of the reception hall as he talked and gesticulated with his long strong sinewy arms. In the end he carried the majority with him. Some action had to be taken. They could not look on while Chiolu carried off their women just like that.

The warriors sharpened their knives, the quivers filled with arrows and something of the enthusiasm shown at the initial stages of the war of the Great Ponds returned.

Wago knew Aliakoro would lose in an open battle with Chiolu and so avoided a direct conflict. He chose to harass Chiolu by making it unsafe for any member of that village to walk the forests and highways at any time of the day or night. He posted men along important paths to kill or capture any straying villagers. At night Chiolu was surrounded by men ready to kill.

The Chiolu villagers took all the precautions they could. They knew very well that Aliakoro would react violently to their last escapade. But they did not know the extent to which their enemies were prepared to go to wreak vengeance on them until an incident occurred. One night a man came out of his house to relieve himself. Carelessly he came out unarmed. A few steps from his house a figure emerged from the deep shadows of neighbouring plaintain trees and rushed at him. He ran back and just as he banged the door shut a heavy blow shook it. He raised an alarm and armed neighbours ran to his aid. The attacker disappeared swiftly. Only the deep knife-cut on the door convinced the neighbours that the man had not been having a vivid nightmare.

After the incident Chiolu took better security measures. Women were heavily escorted to the farms. Children played only in the reception halls and under the noses of their parents at that. Night dances in the arena were discontinued and villagers went early to bed. Women were so afraid of being kidnapped that nothing would entice them into staying up late. They were much more worried over the war than their menfolk. They woke only after the rays of the sun had chased away the last suspicious shadows under the plantain trees. They cooked supper before sundown and sat by their husbands as soon as the crickets announced the first signs of approaching darkness. Widows whose sons were not of age abandoned their deceased husbands' compounds and sought the protection of their parents or fathers-in-law.

There was one widow who had no sons to protect her yet stood her ground. She was Ochomma, the oldest woman in the village. Her husband had died years before and her daughters were all married now. Two of her grandchildren lived with her to attend to her few needs. When Ochomma refused to move, her grandchildren refused to desert her.

'We always shut the door at night,' the children said. 'How can anyone kidnap us? Besides we have grandmother with us.' As Ochomma's compound was right in the middle of the village Diali thought she was comparatively safe.

However, one night invaders from Aliakoro pitched on Ochomma's house. First they buried a charm close to the house to induce a deep death-like sleep on the occupants. Having taken this precaution the men began to carve an opening through the wall. To break open the door would be too noisy and might alert occupants of neighbouring houses. But Ochomma was not asleep. The charms of the marauders did not affect her. Her own charms, coupled with the mysterious powers which her great age had conferred on her, kept her awake. She heard the faint sound of the digging outside and guessed what was happening. Quietly she woke Okatu her

79

3 1303 00152 9511

thirteen-year-old grandson and whispered instructions to him. The boy listened with a thumping heart. He thought of shouting but his great respect for his grandmother restrained him.

Outside, the invaders worked with confidence, secure in the knowledge that their charm was working. Inside a young heart fluttered and raced with intense excitement. Beside it another heart, different by three quarters of a century, beat with little or no excitement, persuading ancient blood to flow through no less ancient arteries.

The hollow sound on the wall indicated that a breakthrough was imminent. Okatu stood by brandishing a knife too heavy for him. Each time an upsurge of fear assailed him he looked at his grandmother whose composure reassured him. Debris falling to the floor of the room announced that a breach had been made. It was yet too small to take a man's body. Even now a shout would have sent the invaders hurrying into the bush. But Ochomma would not shout, nor would she allow her grandson to shout. Okatu strained his eyes to know when to strike at any arm or head poked into the room. Nothing happened. Instead an overwhelming smell, sickly and sweet, filled the room. Ochomma fell asleep almost instantly. Okatu struggled a little longer to keep awake. Eventually he slumped to the ground and slept.

The hole in the wall was widened, and a man squeezed himself into the room. Quietly he opened the door and his companion came in. Okatu was gagged and bound, and carried out. The men looked round for another victim. The feeble red glow from the hearth revealed Ochomma's white hair and heavily wrinkled skin. She was not worth kidnapping, but she was gagged and bound for safety. Their next target was Ochomma's granddaughter, a mat-covered bundle by a corner of the room. It took the kidnappers some time to extricate her from the tangle of mats.

Meanwhile, outside, Ochomma's open door attracted a village sentry. He came near and found the dark bundle that was Okatu. The fresh cold air had revived the boy, but immobilized and gagged as he was he thought he was in the grip of a terribly vivid nightmare.

The sentry acted quickly. He carried him a few paces away and freed him. He whispered something into his ear, undid the gag, and then handed him a club whose end was studded with finger-long thorns. He signalled to the boy to follow him. But the boy went behind the house instead. The sentry swore silently. Little boys could be very stupid, he thought. But there was no time to go after the erring kid. Instead he stood by the door with his knife poised. Over the horizon a big red moon was rising. Its weak, uncertain light bathed everything in a hazy mistiness which deprived objects of their solidity. Presently a man's back emerged, and then the legs of the little girl he was helping to carry out. His companion who was holding the child's shoulders was still in the room when the sentry struck. It was a savage blow packing into it the fury of a whole village. The man crashed to the ground with a few tendons still connecting his head to his body. The other man ran back into the room. Soon afterwards the sound of a club shattering a bone was heard from behind the house. There was a groan followed by Okatu's shrill voice raised in a shout of triumph. Tortured by nightmares of invasion, it did not take much to rouse the villagers from their light sleep, and a large crowd of men gathered quickly. They were treated to a strange sight. In front of Ochomma's house lay the mutilated body of a man. Across the doorway was Ochomma's granddaughter tied and gagged. Inside, Ochomma was laid out in a similar condition. Behind the house was perhaps the most gruesome sight of all – a man's battered head sticking out of the hole he himself had made. Okatu stood staring at the shattered protruding head with some surprise. He still clutched the club whose thorny projections were bespattered with blood. Near the hole in the wall was a coconut shell containing the stuff with the sweet sickly smell. Old men recognized it as the rare and mysterious poison whose smell brought sleep.

The morning was bright and bracing but it did not divulge the secrets of the past night. The warriors kept what had happened to themselves. The women were merely told that some invaders had been scared away, but they guessed there was more to it than that. The atmosphere of rumours and secrecy was intoxicating and gossips basked in it. Several stories were woven around the hole in

Ochomma's wall and the blood marks near it. Some were so ridiculous that the more talkative of the men were inclined to refute them, but then, revealing a village secret was only next to stealing, and they shut up. There was a very interesting angle to this incident – for the first time a boy of thirteen would drink the Wine with the Eagle Feathers. That was old Ochomma's scheme and it had worked perfectly. She had bestowed on her grandson a legacy worth a good deal more than all the rusty manillas stored somewhere under the floor of her room. In later generations Okatu's name was to be a household word, an inspiration to youth.

Two days later Okehi woke to find two corpses by his doorway. They were the remains of Okatu's victims. Shaken, the old man slunk into his bedroom at the sight. His wives and children could not come out for fear and his compound remained unswept long after the heat of the sun had ceased to be a pleasure even to those with fever. The ikoro sounded and the warriors of Aliakoro assembled to be confronted by the two corpses. In spite of the horrors of the battles of the Great Ponds, this sight seemed removed from reality. Even Wago the leopard-killer shuddered. The death of these two men of Aliakoro with the dramatic appearance of their bodies was epoch-making. Dates of past and future events were to be estimated with reference to it in after years. The initial reactions of disgust and sickening horror were unavoidable. But they were quickly replaced by a terrible surge of anger and an unflagging determination of the type common to men at bay. Chiolu had achieved the ultimate in the horror game, Aliakoro had to show that they too could rig up horrors hitherto undreamed of.

Quickly the inter-village fight assumed alarming proportions. Open daylight raids were carried out by both villages and life became a nightmare. Farms were deserted. Those who had barns in their farms suffered heavy losses for their enemies looted their yams and cut down the barns. Starvation was not a long way off. Women kept strictly indoors; no escort of any size offered enough protection. Even water was a problem to some families who depended on the clean sparkling stream hard by. They dared not go to the stream and had to obtain water from wells in their neighbours' compounds.

It was now doubtful whether the wells would cope with the heavy demands. Some women who prided themselves on their great skill in soup preparation stared with dismay at what now passed for soup. How could soup be prepared without egusi, okro, and those wonderful mushrooms? One woman in Chiolu was so worried that she threatened to go to a small farm just behind the compound to gather some vegetables. Her husband restrained her.

'What are vegetables compared to life?' the man argued correctly.

'And what is life without proper feeding, my lord?' the woman answered, hardly less correctly. But she could not disobey her husband and kept indoors. However, when a few days later her husband complained of stomach pains she felt convinced that poor feeding was responsible. Late one morning she slipped off into the farm behind the house after having lied that she was going to fetch water from a neighbour's well. She never came back. Her husband found her headtie during a search and that was the nearest he ever got to seeing her.

As the days lengthened despair and fear gripped everyone. Old men said that even the days of the slave raiders were much better than these. The slave raiders they said were merely out for money. Their minds were not poisoned by that intense hatred which could drive a man to kill another and enjoy the deed. Indeed the slave raiders were not out to kill; they only did so in self-defence. Often when pursued they dropped their victims unhurt and escaped. But these days were different, very different. Death lurked behind every bush. At night the pale moonlight cast dubious shadows which none but the brave dared investigate. When there was no moon the curtain of charcoal-black darkness instilled as much fear into people's minds as if it was one vast insubstantial ubiquitous enemy ready to slay any who left the security of the closely guarded houses.

Even animals began to feel the effects of the deadly conflict. No longer was the arena strewn with white drowsy sheep lured by the moonlight. So many had been killed that the remnants sought the security of their owners' backyards as soon as daylight grew too weak to reveal individual blades of grass. Dogs only barked from the bedrooms of their owners. The old show of bravery was impracticable. Gone were the days when to impress their masters they ran round the compounds and along the village roads barking at nothing in particular. These days an indiscreet bark in the wrong place could invite a barbed arrow.

And so men, beasts and crops suffered. It was a long war, a bitter war, a war of attrition. Negotiations seemed impossible. Even priests were not safe as envoys. Said Igwu the dibia: 'The talisman for invisibility is no safeguard because eventually you will have to appear before the enemy to deliver your message and time may be too short for you to give necessary explanations.'

The war grew so bitter that eventually villages as far away as two days' journey began to feel the effect. The chiefs of these villages warned their people not to go near the two warring villages. Some hunters who defied these warnings ran the race of their lives when they saw arrows flying towards them.

A hunter from Abii ran home one day with a bleeding thigh. He had narrowly escaped death from the hands of Chiolu men. The hunter said to his chief: 'I have never seen such desperate men in all my life. When the first arrow struck the trunk of a tree by which I stood, I thought it was the case of an adventurous headhunter striving to drink the Wine with the Eagle Feathers. I hid behind a tree and made ready to deal with him. Just then three arrows came flying towards me simultaneously and one hit my thigh. Then I knew there were at least three people out for my life. I pulled out the arrow quickly and began to run home. The men ran so fast that in no time at all one of them was within a few paces of me and I began to expect a matchet blow any moment. But my personal gods were with me for one of the pursuers far behind called out to the man just behind me: "leave him alone, he is from Abii". Soon after that the sound of footsteps behind me ceased.' Everyone in Abii agreed it had been a very near miss. The next incident was fatal and the Eze of Abii was very angry. He did not know which of the two villages was responsible. He called his elders and warriors together and after a long discussion the villagers decided to protest to the two villages in turn. They sent out six strong men to Chiolu but the envoys were

84

mistaken for enemies and chased back. They barely escaped with their lives. The chief of Abii held another meeting with his elders and warriors. Were they to declare war on Chiolu? Many warriors thought so and spoke vigorously in support of an immediate invasion of Chiolu.

Abii was a village of average size but her few warriors were famous for their courage and skill in battle. Still the Eze of Abii felt that war with Chiolu was best avoided. He was sure that if only they could get Chiolu to know of the wrongs she had inflicted on them the matter would be quickly settled. But sending another envoy to Chiolu might involve more loss of lives. In the end the elders of Abii decided to contact other neutral villages so that a joint action could be taken. Omigwe and Isiali were among the first to be contacted. Abii soon found that they were not alone in their loss. People had disappeared from some of these villages also.

Isiali being the largest and, as tradition went, the oldest village in the vicinity summoned a great meeting of all but the warring villages. It was an important move which brought eight villages of the Erekwi Clan together for the first time. Before this, these villages had only met in twos and threes during wrestling contests.

The Eze of Isiali spoke first after kola had been broken and served. He called each village by her titles and when the response had died down said:

'Five months have come and gone since Chiolu and Aliakoro began to fight each other for possession of a portion of the Great Ponds. I am ashamed to say – but the truth shines like the moon and must be said – that we lent warriors to Aliakoro at the initial stages of the fight. It was a move I ought not to have made as later events have shown. The fighting has became so serious that both villages are now on the verge of starvation. Their farms are deserted. Children no longer play in the streets nor can women plait their hair in the reception halls in safety. Worse still the war is threatening to spread to neighbouring villages. Truly when one finger picks up oil the others soon get soiled with it. What shall we do?'

Eze Wosu of Omokachi spoke: 'There is only one answer to that question. We shall send arbitrators to the two villages and try to make peace. I am sure they are so battle-weary that they will welcome peacemakers. When two cocks are tired of fighting a mosquito flying between them is enough to stop them.'

The rest of the time was spent in appointing representatives. Elders noted for their impartiality in their various villages were chosen.

Before anything could be done the warring villages had to be notified. As Abii had already learnt, this could cost lives. Forty tough warriors were chosen from the six villages. Elendu of Isiali was to command them. On the day appointed the warriors gathered. Elendu reckoned that it would be wiser to make contact first with Aliakoro, his former allies. They knew him well and with some luck there should be no incidents. Before they set out, Elendu addressed the men: 'We must take all precautions to ensure that no one is killed,' he said. 'That is why I told you to turn up in your best wrappers today. We shall take the widest and most beaten track to Aliakoro and do all we can to make those villages realize that we are a band of peaceful men.'

'Shall we not carry weapons?' someone asked.

'Of course we shall,' Elendu replied. 'Even marriage parties travel armed.' There was laughter.

'I have another idea,' a warrior from Abii said. 'Let us carry drums and sing as we go. None will attack a party of singing men.' This suggestion raised some chuckling among the men but they soon realized it was an excellent idea.

'The whole thing is becoming funny,' Elendu said laughing.

'Yes, but it is better to drum our way to Aliakoro than to get killed,' the Abii man insisted.

'Any drummers among us?' Elendu asked.

'I am a drummer,' the man said again. Others volunteered to perform and six drums were obtained.

'We might as well have some igeles and okwos to enhance the effect,' the Abii man said.

'My friend, one would think you were more of a drummer than a fighter,' an Omigwe warrior sneered.

'If you think you are a better warrior let us step aside for a moment and wrestle,' the man from Abii said.

'I was joking of course, but if you are that worried I can give you a little thrashing to prove I am a better warrior.'

The two men moved towards each other menacingly. Some mischievous men eager for a treat egged them on.

'A little wrestling is not a bad idea,' said one.

'I would never turn my back on such a challenge whether made in jest or not,' said another.

'Looks as if the Abii man is keen,' said a third. Elendu intervened just in time.

'This will not do. No dibia adds pepper to a tranquilizer. There will be time enough for wrestling. I think the idea of drums is not a bad one. Igeles and okwos go with drums and so we shall have the lot. Those of you who can dance should be prepared to take a few turns on the way.'

The men laughed and a friendly atmosphere was restored.

By mid-morning they set out, a colourful party of drummers, singers and dancers. The trick worked. There were no incidents on the way, but the sound of twigs being broken and the movement of bushes being pushed aside by unseen agents reminded the men of what might have been. These little signs showed the intensity of hostilities.

Every path was watched by men whose one desire was to kill. As the shadows began to lengthen the envoys arrived at Aliakoro. They were shocked at what they saw, or rather at what they did not see. There were no children playing anywhere. Reception halls, the haunts of old men, were deserted; the empty three-legged chairs in them seemed to stare back at the drummers in protest. Through chinks in strong fences women and children could be seen huddled in the back-yards and hardly daring to laugh aloud. As for the men there were no traces of them. It was a strange village and it was with considerable effort that Elendu and his men continued their singing and drumming.

They moved into Eze Okehi's compound and filled his reception hall. The singing was stopped and Elendu called out in a clear loud voice.

'Eze Okehi, peace-makers from the Erekwi clan have come to see

87

you. Come out and give us kola and palm wine, we are hungry and tired.' Eze Okehi came out when he recognized Elendu's voice. Elendu was surprised at the change in the old man. He looked much frailer. The lines on is face were now so deep that they held rivers of perspiration as he dawdled towards them.

'Have you brought me the two remaining women?' the old man asked. 'I have suffered much for their sake. Ever since they were kidnapped Ali the earth-god has been angry with me. I have had no peace of mind. An unending series of sacrifices has made me poor. If only my death would end the war I should be too happy to die; I am old enough. My mates are all dead. Every night I dream of them and they beckon me to the spirit world. But I do not want to die and leave a legacy of war to the coming generation. If . . .'

Elendu had to interrupt the rambling old man to get in a word.

'We have come to end the war,' Elendu said. 'We were sent by the Erekwi clan, of which you are part, to arrange for a peace meeting. Come now, let us sound the ikoro to summon the villagers.'

'How do you hope to achieve anything?' Okehi said. 'Our enemies have grown to love killing. Olumba their devilish leader is for ever devising horrible schemes and each day brings with it a different horror.'

'Play your part and leave the rest to us,' Elendu said soothingly.

The ikoro sounded and the haggard warriors of Aliakoro assembled. Elendu explained his mission. There were isolated protests from a few diehards, among them Wago the leopard-killer. But it was clear that the vast majority wanted peace and that quickly.

'We shall be ready to meet Chiolu for negotiations in eight days' time,' Okehi announced at last to the relief of his elders.

'But we shall on no account go to Chiolu. The talks must be held on neutral ground.'

'That is customary,' Elendu said; 'meanwhile all fighting must stop.'

The men passed the night at Aliakoro and set out for Chiolu the next day. They found Chiolu in much the same state as Aliakoro. As they entered the village, Elendu thought of the night raid of five months ago and smiled. He had not forgotten Eze Diali's compound where he himself had kidnapped Chisa the Eze's daughter.

When the party reached the centre of the village, close to the arena, Olumba and Ikechi suddenly emerged as if from nowhere and confronted the men.

'Who are you who come to us with singing and dancing when we are thinking of nothing but war?' Olumba asked in a loud voice. 'Declare yourselves or face death.'

Elendu came forward and said:

'Olumba my strong friend, are you not tired of fighting?'

'We shall never be too tired to fight for our property.'

'We are men chosen by the Erekwi clan to prepare the way for a peaceful settlement.'

'I don't understand.'

'Listen. The conflict between you and Aliakoro has reached a very dangerous stage. You have both begun to kill people from other villages not concerned with the war. Therefore, Isiali, Omokachi, Omigwe, Abii and other villages who speak our tongue have selected us to arrange a peace meeting between you and your enemies, before greater havoc is done.'

'I thought Isiali was involved in the fight,' Olumba said with a sneer. 'You Elendu were among those who kidnapped my wife in a most cowardly manner.' Elendu was an observant warrior. He drew back quickly as he detected the mounting fire in Olumba's eyes.

'You have the face to talk of peace you rogue,' Olumba continued advancing. A warrior from Omigwe quickly intervened.

'Control yourself, Olumba. Do not ruin this attempt to stop the bloody war between you and Aliakoro. If you have any quarrels with Elendu, settle them later. If you attack him, you attack us and if you attack us you attack the Erekwi clan.'

Olumba paused for a while and thought. Then he raised a whoop and several men emerged quickly from bushes on either side of the Erekwi representatives. Elendu and his men were surprised and impressed.

'Aliakoro has agreed to negotiate with you in eight days' time,' Elendu said.

'Where?'

'That will be decided by elders of the Erekwi clan.'

'Let us go to Eze Diali.'

The ikoro summoned the men of Chiolu to Diali's large reception hall. Chiolu agreed to negotiate in eight days' time. 'But we shall on no account give up the Pond of Wagaba, shall we?' Diali asked his people. There was a deafening roar signifying 'No'.

 HOUSEWIVES at Isiali bustled about preparing hills of foofoo and lakes of tasty soup to feed the august assembly drawn from all the corners of the Erekwi clan. The village had never seen such a large assembly of old and venerable Ezes. Curious crowds gathered near the large reception hall of Eze Iwai of Isiali staring at the visitors dressed as befitted their rank. It was difficult to imagine a more splendid display of costly clothing.

Eze Wosu of Omokachi was perhaps the most richly dressed. The colours of his wrapper dazzled the eyes. One woman said: 'Eze Wosu's wrapper should provide enough bride price for four wives.' Massive rings of gold graced the Eze's ten fingers. His heavy flowing shirt with an inner lining of purple was made of that costly stuff known as Opukapa. It was a very rare material found only in the treasure chests of those who had traded with the white men from across the roaring Abaji now known as the Atlantic. Eze Wosu's walking-stick was a real wonder. The gold head was so intricately worked that it defied description. The little boy who said that the head resembled a vast collection of wrestling earth-worms perhaps got farthest in describing it. Wosu's hat was tall and charcoal-black. The eagle feather gracing it needed no explanation.

Eze Diali and Eze Okehi were not gorgeously dressed but each wore a heavy ancient sword probably to indicate that they were at war. These Portuguese swords were apparently not functional. No one had ever been known to use them in actual fighting. They were blunt and attempts to sharpen them had never really succeeded; but they were costly and rare and Ezes wore them on occasions for prestige.

After the midday meal the main business of the assembly began. The warring villages stated their case quoting ancient history which none but the very old could grasp. Eloquence was not lacking on either side and the assembly was hard put to arrive at a decision. Who really owned the Ponds of Wagaba? The answer was anybody's guess. Both parties had at one time or the other fished in the famous pond. Before the present war Chiolu was the current owner but did that establish absolute ownership? Arriving at a decision was made more difficult by vehement declarations by both sides that any decision not favouring them would be ignored and war resumed.

The Eze of Aliji spoke before the assembly broke up for a recess. He said: 'Warriors of Chiolu and Aliakoro, listen to me. You have come to this meeting because you have faith in your brother Ezes of the Erekwi Clan. You should be happy that for your sake the Ezes of the Erekwi clan have assembled together for the first time ever. Ezes are not to be trifled with. At least I personally cannot afford to waste time over two people who want to kill each other by all means. Before we go on we Ezes want to feel that you will abide by whatever decisions we arrive at. Weigh any amount of fish against your wives and children and you will see immediately that you are behaving like the tortoise who clubbed his wife Aliga to death in an all-out attempt to kill a tse-tse fly that had perched on her head. A fool exhausts what he has in hand before he grows wise. But you are no fools.'

The Assembly broke up and the Ezes with a few chosen elders went into a separate room to confer. Decision was not easy.

'Let us split the pond between them,' the Eze of Abii suggested.

'That cannot be a lasting solution,' Eze Iwai replied. 'Very soon boundary disputes will flare up.'

Eze Wosu said: 'Suppose we let them fish in alternate years?'

'You will find some years longer than others,' the Eze of Abii answered. The men laughed.

'There is only one way,' Iwai said, 'and that is to let one village have the Pond.'

'But who really owns the Pond?' someone asked. 'A decision like that will amount to no decision at all. Each village made it clear that she would not let the pond go.'

It was not easy. The old men racked their brains in vain for a solution.

'This is like digging the grave of a hunchback,' Eze Iwai said. 'It never fits.' Someone suggested an inspection of the Ponds. For the old men the march to the Great Ponds would be enervating but they agreed to go. The next day young warriors volunteered to carry the old Ezes to the Great Ponds. On arrival the ponds were carefully inspected. Back at Isiali the problem of arriving at a decision was as difficult as ever.

'There is only one way out, the gods must decide,' Wosu said

'How?' Eze Iwai wondered. 'A whole village cannot swear.'

'A whole village cannot swear of course, but a representative from either of the villages can swear on behalf of his village.'

It looked like a way out and the next day when the assembly met again this decision was announced by Eze Iwai. The decision was welcomed but each village insisted that the other should do the swearing. After much wrangling, Eze Diali spoke out:

'I am prepared to swear on Chiolu's behalf. Name the god I shall swear by and set the time limit. The Pond of Wagaba is ours. My fathers fought for it. I fought for it. My son fought and died for it. I know that the gods will uphold our claim.'

A hush fell on the assembly. Then Aliakoro asked for permission to move apart and confer. Soon afterwards they came back.

'We are glad that Chiolu is prepared to swear,' Okehi said. 'According to custom it is our right to choose the person to swear and the god he will swear by. The traditional time limit is six months, we don't dispute that.'

Eze Iwai and the other arbitrators conferred in whispers.

'Choose your man then,' Eze Iwai said.

92

'We choose Olumba,' Eze Okehi announced firmly. Another hush fell on the assembly.

'And your god?'

'We choose Ogbunabali, the god of the night.' A low hum issued from the assembly. Olumba sat motionless where he was. His muscular arms were folded across his chest and he worked his jaws slowly as he ground his teeth. Eze Diali looked apprehensively at Olumba. What if the great warrior refused. His doubts were dispelled when Olumba stood and said laconically:

'I agree to swear by Ogbunabali on behalf of Chiolu.'

The awe-inspiring shrine of Ogbunabali was at Isiali. The priest was contacted and he promised to make necessary arrangements for the swearing the next morning. Chiolu and Aliakoro contributed towards the sacrifice necessary to invoke the god. There was not much to it – just two black hens and some odds and ends.

Ogbunabali was one of the powerful gods in the Erekwi clan. There were shrines for it in some villages, but the shrine at Isiali was the biggest and the priest there was recognized as its chief priest. Ogbunabali had the pecularity that it killed mostly by night. He had neither the dignity of Amadioha the god of thunder and of the skies nor the popularity of Ali the earth-god, but he had a sombre reputation all his own.

Early in the next morning the Ezes and the elders trooped to the dark shrines of Ogbunabali the god of the night. An image of the god was unveiled after sacrifices, libations and lengthy incantations. Olumba stood before it naked but for a narrow strip of loin cloth. This was to make sure he carried no talismans or other charms that might fight the powers of the god. Then in a solemn voice he repeated after the priest.

'I swear by Ogbunabali the god of the night that the Pond of Wagaba belongs to Chiolu.

'If this is not true let me die within six months;

'If true, let me live and prosper.'

The image of the god was waved around Olumba's head three times and the ceremony was over. If Olumba died within six months, the pond was Aliakoro's, if he survived it was Chiolu's.

Eze Diali spoke: 'Before we go it is necessary for Aliakoro to assure us that they will not try to harm Olumba by physical or spiritual means.'

'That is reasonable,' the priest said, grabbing a drinking horn and saying solemnly as he poured out libations.

> '*Those who would harm Olumba*
> *By the knife or the barbed arrow,*
> *By strange charms or witchcraft,*
> *Kill them Ogbunabali King of the Night,*
> *Kill them and show signs.*'

This was the customary protection offered to those under oath. No one ever tried to kill anyone under oath and so no one knew how protective these pronouncements of the priest really were.

'The new moon is just out,' the priest said. 'I want everybody present to remember this fact to avoid confusion if and when we shall have to release Olumba from his oath.'

Olumba came out of the shrine dazed. The whole thing had happened so quickly that it seemed unreal. But his loin cloth, his fellow villagers surrounding and encouraging him and the chief priest of Ogbunabali who walked ahead towards Isiali were real enough. The men of Aliakoro who looked at him strangely were also real, very real. He walked back to Isiali quietly with the rest of the swearing party. His feelings were numb and his thoughts scattered.

Back at Isiali the Ezes of the Erekwi clan and their entourages made ready to go. Their costly dresses were carefully folded and put into special caskets. Once in their travelling dresses they headed for their various villages and within a short time Isiali, though a populous village, seemed deserted by contrast. Groups of children with their insatiable curiosity dogged the visitors, trying to steal a last look. They trailed them until the village could no longer be seen. They stopped only when the familiar fruit trees, bushes, nooks and corners and favourite play spots were replaced by little-known giant trees whose secrets the children had never dared to explore. The very climbers harassing these trees were strange and their exotic flowers caressed by weird insects conjured up frightening fairy tales that sent the children scampering back. The older children were the last to turn back. They stared for long at the last far bend at which the visitors had disappeared and wondered what things were beyond.

Eze Diali walked by Olumba who had been silent up till now. The warrior looked up as usual but one could see that this posture was maintained by sheer habit. The care-worn face would rather look down.

'We shall eat new yams in six months,' Diali said.

'Yes, we shall celebrate Olumba's release from his oath along with the new yam festival,' Chituru replied. He looked at Olumba trying to lure him into a smile, but he failed. Silence fell again on the party after this feeble attempt at conversation. Diali realized that Olumba was best left undisturbed. He knew how he felt because before he became Eze, he himself had once sworn by Amadioha in order to take possession of a fertile strip of land over which he nearly fought with a neighbour. He claimed the land in the end but he reckoned those six months among the worst he had ever spent in his life.

The walk was doing Olumba a lot of good. His thought became clearer as the blood flowed freely through his body and perspiration poured out in rivulets. The Pond of Wagaba – who were its rightful owners? It was one thing to argue eloquently in public in favour of his village, and another to stake his life over the truth of his arguments. If the pond belonged to Chiolu, he would be all right. If not . . .? He tried to recall all he knew about the Great Ponds. He remembered Eze Diali's speech during negotiations with Aliakoro. The chief had said: 'Time obscures many things, but time also establishes many things. That you have not challenged us for thirty years is proof enough that the Pond of Wagaba belongs to us.' Olumba wondered whether Ogbunabali the god of the night would recognize this time factor. How did the gods reason anyway? True, they dispensed justice impartially, but this impartiality was based on arguments which at times could be untenable from the human point of view. Olumba recalled how a sick man who once went for a divination was told that he was being attacked by his dead grandfather's spirit because his grandfather had not been given a decent second burial ceremony. The man was quite young when his grandfather died and was not in a position to do anything then. His father who ought to have performed the ceremony was a palm-wine drinking imbecile who always said to everyone's surprise and sometimes amusement, that he was so poor that the gods and spirits ought to contribute towards his upkeep. For all his irreverence he had never been known to be seriously ill. Some said he was so foolish that spirits thought it beneath them to bother about him. So, his father's spirit pounced on his son instead, a decade later, and killed him in the long run, despite the young man's frantic efforts to offer the prescribed sacrifices. Olumba turned this incident round and round in his mind. If gods could reason that way then anything could happen to a man under oath. He started sweating profusely and his eyes grew dim. His legs wobbled and he stumbled. Those immediately before and behind him stared at him but he straightened up quickly and walked on. Reassured, his companions moved on.

They came to a stream spanned by a one-log bridge. It was a huge log and walking across did not call for much strain in balancing. At midstream Olumba's quaking legs slipped and he fell with a mighty splash into the stream. Two men jumped in to rescue him but Olumba did not need their help. He stood in the chest-deep stream and slowly bathed his head with the clear liquid chilled in the cool belly of the forest. Eze Diali and his villagers watched him aghast. Was he well? He moved out of the water to the opposite bank and sat down.

'What is it?' Diali asked trying to mask the anxiety in his voice.
'Nothing.' Olumba replied.
'Do you want to rest? We can wait.'
'No.'
'Get up then.'
'March on, I shall follow.'
'You know we won't allow that.'
'I want to be alone for a while.'
'No,' Diali said firmly. 'We will not let you. Right now your life is our most precious property.'

'I must be alone for a little while.' Olumba replied.

Chituru said: 'Do you mean we should leave you behind?'

'No. I shall walk with you. The only thing I ask is that I stay right behind.'

'Well there is no harm in that,' Chituru said. Eze Diali gave way. The villagers marched on with Olumba in the rear. The warrior began to feel he had been a fool to have agreed to swear. The gods may not be fools but their way of thinking was strange. He dwelt for long on the man who was killed by his grandfather's spirit. Then suddenly a light dawned on him. The spirits of dead men behaved almost exactly like men. If a man was cruel, his spirit would be cruel after death. It would molest innocent folks and compel them to offer heavy sacrifices. These spirits were not to be compared with gods who were higher and nobler. Olumba's mind cleared somewhat, his steps became firmer.

Fowls were going to roost when the men of Chiolu reached home. Anxious villagers who had been at home gulped down the news. The women were thrilled by the descriptions of the fantastic displays of dresses by the Ezes of the Erekwi clan. They were also relieved by the news of the temporary truce. Still it was two market days before they were able to go to the nearer farms unescorted to collect vegetables and cocoyams.

For all her restraint Nyoma, Olumba's first wife, could not help crying when Olumba related the part he had played in the negotiations.

'My lord, what shall we do?' she said making a brave attempt to restrain her tears.

'Nothing,' her husband said.

'Which god did you swear by?'

'Ogbunabali.'

'Ogbunabali!' the woman echoed under her breath.

Husband and wife were silent, their thoughts racing.

'I have never grudged the smallest gods a sacrifice,' Olumba said more in soliloquy than in conversation. 'You have never,' his wife agreed. But as she spoke a disquieting thought occurred to Olumba: in his medicine house he had no shrine for Ogbunabali. He was not to blame really. This god was unpopular in Chiolu. It had no priest in the village and only a few households had shrines for it. How Olumba wished he had been one of the god's few worshippers. He thought of erecting a shrine, but shrank back at the idea as soon as it occurred to him. Should he consult the dibia? Time enough for that.

'We have no shrine for Ogbunabali,' Nyoma said. Olumba was startled at the coincidence of their thoughts.

'That is true,' he mumbled.

'Let's erect one,' she said.

'It is not wise.'

'Why not?'

'I don't know.'

'Let us ask the dibia.'

'I shall do so in due course,' the man said.

'Can't we see him this evening, my lord?'

'No.'

'We should not delay, my lord.'

'I know.'

'Let's go this evening then.'

'Don't worry I shall not die tonight,' Olumba said, an indescribable grin torturing his face.

'Of course you will not, my lord,' the woman said her eyes threatening to overflow again.

'Go into your room,' Olumba said to avert the imminent sobbing. Nyoma rose and as she walked away a heavy sob shook her hunched shoulders.

'Stop it,' Olumba suddenly flared out. 'I am not dead yet and I am not going to die! The gods are wise and will always protect the innocent.'

But were the gods wise? It was almost as if someone near by was asking the question; so clearly did it pop up in his mind. Rather than attempt to answer it Olumba sought the refuge of his medicine-house. Solemnly he graced the many shrines with bits of kola and white chalk beginning with Amadioha the god of thunder and of the skies.

The next day Eze Diali summoned a meeting of the elders and some top warriors.

'This meeting,' the chief began, 'is in connection with Olumba. His life is public property now and we have to keep it safe. What steps shall we adopt to achieve this?'

There was a flood of suggestions.

'He must not travel.'

'He must not climb trees.'

'He must eat only what his first wife cooks.'

'He must not go to the farm alone.'

'Some even suggested he should not leave his room. Eze Diali restored order and methodically the various suggestions were considered. In the end the villagers drew up a code for Olumba. Diali made the final pronouncement.

'Olumba, what we are going to tell you now is bound to be uncomfortable in some ways, but we are sure you understand the situation. You fought bravely for the Great Ponds and now you have staked your life to ensure total victory. We do not want all these efforts to be in vain. You have heard the decisions of the elders but let me sum up to make sure you don't forget. You are not to travel out of the village. You will eat only what your first wife will cook for the next six months. You will not climb any tree no matter how short. You must minister regularly to your household gods; their shrines must never lack kola.'

Diali paused and all eyes were focused on Olumba.

'Elders and people,' Olumba said, 'there is no doubt that you are doing the right thing. However, I have two points to raise. Firstly I shall have to tap the few palm-wine trees in my compound and that will involve some climbing. Secondly I shall work on my farm which is far from the village.'

Discussions were resumed and it was some time before solutions were arrived at. It was Chituru who spoke this time.

'Ikechi,' he called.

'I am here,' the young man said.

'You will tap Olumba's palm-wine trees for him.'

'It is well.'

'Olumba, the village will organize communal labour for your farms', Chituru further explained.

'You have turned me into a woman,' Olumba said with a short laugh.

'It will not be for long,' Diali said.

The elders went away. Olumba and Ikechi remained to chat with Eze Diali.

'The important thing is not to be afraid,' Diali said.

'I am not afraid,' Olumba replied.

'The gods are wise,' Diali said studying the ground.

'Very wise,' Olumba echoed absent-mindedly.

'I am sure Ogbunabali will in fact protect you.'

'I think so too.'

'Have you a shrine for it in your house?'

Olumba suddenly looked up. 'No,' he said.

Diali said soothingly:

'It does not matter; one cannot have shrines for all the gods.'

'I wish I had one for Ogbunabali, though.'

'Yes but don't let that worry you. You must dismiss any thoughts that tend to introduce fear into your mind.'

'You are right, Eze Diali.'

'Remember also that there are other gods looking after you. Amadioha is an ever-present powerful god. Ojukwu and Ali are there too.'

'You can also count on the spirits of your ancestors whom you worship so well.'

'You are right, Eze Diali. My father was a brave fighter. He should be a greater fighter in the spirit world.'

'Your father was a great fighter indeed. His bow had so many notches on it that he lost count.'

'I still have that bow,' Olumba said with pride. 'It is my ambition to have as many notches as he had.'

'You may not have the chance now that the pond issue is going to be settled once and for all.'

'You never know what other village will fight us in future.'

'Quite true.'

'We may even do battle with Aliakoro over another issue, a land dispute for instance.'

'That is possible. However the Ezes of the Erekwi clan are learning to come together, and may in future settle all inter-village disputes before they flare up into real fighting.'

'I wonder what would happen then?'

'There would be peace.'

'Yes,' Olumba said, 'and boys would grow old without ever tasting a fight.'

'That is true,' Diali said smiling.

'What a weak generation that would be!'

'They would not be as weak as you think. They would be taught the art of fighting all the same.'

'It takes a real war to make a fighter, my lord. Look at young Ikechi for instance. One can now call him a fighter. Others in his age-group who have no notches on their bows are still women as far as fighting is concerned.'

'Whatever we do,' Diali said thoughtfully, 'a time will come when there will be little or no fighting. Every generation, unless it meets fresh enemies, does less fighting than the one before. Apart from men like you, fighters in your age-group cannot be compared to the great warriors in our age-group. In the same way Ikechi's age-group may never produce a single warrior as good as you are; not because the boys are weak or cowardly but because the opportunity for development is lacking.'

Olumba nodded in agreement.

'Gone indeed are the days of great wars fought by great warriors, warriors so strong that they did battle with spirits and beat them.'

'They were really great if they could fight spirits,' Olumba said. 'As for me I would rather face a whole village single-handed than fight with a spriit.'

'You have always said so, Olumba.'

'But I am fighting with a spirit now,' Olumba said thoughtfully.

'You are not, my son,' Diali said quickly trying to erase this trend of thought from Olumba's mind.

'I am.'

'You are not.'

'Yes, my lord, I am fighting with a god at last. What a man works hard to avoid always hits him. I have done all I know how to satisfy the gods, yet here I am fighting with one.'

'Don't view it that way,' Eze Diali said, uneasy over Olumba's changing mood. But the man was already on his feet ready to go.

All through the dialogue Ikechi had said nothing. He merely listened. He very much wanted to help Olumba but as things stood there was nothing he could do apart from tapping his palm-wine trees as the elders had ordered.

Back in his compound Olumba sat down in his reception hall. His wives and children surrounded him but he scarcely saw them as he sat deep in thought.

'We must not weep or show any signs of sorrow,' Nyoma told the other woman.

'I shall do my best, but it is so very difficult,' Wogari, Olumba's second wife replied.

'Crying attracts evil spirits, remember.'

'That is true.'

'Laughing makes the spirits of our ancestors happy and more disposed to help us. I remember when my first baby died. I was so sad that eventually I fell ill. When our husband thought I was dying he called in the dibia who divined that my dead mother's spirit was responsible for my illness. The spirit, the dibia said, could not bear to see me suffer so much and had decided to take me to the spirit world to end my pains. After the necessary sacrifices the dibia warned me to laugh and feel happy as much as possible. I obeyed and recovered rapidly.'

The younger woman listened attentively and at the end said: 'If the spirits of our ancestors love to see us happy, then they should help to keep us happy. They should prevent our children from dying and ward off other such misfortunes.'

'They do just that, but bad spirits at times overpower them and carry out their evil schemes on us.'

'But what can we do to keep him happy?'

'We will laugh and sing as much as possible.'

'How can we laugh when there is no cause for laughter?'

'We can. Come, let us sing.'

Nyoma raised a tune and the younger woman joined. It was a melodious happy tune and as they clapped their hands gently to keep the beat, their husband turned round in surprise to look at them. Gradually he came nearer. As he watched the two women singing, clapping and smiling the mask of doubt on his face fell off and he smiled. Nyoma rose to dance. Deliberately, she danced awkwardly and Olumba burst out laughing.

'Nyoma,' he said, 'is this a new type of dance?'

'It is, my lord,' she said beaming.

'What is it called?'

'I cannot tell you; the women are still keeping it a secret. We want to surprise the men during the next new-yam festival. You are very lucky to have a glimpse of it now.'

'Wogari, can you dance it too?'

'Yes, my lord.' The younger woman got up and imitated Nyoma's improvised steps as much as she could and danced even more awkwardly. Olumba sat back and laughed. It was his first hearty laugh for some time.

10 'MY lord, the new moon is out,' Wogari said pointing skywards at the barely visible crescent. Olumba came out of his reception hall where he had been resting and searched the sky.

'Follow the direction of this finger,' his wife said as he turned this way and that trying to locate the moon.

'You are right,' he said at last, 'I have seen it.'

'One end of the moon is pointing upwards, my lord.'

'That is true.'

'That means good luck.'

'Yes,' Olumba said thoughtfully.

One long month was gone. Olumba after intense internal struggles was able to keep his fears down. What bothered him was the compulsory state of idleness to which he was subjected. A man who could not hunt, tap palm wine and go to the farms was hardly alive. The best exercise he could get was to walk from one end of the village to the other. After a few days he discontinued this practice because of the fuss people made over him. For instance old Ochomma on seeing him one day said: 'My son, Amadioha and Ojukwu will preserve your life. I have heard what you are doing for the village.' Olumba mumbled something in acknowledgement. The ancient woman went on: 'When you go to bed put some owho sticks outside your door to prevent evil spirit from disturbing you at night. Ogbunabali will not hurt you because the Pond of Wagaba is ours; it is the wicked roving spirits we have to fear.'

'I am sure the gods will protect me, mother.'

'No doubt about that, but do as I tell you. Even Amadioha can be careless at times, but I have warned him to see you through this or face my contempt.'

Olumba had never heard anyone speak of Amadioha in such tones. Ochomma spoke as if Amadioha were her son. She went on in her quaking voice:

'Amadioha, god of thunder, proud ruler of the skies, who begat Onunwo who begat our great grandfather: do not disgrace yourself. We see your might in lightning, thunder, rain and sunshine, in the death of the wicked and the protection of the innocent; show your power now.'

Demonstrations like this made Olumba feel reluctant to move about. Everywhere he went, instead of the usual smiling faces, he was confronted by faces heavily lined with pity and fear. So he stayed indoors as much as possible.

One evening Ikechi came as usual to tap the two palm-wine trees just behind Olumba's compound.

'Olumba.'

'Ikechi, how is your father?'

'He is well. He sends his greetings.'

'Greet him when you get back.'

'That tree,' Ikechi said pointing to a huge palm-wine tree, 'is getting tired.'

'You are right. Yesterday I observed that it's supply did not fill the pot as usual. No matter, there are many more trees waiting to be tapped.'

'Where?'

'There are two mature trees behind the ones you are tapping now.'

'I have not noticed them.'

'Trees and bushes are in the way.'

'When can I start tapping them?'

'Tomorrow if you like.'

'Can't I see them now?'

'Yes if you want to,' Olumba said, glad of a chance to get about. He disappeared into the house and reappeared a moment later with his knife. He slashed his way through the bushes.

'Here they are.'

'Hei, they are huge and should produce a lot of wine.'

'I doubt it.'

'Why?'

'The soil is not very good. Trees here are usually poor producers.'

The two men stood and sized up the two trees.

'We might as well clear the bushes around them,' Olumba said, his matchet already at work. Ikechi helped him and quickly the thick undergrowths disappeared. They set to work on the climbers hugging the trees.

'Hei, look at that?' Ikechi said pointing to the top of one of the palm-wine trees.

'What is it?'

'Take another look.'

'A nest of wasps!'

'Yes.'

'Do you know how to deal with it?'

'No,' Ikechi said.

'I shall help you.'

'Olumba, remember you are not to do any climbing. Leave me to deal with it.'

'How will you deal with it?'

Ikechi thought for a while. 'I shall hurl stones and clubs at the nest to dislodge it,' he answered.

'That wouldn't do. They would leave their nests and settle all over the tree."

'They should clear after a day or two.'

'Probably. But I have a neater way of doing it. I'll show you when you come tomorrow.'

'Will it involve climbing?'

'Yes, just once.'

'Let me do it my way then.'

'You don't mean I'll die at this single attempt at climbing. I have never had a fall yet.'

'I still don't think it is wise.'

'I will show you anyway.'

After supper that night Ikechi went over to Diali's compound.

'Olumba wants to climb a palm-wine tree,' he announced curtly. Eze Diali studied the floor of his reception hall for some time.

'Only one month and he is bored; just as I feared.'

'Dede, we should stop him.'

'Yes, my son.'

'You will come with me tomorrow and speak to him.'

'Yes I shall.'

'That should stop him.'

'For now, yes, but we have five months to go, my son.'

By the afternoon next day, Olumba was sharing some kola with Diali.

'Do you want to undo all you have done?' the old man asked.

'No.'

'Then don't climb. After five months you can climb iroko trees if you want.'

Olumba laughed.

'So you betrayed me, Ikechi.'

'Don't blame him,' Diali said, 'he did exactly what was expected of him.'

Diali went away and Ikechi went to see to the palm-wine trees. Olumba followed him. Ikechi hurled a club at the wasps' nest and missed. He tried again with no result.

'This is clumsy,' his companion said. 'Wait a moment and I shall show you.' Olumba dashed back to the house and brought a strong new bamboo ladder. He placed the ladder against the tree firmly. He looked around, plucked some leaves and stuck them to his hair.

'What do you want to do?' Ikechi asked.

'Just watch. I shall cut off the climber to which the nest is attached and bring down the wasps and their nest intact. Only few can do it; it is an art you ought to learn.' Ikechi protested but Olumba knew his young friend was getting curious and began to climb.

'What leaves have you in your hair?'

'I will tell you when I come down; meanwhile watch me.'

Ikechi could not recall exactly how it all started but he had a feeling that it was a bird flying past that disturbed the nest of wasps. Suddenly the insects swarmed round Olumba stinging him fiercely. He groaned as he tried to suppress a cry of pain. He waved his matchet about in a bid to ward them off, but they came on swarming all over his head. He held the ladder with one hand, protected his eyes with the other and began to descend two steps at a time. Half-way he missed a step and trod the air. Ikechi shouted as Olumba crashed heavily to the ground. He rushed to his aid. Olumba was breathing with great difficulty and blood was trickling from his nose. Ikechi was hysterical. He shouted again and the evening breeze carried the message to neighbouring compounds.

When the neighbours arrived they were so shocked that for a moment they hung back apparently ignoring Ikechi's suggestion that the injured man be carried into the nearest house. Those who finally helped moved like dream-walkers, their minds vacant. Olumba of all people! Inside his room the injured man was unconscious. His two wives raised a terrible yell. Chituru who was the first elder to get to Olumba's compound quickly ushered the dazed women into a room and pleaded with them to make as little noise as possible. Their husband was not dead, and would probably not die. Until he recovered it was necessary to keep the affair secret so that their opponents would not have cause to hope. These arguments were reasonable of course but in their despair the women would not see reason. They wailed with such passion that within a short time their voices were hoarse and barely audible.

The news spread through the village very rapidly. Men ran down to Olumba's compound. Diali walked down with Ikechi who had brought him the news.

'What happened?' he asked.

'He climbed that palm-wine tree.'

'The wasps stung him?'

'Yes, dede.'

'I knew he would not listen, I know him too well. Olumba is not the man to remain idle for long.'

'But he ought not to have tried a dangerous thing like that. If he had climbed a tree without wasps nothing would have happened to him.'

They got to Olumba's compound. The crowd made way for the chief. He entered the room where the injured man was laid out and studied him for some time. Then he turned to Chituru.

'There is only one dibia I know of who can deal with this?'

'Anwuanwu of Abii?' Chituru asked.

'That's the man.'

'Shall we carry him to Abii or send for Anwuanwu?'

'It will be better to carry him straight to Anwuanwu,' Diali replied. Twenty strong men were quickly chosen and a light bamboo bed procured. Olumba was covered with wrappers and the carriers headed for Abii. It was a dark night, the moon had long gone to bed. The sweating carriers stumbled along hardly caring for the bruises they sustained, so fixed were their minds on their destination.

On his bamboo hammock Olumba moved once in a while. These movements were welcome because it saved the men the trouble of checking from time to time whether their charge was still alive. The squeaking bed broke the silence of the night.

'We want to be relieved,' one of the carriers said.

Eziho the leader ordered the company to stop. Olumba's couch was lowered and his heartbeat felt. He was alive but still unconscious. His breathing seemed to be improving but it was not easy to tell. They adjusted his displaced wrappers to give him maximum protection from the cold night breeze and moved on.

'He will not die,' Eziho announced trying to instil some confidence into the men. But everyone knew that the situation was grave. Ogbunabali killed mostly by night and if the god was behind this then Olumba's life was not worth much. The carriers were particularly worried because carrying a dead body without wearing the right charms was a dangerous thing and, for all they knew, Olumba might turn into a corpse any moment.

After midnight the fourth set of carriers brought Olumba to Abii. When they came to Anwuanwu's house they found it open. Inside the dibia seemed busy sorting out bundles of herbs. Eziho knocked at the open door.

'Come in,' the dibia said.

'Thank Amadioha you are at home,' Eziho said. 'Anwuanwu we are in great trouble.'

'I know,' the dibia said. 'I have been expecting you. Bring in the injured man.'

'Who brought you the news?'

'There they are,' Anwuanwu said nodding towards a corner of the room.

'Where?'

'One of them is standing right in front of you.'

'I can't see anyone.'

'Then don't ask for beings you can't see.'

Eziho ordered the carriers to take in Olumba.

Shortly afterwards Anwuanwu's divination cowries were chasing one another on the floor. After several throws the dibia looked up.

'Ogbunabali has no hand in this,' he said peering closely at his mystical cowries, 'but men are at work.'

'Men?'

'Yes, men.'

'What men?'

'I shall answer that question later. Now we must work fast to save Olumba.'

He made a move to pack away his cowries.

'Wait,' Ikechi said, 'I want to ask a question.'

'Yes?'

'Will Olumba ever be killed by Ogbunabali?'

Anwuanwu laughed: 'No dibia is given the power to predict with certainty when and how a man will die, not even the great dibias at Eluanyim. I can only deal with the present situation, my son.'

The dibia ordered the men to construct a high trestle to support Olumba's bamboo hammock.

'Where can we get forked sticks at this time of the night?' Ikechi asked.

'They are already here,' the dibia said. He led the way outside and showed them four freshly cut forked sticks.

'You seem prepared,' someone said.

'Every dibia should be,' Anwuanwu replied.

The trestle was constructed outside and Olumba's hammock was placed on it. Anwuanwu stretched out the injured man and massaged him all over taking note of painful points. He soon realized that the man had fallen squarely on his back. The dibia made a small fire under Olumba's bed. He tended it, regulating its flame. Carefully he threw in different herbs into the slow fire. The onlookers drew back at the resulting pungent smell. Many thought they had never smelt anything quite like this exotic combination of aromatic herbs. The fire gathered strength and then Olumba began to feel uncomfortable. Anwuanwu resumed his massage until his patient opened his eyes.

'Where am I?' he asked feebly.

'At Abii,' the dibia replied evenly.

'Why?'

'For treatment. You fell from a palm-wine tree.'

'My back aches.'

'You will be all right, my son. Lie still.' The dibia rubbed his patient's face shoulders and chest with a whitish lotion with a touch of pepper in it.

'That should deal with the stings,' he announced confidently.

While Olumba was wriggling on his hot bed Anwuanwu collected materials for a sacrifice and put them into a broken clay pot. He moved a few paces from the men and turned about to face the wall of darkness beyond the circle of feeble light formed by the smouldering healing fire. He mumbled some incantations and turned round again.

'Olumba can you hear me?' he asked.

'Yes,' came the reply.

'Can you talk?'

'Yes.'

'Then repeat after me.'

In a muffled drowsy voice Olumba repeated after the dibia:

> 'Ogbunabali, king of the Night,
> Let not evil spirits rejoice,
> Nor men accuse you of injustice:
> I know your hand is not in this,
> Heal me and clear your good name.'

Three men bore the sacrifice to a road junction.

'Anwuanwu, we don't know how to thank you,' the leader of the Chiolu party said.

'Your man is not well yet,' the dibia reminded them.

'We are sure he will be all right.'

'You are right,' Anwuanwu said.

'Tell me, Anwuanwu,' Eziho said, 'what made Olumba climb that tree? He saw the wasps and he knew how precious his life was.'

'That question brings us to the second phase of our divination,' the dibia said. 'Hold on until I am through with Olumba.'

The dibia resumed his message, stroking Olumba gently from head to toe. Soon the injured man closed his eyes and his regular quiet breathing showed he was asleep. Eziho and his comrades studied him thoughtfully. How different this sleep was from the previous fearful state of unconsciousness.

The slow fire under Olumba's bed died down and the men began to feel the coldness of the dewy night air. Olumba was carried into Anwuanwu's hut and made as comfortable as possible.

'Let's hear the second phase of your divinations,' Eziho said.

'Give me two manillas,' the dibia said stretching out his hand. Ikechi brought out two manillas from a bag he had been carrying all the night and gave them to the dibia. The cowries, worn smooth with long use, rattled as the dibia endeavoured to see through them. For an unusually long time he said nothing. The clink, clink, clink of the cowries eventually roused those of Eziho's party whose chins had sunk to their breasts in sleep.

'Men are at work,' the dibia announced at last. The announcement seemed to have cost him some effort.

'What men?' Eziho asked.

'Hold on!' Anwuanwu said almost in rebuke.

The men watched him silently while he wrestled with whatever forces were opposing him. Suddenly he abandoned his cowries and rummaged in his old sooty medicine-bag over the fire-place. He brought out a small calabash, uncorked it and decanted some of the contents on to his left palm. He rubbed some of the stuff over his eyes which soon filled with tears. He went out and blew the remainder of the brown powdery stuff into the air. He came in again with some haste.

'Now we shall see who is greater!'

His audience said nothing. The dibia was behaving queerly and it was not easy to choose the right words.

'Ha-ha!' Anwuanwu laughed mirthlessly, 'I thought so. Now you reveal yourself, you unscrupulous fellow.'

Eziho and his men began to grow uneasy. Was that last remark meant for them?

'Your opponents are behind Olumba's fall. They have employed a powerful dibia whose work is two-fold: firstly to work on Olumba's mind and make him careless of his safety, secondly to prevent any other dibia from finding out what is happening and taking counter measures. However, I have laid him bare. There he is at last, the mischievous fellow,' Anwuanwu concluded, laughing and gazing at his cowries.

'Do you mean that our opponents have employed a dibia to work against us?' Ikechi asked with a sinking heart.

'Yes, my son.'

'But the priest of Ogbunabali pronounced a curse on anyone who would attempt any such thing.'

'That may be true, but tough dibias can do many things.'

'Can dibias fight against spirits and gods?' Eziho asked his jaws dropping in perplexity.

'Yes.'

'How can a dibia be more powerful than a god?'

'Dibias are weaker than even the weakest ghosts, but they can set a powerful spirit against a weaker troublesome one and so stop the latter's actions. The dibia involved in this case hopes to pit other gods against Ogbunabali if the latter attacks him. Actually if the Pond of Wagaba belongs to Aliakoro, Ogbunabali will ignore your opponents and deal with Olumba.'

'And if the pond belongs to us?'

'The god will do justice. He is a powerful god and should not be trifled with. No true dibia ever tries to interfere with the gods in matters of this nature. The great dibias at Eluanyim teach that such interference is not only wrong but dangerous. A god may be put off once but he never forgets. Decades later he may try a second visitation and strike down not only the dibia but all his relations also. For instance, there were originally twelve family groups here in Abii. Many years ago, no one living knows how many, one family was completely wiped out because of this type of thing. The members of this family, young and old, suddenly began to die in twos and threes. Dibias who attempted to arrest the situation fell ill and recovered only when they withdrew their help. The last survivor of the family ran away to Aliji but the god was after him. After dining with his host he was found dead the next morning. Many thought his host had poisoned him but the innocent man was so angry at this insinuation that he called for a public inquiry into his guest's death. The elders of Aliji went for a divination and the truth was out.

'Even now, when Abii families have anything to share, it is divided into twelve parts. When eleven portions have been selected, the twelfth portion – known as "the share that vanishes" – is subdivided among the other families.'

'Anwuanwu, what shall we do?' Eziho's voice was all doubt and fear.

'That is for your elders at home to decide. When you go back, let them know my findings. If they are interested let them consult me again. Meanwhile I shall see that Olumba recovers from this particular mishap.'

At dawn Ikechi and another man were left behind to help look after Olumba. The rest returned to Chiolu. As soon as they arrived, Eziho went straight to Olumba's compound. Although the sun was up, Olumba's compound was unswept. A thin column of smoke somewhere in the backyard was the only indication of life in the compound.

'Nyoma! Nyoma!'

A door was timidly opened and Olumba's first wife came out trembling. She could not ask the urgent question burning on her lips, the voice to carry over the question was hoarse with continuous crying.

'Your husband is alive. He should be back in a few days. Anwuanwu is a great dibia. It was lucky we sent him there without hesitation.'

The woman fell on her knees facing the shrine of Amadioha. 'Amadioha, I thank you. Ojukwu, you too. Stand behind your son and sustain him lest any man should accuse you of injustice.'

Eziho was struck by the last sentence. Was that not what Anwuanwu made Olumba repeat after him?

Eziho went to the backyards to see Wogari and the children.

'I hope you are all well. There is nothing to worry about. Olumba will be back shortly. While he is away you can count on me to do all that he would do for you if he were here.'

'Eziho, we thank you,' Nyoma said.

'No need to thank me; your husband would do the same for me and more. Is there anything you want me to do right now?'

'Nothing,' Nyoma replied.

'As Ikechi is away who will tap the palm wine?' Wogari asked.

'I shall do that,' Eziho said. 'I shall go to make ready and come back as soon as possible.'

He did not come back soon for the discussions he had with the elders were elaborate. There was much concern over Aliakoro's mean manoeuvres.

'The gods see everything; let us leave matters in their hands,' Diali said.

'I think we should get Anwuanwu to oppose whatever dibia is working against us,' Chituru replied. 'The gods will no doubt help us, but we should also do something for ourselves. While a dibia fights to save a sick man, the sick man also fights to save himself.'

In spite of Chituru's observations many of the elders felt that it was enough to have the gods on their side and the move to invite Anwuanwu was turned down.

Although Olumba's wives were not aware of the elders' decisions – all such decisions were top secret – they privately invited Achichi the local dibia to help in the fight for their husband's life. Achichi was able to divine that Ogbunabali, the god of the night was not responsible for Olumba's present plight but he could not tell who or what was responsible.

He offered routine sacrifices to ward off evil spirits. More important, he instilled the much needed confidence into Olumba's two wives. They began to sweep their husbands's compound and to run the household as if Olumba were around.

Five days after Olumba's fall Diali and some elders were listening to the latest reports on Olumba; it was a daily ritual now. Three men walked into the Eze's reception hall and saluted him. Diali looked them over. They were from Aliakoro.

'My lord,' the leader of the delegation said, 'we bear important messages from Eze Okehi.'

'Sit down, my son,' Diali replied graciously, 'and let's have some kola first. There is time enough for any discussion.' '

Kola was served and while the crunching was still going on, the spokesman of the envoy opened up again with unconcealed eagerness:

'What we have to say concerns Olumba.'

There were only three other Chiolu elders apart from Diali.

'Wait, my son,' Diali said and sent off two of his children to call other elders. The elders hurried down as soon as they were told that Aliakoro's representatives had come. In a short time Diali's hall had little room to spare. Ikechi was among those present. His enthusiasm over village affairs and his attachment to Olumba had won him a place in exclusive village talks of this nature.

'Let's hear you, my son,' Diali said. 'By the way what is your name. I recognize you very well but the name has escaped me.'

'I am Wago, Wago the leopard-killer.' Wago's deep-set eyes surveyed Eze Diali.

'What messages have you brought us?'

'Eze Okehi and the elders of Aliakoro have heard of Olumba's death. They sent us to discuss when the Ezes of the Erekwi clan will be summoned to pronounce us the rightful owners of the Pond of Wagaba.'

Eze Diali allowed himself a short laugh, while other elders merely smiled. In conferences of this nature both speech and laughter were properly controlled for a laugh that was out of place could jeopardize the village.

'You seem to know more of our affairs than we do ourselves.'

'Well, my lord, certain things cannot be hidden; this is one of them. Also we have been very vigilant. When a man has some yams in the fire his attention is not easily distracted.'

'Elders, what answer shall we give?' Diali said facing his counsellors, an amused expression on his face.

'It is simple,' Wezume said. 'Without resorting to any parable we should point out that Olumba is *not* dead.'

'You hear our answer?' Diali said turning to Wago and his men.

'We must say that this statement is not true. One can convince a blind man that there is no oil in the soup and get away with it, not so with pepper and salt.'

'What are you talking about?' Diali asked enjoying the situation.

'The fact is that after Olumba had fallen, he disappeared. If he is nowhere, he must be dead.'

'How do you know he is nowhere? Do you live with him?'

'No, my lord, but we are vigilant.'

'Your vigilance is not very effective,' Diali said raising general laughter.

'Where is Olumba?' Wago persisted.

'We can't tell you.'

'Because he is dead.'

'Have his wives shaved their hair? Have you seen any new grave in his compound? When a man like Olumba dies don't you think he will be buried in the middle of his compound?'

'Not in a situation like this,' Wago replied, convinced that Chiolu elders were putting on an act.

'Go back and tell Eze Okehi, my brother Eze, that Olumba is alive. If he doubts it, he can send his elders to verify.'

'We want to save them the trouble.'

'No you can't. This is a big issue. Death, if it comes, will be certified jointly by your elders and ours.'

'When do you want the elders to come?'

'Eight days from now.'

'I believe we can wait since time won't make much difference now.'

Wago and his men left. Diali and the elders enjoyed a long laugh afterwards. It was probably the best laugh Diali's hall had heard since the first battle of the Great Ponds. With unusual good humour the elders planned a long interview calculated to fool and confound the elders of Aliakoro if they were foolish enough to come up.

They did turn up after eight days. Eze Okehi thought it was his crowning triumph and made the journey despite his lingering illness. After much wrangling and simulated anger Chiolu produced Olumba dramatically.

11

IGWU was not very interested in fishing. During the fishing season he went once or twice merely to exercise his right as a son of the village. Like other villagers he had a vague feeling that the Pond of Wagaba was Aliakoro's but he felt it was not worth fighting for. He deplored what to him was a stupid exchange of fish for human lives. He never expressed these opinions to anyone for fear of being labelled a traitor to the cause of his village. In fact he did what he could in the way of charms and sacrifices to help his village win the war. He did not fight; nor was he expected to. But he was a strong well-built man and by no means a coward. Indeed when he was younger, he had aspired to have as many notches on his bow as possible. His shooting was good and he wielded his matchet with more than average dexterity. He was once a budding wrestling champion for he had maintained two years of unbroken victories. If he had done five more years without being beaten he would have become a champion.

Then the blow came. His personal spirits or agwu that had been kept at bay for some years suddenly became dangerously active. Igwu became irresponsible. He neglected his farms and developed very rude manners. He could not keep money and his personal appearance became loathsome. His father was obliged to thatch his house when the rains came for no one could persuade Igwu to mend his own roof. There was only one way to pacify his agwu – Igwu had to become a dibia. At first the young man refused to accept this recommendation and fought with the dibia whom his parents had called to deal with the situation. But the longer he held out the worse his condition grew until his sanity became questionable. Fortunately he gave in at this point. For a start he stayed in the forest without proper food for eight days and eight nights. After this the dibia who was looking after him took him to Eluanyim to learn the ways of the spirits. After a few months (some say he did not complete the course) he came back bringing with him his famous divination drums. The spectacular accuracy of his divinations, and the fact that he was then the only known dibia who employed drums for seeing beyond this world, built up his reputation quickly.

As was expected, Igwu's eccentricities vanished as soon as he became a dibia. He established shrines for his agwu and found peace.

That was twenty years before. Igwu now a middle-aged man was not behind in his profession. His name was mentioned along with famous names like Anyika, Anwuanwu and Agwoturumbe. He chose to remain unmarried for a long time in a bid to achieve high proficiency. But he was not a recluse and his relationship with other villagers was normal. He took part in those activities which did not go against his professional rules.

After that severe battle with his personal spirits, Igwu developed a great respect for spirits and gods. Of course this was to be expected from any dibia, but Igwu's direct personal experience deepened this attitude. When therefore the elders of Aliakoro asked him to do something about Olumba he refused at first.

'There is a curse on anyone who tries to hurt Olumba,' he pointed out.

'Yes, but we don't want you to hurt him,' Wago replied.

'What am I expected to do?'

'Make him careless.'

'So that he may run into danger?'

'Well, yes.'

'That means hurting him.'

'Not directly.'

'Ogbunabali is a strong god and should not be trifled with.'

'You will only be helping him to do justice because the pond belongs to us.'

'Do you doubt that?' Eze Okehi asked knowing that the dibia could only give one answer.

So Igwu found himself working to destroy Olumba's sense of self-preservation. At the same time he did all he could to protect himself from the possible fury of Ogbunabali, god of the night. Some eight days after, Olumba had fallen off the palm-wine tree. Although Olumba had not died the incident had showed quite clearly Igwu's capabilities.

When the elders who had gone to check on Olumba's death

returned disappointed they held another meeting, in which they decided to persuade Igwu to go all out for Olumba's life.

For days Igwu maintained the stand that to interfere with Ogbunabali would be very dangerous and refused to do anything. After the general meeting to which he was invited, the elders went singly and in twos and threes to plead with him. Igwu did not budge.

'We shall give up the idea,' Eze Okehi told Wago. 'Igwu has refused to help us. Let us leave Ogbunabali to judge.'

'Why should he refuse?' Wago said. 'He is a member of this village and he does not need to be persuaded to help.'

'See what you can do; as for me, I shall not plead with him any more.'

'He will help,' the leopard-killer grumbled and walked over to Igwu's compound.

The dibia was indoors. He was lying on his bamboo bed resting. Wago knocked, wiped his brow and entered. He sighed with pleasure as Igwu's hut cut off the scorching rays of the midday sun. Wago sat down. Igwu did not rise from his bed. His face was a mask of sullenness.

'Igwu, you know why I am here,' Wago said.

'Yes, I do.'

'What do you say?'

'The same thing.'

'Why?'

'For the same reasons you have heard twenty times over.'

'Are you afraid?'

'Yes.'

'Of whom?'

'Of Ogbunabali, god of the night.'

'But the pond is ours.'

'Why did you not volunteer to swear at Isiali?'

Wago thought that over for a moment.

'You see I am a hunter and can die any time.'

'Is Olumba not a hunter?'

'Hardly. He has never killed a leopard; I have three skins.'

Igwu did not reply. His toes twitched as he studied his roof.

'There is one thing you forget,' Wago said.

'What?'

'That whatever you do is the responsibility of the village. If Ogbunabali ever gets angry, his fury will be on the whole village, not on you alone.'

'You don't know the ways of the gods.'

'I think I do.'

The dibia turned his head sideways and looked at Wago. He smiled and resumed his study of the ceiling.

'What can you claim to have done for your village?' Wago asked. 'Two cousins of mine have died in this war, and my daughter has been kidnapped and perhaps killed. I myself have come face to face with death so many times. What have you done? You merely sit here concocting charms that do no one any good.'

'Why do you now think my charms can work against Olumba?'

'Well, we are not sure. We just want to get you to do something for once.'

Igwu got up slowly and faced the shrine at the head end of his bed. Then he turned round slowly to face Wago. It tasked Wago's manliness not to retreat a step or two.

'Listen,' the dibia said slowly. 'A bird that flies too fast may fly past its nest. Wago, you think you are upholding this village but in fact you are wrecking it. No one wanted this stupid war in which so many magnificent young men have died. It was all your doing. But you are not content with that. You now want to bring the anger of the gods on the whole village. Pfff!' Igwu spat on Wago. 'You are worse than a goat.'

'You spit on me? Your eyes will grow dark now!'

Wago roared with rage. He made ready to spring on the dibia, but the latter said coolly.

'Do not fight here or you will be dead by tomorrow. You are a good wrestler, a leopard-killer and all that, but I am prepared to wrestle seven times with you on the arena tomorrow. I want to test this strength of which you are so proud.'

Wago laughed in spite of himself. 'You say I am a goat but you are much worse. Why can't you think before throwing a stupid challenge like that? All the charms in the world will not help you. I shall throw you down as many times as we shall wrestle and you will probably develop a hunchback at the end of it.'

'I shall use no charms; that would be making it too difficult for you. But you may come with all the charms I have prepared for you,' Igwu said grinning.

'Before we start I shall hand over all your useless charms to you. I have thrown some of them away and I am none the weaker for it. Igwu, you are useless in this village if you cannot do the one thing you claim you can do to help your village. I know why you don't feel the effects of the war; neither you nor any of your relations have done any fighting at all. You are a cowardly stupid lot.'

'You ought to have lost your entire family, you mad dog,' Igwu retorted.

'I am not surprised,' Wago sneered. 'Only a man who has no wife and children can talk like that. The cry of a baby means nothing to you.'

'I know I am a lonely man. I have no household, yet I care more for the lives of people than you do. You love your wives and children and yet you started the war.'

'I would rather fight than swallow an insult. Only imbeciles like you can choose otherwise.'

'Wago, I am a man like you!'

'You are a woman and a weak one at that!'

'Let's get out now and wrestle.'

'I am ready.'

The two men strode out and walked towards the arena. On the way Wago called some other men to come along saying: 'I do not want to give him any chance to deny anything afterwards.'

Soon many villagers particularly the children were rushing to the arena excitedly. As soon as Eze Okehi heard this he went off to the arena with two other elders who had been chatting with him in his reception hall. When he got there he saw Wago adjusting the tails of his wrapper.

'What childishness is this?' Okehi said angrily. 'Wago and Igwu, are you out of your senses?'

'He challenged me,' Wago said.

'Igwu, is that true?'

'Yes. Wago's much vaunted strength has made him drunk. I want to disillusion him for once.'

'But you are weak, that is the truth,' Wago said grinning and apparently keen on the match.

Igwu grew angrier and pushed aside all who tried to stop the contest. Still Eze Okehi and the elders would not let them. But Wago continued his taunting until Igwu thought he had had enough.

'I shall wrestle with Wago,' he roared. 'If you touch me you do so at your peril! Wago get ready!'

'I have been ready for quite a while!' Some young men and children giggled.

The two men closed in. Wago, all smiles, made funny passes at Igwu making him look foolish. Wago feinted to the left and stopped abruptly. Igwu rushed to the same direction only to find Wago not there. The growing crowd laughed. Igwu bit his lips and made a desperate swoop. He came so fast that he was able to hold Wago's two legs. As he poised for what would have been a classic throw his right hand slipped and siezing the chance Wago extricated himself. The noise from the crowd died down as Wago struggled free. Then the smile on Wago's face was replaced by a look so sinister that the spectators held their breath. Wago was on the offensive. He pushed this way and that looking for an opening. None was forthcoming. It looked as if Igwu had not forgotten his tactics. So far he was holding his own; but only that far, for in the next moment Wago gave him a sudden vigorous push and as he staggered backwards kicked his legs together. Igwu fell in an untidy heap and the crowd gasped. The dibia picked himself up smartly and moved into the attack again. But his heavy breathing showed he was getting tired. Wago on the other hand seemed to be gathering strength. He threw down his opponent twice more and the elders held him.

Igwu, though brown with dust, held his head high.

'I lack practice, that is all. I don't think you are much stronger. The elders know I would have been a champion but for my agwu. So while others wrestled with men, I wrestled with spirits. But I will show that these years have not been wasted.'

'If you are that much a dibia why don't you help the village? You are a good-for-nothing,' Wago said haughtily. Wago's relations were afraid. 'You don't talk to a dibia like that,' they warned.

'Nonsense, he is good for nothing.'

'We shall see,' Igwu said and went home, shaking off the sands of the arena still clinging to his back.

Two days later Wago was ill. He could not eat and his sleep was one long nightmare. There was no doubt what was wrong with him. His wives and relatives went straight to the dibia to plead for his life.

'I am not responsible for his illness,' Igwu said with feigned unconcern. 'I am good for nothing, how can I harm him?'

'Please don't take Wago's words seriously,' Wago's people pleaded. 'What shall we pay to induce you to restore his health?'

'Nothing.'

'Do you want him to die?'

'No.'

'Then what?'

'I shall release him from his illness only if he comes here himself.'

'Can't we . . .'

'That is all,' the dibia said with finality.

Back home Wago roared: 'I shall rather die than go to Igwu's house to beg for mercy.' His wives pleaded in vain. In the end Eze Okehi came to plead with him.

'It is futile and foolish to pit yourself against Igwu. He is a dibia and when it comes to the supernatural we have to accord him due respects. You have shown you are better at wrestling, now it is your turn to admit defeat.' Not Wago, the leopard-killer. He refused to move and threatened to fight with anyone who repeated the suggestion. But he got no better. By the fourth day his wives were seriously alarmed. They dashed back to Igwu.

'The fact is,' the dibia pointed out, 'he can only recover if he sits by the shrine in my house while I give him medicines.'

By the sixth day Wago was dying. He was unconscious for the greater part of the day. Towards evening his relatives carried him to the dibia's house without trouble. He was far too weak to resist. He spent the night in Igwu's house. On the morrow he felt stronger and asked for food. He ate and slept heavily until evening. When he woke he looked round and asked where he was. No one answered him. When eventually he knew where he was he rose angrily to go. He was too weak to walk yet, and he staggered into Igwu's arms when he got to the door.

'Let me go,' he said as vehemently as his illness would let him.

'I should rather die than beg you for my life.' Igwu said nothing, but held him down by sheer force. From then on, Wago refused to take any more medicines.

'Take him home, he will be all right,' the dibia said quietly. 'I wonder why I bothered about him in the first place. He who immitates a left-handed man often hurts himself.'

'It is not enough for him to get well,' Wago's first wife said. 'We must settle this quarrel between you.'

'As far as I am concerned the quarrel is over. I have been a fool, that is all,' Igwu said.

'I am not prepared for any settlement,' Wago said.

Wago's quarrel with the dibia generated a lot of tension in the village. Eze Okehi knew this was undesirable particularly now that co-operation among the villagers was so vital. So he called a meeting of the elders to straighten out differences between the two men.

'I don't regard this as a quarrel,' Igwu said with a smile. 'Some people require firm handling now and then to bring them to normal, that is all.'

'My illness soon after the wrestling bout was a mere coincidence,' Wago said. 'If you want to brag about it, you can go ahead. You are like the troublesome wife who is always ready to fight with her husband but runs away from other women in the streets. For days we have begged you to help us, and like the coward you are you have refused. Now you have the face to say you are responsible for my illness. Are you not ashamed? Of what use are you in this village?'

Igwu was stung. All eyes were on him. No one said anything.

'Wago,' the dibia replied rising, 'I am not your match in words.'

'Nor are you in deeds,' Wago the leopard-killer interrupted.

'I will now show that I am more than a match for you in deeds. Elders, I am prepared to do whatever you want. Take note however that I shall take no blame for the consequences. I have nothing to lose. I have no household. I am as lonely as a knife-blade without a handle.'

'Sit down, Igwu,' an elder said. 'Let's do one thing at a time. Whether you help us or not is not what we are here for. We are about to emerge from a war. We do not want to plunge ourselves into internal disagreements which can at times be more uncomfortable than an inter-village war. Let us resolve your differences now.'

Okehi and the other elders echoed these sentiments. They also took note of Igwu's long-sought promise of help.

After further talks the two men came forward and embraced each other to demonstrate their reconciliation.

'Now that we are through with this,' Okehi said, 'we can discuss any other matters. Igwu, I take it that your offer to help was made in anger?'

'No, I meant it.'

'Good. Tomorrow we shall hold another meeting about that. Elders, are you in agreement?'

'Yes,' came the chorus.

The assembly dispersed leaving Eze Okehi and Wago the leopard-killer.

'Wago, I must say you have behaved badly,' Okehi said gently.

'I have got what I wanted. I am mainly responsible for the war of the Great Ponds. I am determined to see that we win in the end, for otherwise all the lives lost, including my daughter's, would be in vain.'

'That wrestling was ridiculous.'

Wago laughed mischievously. 'Serves him right. His words stung me into accepting the challenge.'

'Go to him when you have the time and apologize. That will be more effective than all that we have said in this hall today.'

'I can't do that, my lord.'

'Why not.'

126

'Igwu is proud.'

'Are you not?'

'I am.'

'Will you go to him?'

'I say I won't,' Wago said, his eyes flashing.

'But you've got what you wanted.'

'That is true. However, you have settled our differences and I don't see why I should go to beg him. After all we embraced each other in public.'

'You see, to work well, he must have a calm mind. He made that promise in anger as you could see.'

'When people press me too hard they say I am mad. Why can't he apologize to me? A dibia is only a man, no matter what his powers are. If any other man had made this suggestion I should have fought him outright.'

Okehi laughed and said: 'Wago you are mad.'

'My lord, I mean it. Don't suggest it again, don't, don't!'

'As you please, my son,' the old man said thoughtfully and walked towards his house.

The next day a few chosen elders met again, this time in Igwu's house. Methodically Igwu gave the details of the processes involved. Then he added: 'There is one important point. I shall need a fragment of Olumba's clothing or anything that he has touched. How can we get that?'

'That won't be easy,' Okehi said, 'but what must be done will be done. We shall assign the job to one or two young men.'

Just then, Igwu looked at Wago. Wago thought he read a challenge in Igwu's eyes and rose abruptly: 'I shall get a bit of Olumba's clothing or whatever else you want,' the leopard-killer announced briefly. The elders sensed the tension between the two men but did not betray their amusement.

Nothing could be done until Wago fulfilled his promise. The elders dispersed to reassemble when Wago came back from his mission.

By the afternoon of the next day the warrior left for Chiolu and arrived by night. He did not risk taking the main village path. He

127

walked through the bush keeping the village to his left. He did not feel lost for he had taken the same path several times at night when the war was on.

His plan was simple. He would hide near the fenced-in enclosure in which Olumba normally had his bath and wait for an opportunity to cut off a piece of his wrapper. The cutting would not present much difficulty because Olumba would normally spread his wrapper on the fence with one end overhanging.

For two nights Olumba chose to bathe in the daytime. Wago began to feel uncomfortable. His stock of food was running out and any attempt to replenish it might give him away. On the third night things happened perfectly. Olumba heard only a slight rustling as Wago's sharp matchet nipped off a tiny fragment of his wrapper. A dog barked as Wago scampered off with his prize but no attention was paid to it.

The next day, Igwu set to work. The chosen elders watched in fascination as Igwu assembled his ingredients.

'I hope I shall never do this again,' the dibia said rather sadly. 'The great dibias at Eluanyim taught me this particular art reluctantly just before I left them. One very old dibia said to me: "If you use this sparingly or not at all, you will be a successful dibia and die happily."'

The elders said nothing but looked on with awe.

'My lord,' Igwu said addressing Okehi, 'the ingredients are all here. Leave me now and I shall do the rest.'

The elders dispersed and the dibia began a long complicated ritual almost defying description. In brief, he set a huge pot of water boiling. Into this he first cast the fragment from Olumba's wrapper, then the various ingredients the elders had collected, among them thorns, a scorpion and the skin cast off by a viper. All the while Igwu mumbled incantations, now facing the east, now the west. The last item to get into the pot was a short chunk of plantain stem carved like a man. Before it was thrown in, Igwu called Olumba's name three times. As the concoction boiled the dibia poked at the carved plantain stem with a long thin knife, piercing the face, the stomach and other vital parts.

128

12

AFTER his bath Olumba went in for supper. The rent in his wrapper was so small that he did not notice it until the afternoon of the next day. He was sitting in his reception hall making thatch.

'I wonder when this was torn off,' he said studying the rent. Wogari was putting Olumba's son to sleep. She looked up and asked: 'What is that, my lord?'

'One corner of my wrapper is off.'

'Must be rats.'

'Must be, they are multiplying fast. One was nibbling at my toes the other night.'

'That reminds me I must fill up these holes in your bedroom and plaster the walls and the floor.'

'You had better or I shall have no wrappers left. You have left it too long.'

'That's because I want to do the plastering with red nchara mud. Ordinary mud won't do.'

'Why not?'

'The new yam festival will be celebrated soon. Also you will be released from your oath at about the same time.'

His oath. Silly woman to remind him of it. It had been off his mind since morning, and what peace of mind had been his for that brief period of forgetfulness! Now his mind was full again; the first battle of the Great Ponds; the fight with Wago the leopard-killer; the second battle with its ambushes, negotiations and snatch parties; Ezes of the Erekwi clan; Ogbunabali the god of the night. This train of thought was now a part of him. It always ended with grave doubts for the future.

Olumba tried to concentrate more on his thatches to arrest his thoughts. It was no use. He could see the face of the priest of Ogbunabali right there on the thatch in hand. He dropped the half-finished thatch to think. If the god had not struck in three months, the Pond of Wagaba must be theirs. Why should Ogbunabali wait so long if he meant to strike?

'The god may strike on the last day.'

Olumba was startled. That voice again. It was getting louder.

Was it his mind working or was the voice really outside him? Each time he tried to reassure himself something in him always opposed his views. At first it was merely a question of a mind doubting its own deductions. But later Olumba began to think it was rather more than that. At times the voice was so loud that he actually looked round to see if there was someone else near. Always it succeeded in forcing its fears and gloomy views on him. After three months he took to answering back audibly.

'No, the god will not strike on the last day,' he muttered.

Wogari looked up.

'Were you speaking to me, my lord?'

'No.'

The woman redoubled her efforts to put the child to sleep. It was also an attempt to hide the fear clearly etched out on her beautiful face. Ever since Olumba started muttering to himself the women had had to resort to devious ways to hide their fears and tears. From her childhood Wogari had associated this type of muttering with the mentally ill and the death-bed cases. But here beside her was a case that was neither. It frightened her more than anything else.

Fed up with his mental battles Olumba put away the thatches and began to stroll towards Diali's. On the way a brightly coloured snake crossed his path. Olumba stood rooted to the spot. That was azigwo the snake of ill omen. He watched it disappear on the other side of the road and turned back. As soon as he got home he told his wife about it.

'I have just seen an azigwo.'

'Amadioha forbid!'

'Let's go to Achichi.'

Achichi had gone off to farm. The couple tried again in the evening.

'It is merely a warning that you should be careful,' Achichi said during the divination.

'Who is warning me?' Olumba asked.

'Amadioha.'

'Any sacrifices involved?'

'Nothing much. Just a few trifles to thank the god for his warning.'

'How am I to be careful?'

'Avoid climbing trees and things like that,' Achichi said, a wisp of a smile on his face.

'I know all that,' Olumba said with slight irritation. 'I am wondering if there is any specific thing or person I should beware of.'

'Nothing in particular,' the dibia said.

The single sacrifice was performed that evening. Olumba went to bed with some relief. If Amadioha the god of thunder and of the skies was good enough to warn him, things would turn out well.

Near midnight he woke with a start. He was sweating and trembling. He went into the next room and woke Wogari.

'Did you call me?'

'No, my lord.'

'I thought I heard my name three times.'

'Did you answer?'

'I think I did.'

'Amadioha forbid! It must have been a vivid dream.'

'I doubt it.'

'What can it be?'

'I don't know, but it was so . . .' He wanted to say frightening but checked himself. That was the wrong thing to say before his wife.

'Go and sleep, my lord. I am sure it was a dream.'

Olumba went to bed but it was no use. The room was unbearable. Why, he could not tell, but he was sure he could not stay in there one moment longer. He felt very hot and the air was stifling. He hardly knew when he moved over to the other room and lay beside his wife.

'Chei! My lord, you are hot,' she said a moment later in alarm.

'Wogari, I don't feel well.'

'What is it?'

'I don't know.'

'Should I light the lamp?'

'Yes.'

The woman went into the kitchen and brought a glowing firebrand. With this she lit the oil lamp. The yellow flickering light revealed her husband's shocked features. Before her very eyes

Olumba's condition was deteriorating at an astonishing rate. Frightened, she walked over to the other house and woke Nyoma.

'Come and see what I am seeing,' she said tearfully. Together the distraught women went back to Olumba. His eyes were now closed and his breathing was laboured. Perspiration ran down his muscular body in rivulets. Without another word, Nyoma went off to call Achichi. Normally she would have been frightened to step out alone in the small hours of the morning. But now the usual feminine fear of the dark left her. She could not tell which of the many possible routes she took to Achichi's house. She found herself knocking frantically at the dibia's door.

Achichi came to Olumba with Nyoma and tried a quick divination, but he failed for the first time in his career. He saw nothing. He tried again and again. All was blank. What now? Was he to confess his inability to divine anything? It was unheard of.

'Olumba's father's spirit is angry,' he told the women off-hand.

'Why?'

'Some neglected sacrifices.'

Achichi was ashamed to deceive his clients but there was no other way out. If he spoke the truth no one would have faith in him any more and that would be too bad for the village. He chose to deceive a single client instead.

As he expected Olumba got no better. By the evening of the next day the warrior was critically ill. Eze Diali came to see him.

'Where do you feel pain,' he asked.

'Everywhere,' Olumba moaned. 'My head, my chest, my stomach. Chei! I am burning!'

Diali studied the sick man for a moment. He thought there was no time for a meeting. On his initiative he sent Ikechi and another young man to fetch Anwuanwu from Abii. As soon as the young men got under way, he held a brief meeting with the elders who had already gathered in Olumba's compound.

'I have sent for Anwuanwu. I don't think Achichi can handle this,' he told the elders.

'That is right,' they agreed.

Waiting for Anwuanwu to arrive proved a nerve-racking affair.

Olumba sickened at a rate that made everyone panic. The whole village was hushed. Achichi bustled about doing whatever came to his mind. He hung charms across the doorway, rubbed the sick man over with medicine and gave him potions to drink. The obvious futility of his efforts was frightening. People would have felt better if he had done nothing. Behind the old men's mind was one uncomfortable fact. If Ogbunabali, god of the night, was at work then Olumba might die before Anwuanwu arrived. If Olumba could hold out till morning then the dibia would have perhaps one whole day to battle for his life.

Olumba survived the night. Anwuanwu arrived by mid-morning. He cleared everyone, except Diali and two elders, from Olumba's room. He looked at the sick man and let out a short mirthless laugh from the back of his throat. The old men watched him puzzled. The dibia brought out his divination cowries and threw them hither and thither on the floor. He laughed again.

'I thought so,' he murmured.

'What?' Diali asked.

The dibia ignored the question and fished in his medicine-bag. He brought out a black horn and poured some black powder on to his palm. He went outside, faced the direction of Aliakoro and blew the powder into the air three times. He ran into the house again, picked up a huge talisman and dashed out. Once again he faced Aliakoro and shouted:

'Taaa!'

He waved the talisman round his head three times, spat to the left, and to the right, and went into Olumba's room. Once more his cowries rattled and he studied them intently.

'Olumba is being cooked,' he announced.

'Cooked?'

'Yes. Also the dibia responsible is working hard to prevent other dibias from finding out what is happening. At first my cowries were dumb, but I have now cleared the way.'

'Who is doing the cooking?'

'Your enemies at Aliakoro. Olumba, did you hear any call at any time?'

133

'Yes,' the sick man murmured.

'Are any of your wrappers missing?'

'No.'

'Any torn off?'

'No, but rats ate a corner of the one I have on.'

Anwuanwu examined Olumba's wrapper and smiled.

'This rent could not have been made by rats. The cut edge is even. That shows that a knife was employed.'

'Are you saying that someone from Aliakoro came here and cut off a corner of Olumba's wrapper?' Diali asked incredulously.

'Exactly.'

'What for?'

'For the cooking process.'

It sounded a tall tale. Diali thought it wise to swallow it. There was so little time for arguments.

'So there is no god behind all this.' Diali said.

'Let me see,' the dibia replied and studied a few more throws.

'No god is involved,' he said confidently.

The old men were reassured.

'You can deal with the situation?'

'Yes,' the dibia said simply with a smile. All through the morning Anwuanwu battled for Olumba's life. Towards evening his patient's condition showed some improvement. Meanwhile the elders collected materials for a great sacrifice. The spectacular part of the many rituals performed that night was the burying of a big he-goat alive. According to the dibia Olumba's spirit had already travelled half-way to the spirit world. The only way to persuade the spirits to let him go was to offer them a he-goat's life. The he-goat was buried with all the ceremonies normally accorded to a dead man. It was washed and a new wrapper was tied round it before burial.

In two days Olumba was well again. His recovery was as rapid as his illness had been sudden. The elders paid the dibia's fees without question. Anwuanwu thanked them.

'Don't thank us,' Diali said. 'We owe you all the thanks. Money is nothing compared to Olumba's life.'

'That is true.'

'Anwuanwu, we want to strike a deal with you. We want to retain you for Olumba for the next three months. You can see for yourself that we have no one else to fall back to.'

'I am prepared to work for you as long as you like.'

'Good. We shall find you a nice house in the village.'

'I won't need one.'

'Why?'

'I shall not stay here. I can work quite effectively from Omokachi.'

'You don't say you are leaving us now?'

'I shall stay for four more days to complete my work. Olumba is well but the dibia at Aliakoro is still on the offensive. His pot boils yet. My job is to render that pot ineffective as far as Olumba is concerned.'

The next four days were very busy ones for Anwuanwu. He did so many strange things that no one cared to come near the room in which he was working. At night strange noises were heard. Huge night birds flew past Olumba's compound flapping their wings ominously. During the day animals which normally avoid man strayed into the compound with impunity. Anwuanwu had warned everyone not to attempt to kill any wild animals he might see. He did the killing himself. A tortoise appeared first in Olumba's reception hall. Elders who were sitting in the hall thought the dibia had brought it along. When Anwuanwu explained that it was a wild one straight from the bush everyone was shocked. The reception hall was deserted and strange tales of many wild animals taking over Olumba's hall spread through the village. It is difficult now to say which stories are true. The case of the tortoise is well authenticated but it is not easy to dismiss Nyoma's assertion that she saw a viper and an owl after the appearance of the tortoise. According to the woman, Anwuanwu killed the animals as they appeared and carried them into the room allotted to him. What he did with these creatures no one knew.

Today Chiolu villagers still talk of those four hectic days Anwuanwu spent in their village, trying to overcome the dibia at Aliakoro.

After the four days Anwuanwu went back to Abii. Olumba was

now well protected with charms and he knew what to do in an emergency. However the strain told on him. He lost weight and shadows crept under his eyes. His first wife thought she saw a few more grey hairs on his head and she pulled them out as her husband relaxed in his reception hall.

Although Anwuanwu had put Olumba on his feet again the villagers of Chiolu, especially the elders, were worried. Why should Aliakoro resort to such practices? Diali called a meeting of the elders. It was a rowdy meeting; everyone was angry. Several elders suggested a counteraction.

'Let's show them that we too can do some cooking,' Chituru said. This suggestion was adopted and Anwuanwu was sent for.

'Tell Eze Diali,' Anwuanwu told the messengers, 'that I shall do no such thing. If he insists let him get another dibia. The gods are wise; they know what to do.'

Anwuanwu's attitude irritated the elders, but there was nothing they could do. By now they had a great respect for the dibia and they thought it wise to accept his decision. As an alternative a protest delegation was sent to Aliakoro but Eze Okehi denied being responsible for Olumba's illness.

'This is funny,' the old Eze said. 'Your man is under oath and should die if the pond is ours as in fact it is. He falls ill and you turn round to accuse us. Do you think Ogbunabali is asleep? He is doing his work, for the time has come.'

Chiolu could not argue. There was no strong evidence to support any argument. Aliakoro elders laughed when a Chiolu delegate pointed out that a fragment of Olumba's wrapper had been cut off.

'Let Olumba build a new house,' Okehi said. 'Rats have taken over his present house.'

Okehi and his men continued their discussion after the embarrassed Chiolu delegates had left.

'Wago, what is Olumba's present condition?' an elder asked. Wago had been spying incessantly on Chiolu.

'Soon after Igwu's action, Olumba became very ill. Achichi their dibia could do nothing. Fortunately for them they sent for Anwuanwu who came and arrested the illness. Olumba is now well though very weak.'

'Of course,' someone said, 'anyone who wrestles with a gorilla must have a dusty back.'

'What is to be done now?' Okehi asked.

'Igwu can advise us, let's go to him,' Wago said. Eze Okehi, Wago, and three other elders went to see Igwu. The dibia was in front of his house cooking some yams. When it was hot he preferred to cook in the shade of the tree in front of his house. He ushered the visitors into his house and poked at the yams in the pot with pointed stick. He fished out a small piece and tasted it. It melted even before his strong teeth closed on it. He carried the pot of yams into the house.

'Igwu,' Okehi said, 'we must thank you for your efforts so far. Olumba nearly died four days ago, but for Anwuanwu's timely intervention.'

'You don't need to tell me, I know it all. The past four days are the worst I have ever spent. Even the eight days I spent in the forest just before I became a dibia are nothing compared to these four days. Anwuanwu is a great dibia. If I had not been vigilant I should have been dead by now. It was a trial of strength I shall never forget. At one stage this room was filled with snakes and scorpions. Fortunately I anticipated this move by staying outside'

'Who won?' Wago asked grinning in unbelief.

'Olumba is well now, so that question answers itself. Anwuanwu had the advantage that he was opposing evil. As I have told you, what I have been doing is not expected of any dibia trained at Eluanyim. Trying to cook anyone is not only difficult but dangerous. At any stage the wicked spirits you are invoking can turn against you. So you spend half your time and resources trying to shield yourself.'

Igwu spoke frankly and even Wago the leopard-killer was impressed. Still something had to be done. The fourth month was in and the Pond of Wagaba had to be won. Okehi spoke: 'Igwu we are sorry to put you to all this trouble. But you should understand our position because you are one of us. Is there no other way in which you can help us?'

137

'Give me two days to think,' the dibia said. After two days he spoke to Okehi:

'Tell me,' the dibia said, 'does the Pond of Wagaba belong to us?' There was just a moment's pause before Eze Okehi replied.

'Yes, but why?'

'I want to offer a series of special sacrifices to Ogbunabali god of the night and pray to him to expedite judgement.'

'That is a good idea, go ahead.'

'I shall let you know what help you can give me in the way of materials.'

'It is well. Remember the sooner the better,' Eze Okehi said.

Eze Okehi had to be content with that, but Wago was disappointed. He said later: 'If he decides to sit in his house and do nothing we shall not be the wiser for it. If nothing happens he can always argue that another dibia is operating against him.'

'Wago,' Okehi said, 'we can't force Igwu. He is not a child. He is a man like any of us and we ought to give him what respects are due to him. Twice he has demonstrated his powers. If we don't pester him, perhaps he will do more.'

13 A SURE way to enhance Olumba's peace of mind was to find his lost wife, the mother of his only son. Eze Diali realized this. He organized a search-party. He knew it was unlikely the women would be recovered, but it would keep Olumba's spirits up. Ikechi was one of the four men chosen to search for the women. At first he was excluded, because the elders felt he had had more than his share of adventures in the past few months. But when he swore he would go off on his own, he had his way. Before they left, Diali had a talk with him. The chief said:

'Do your best, my son, you know how important those two

women are to this village. Oda may make the difference between losing and acquiring the Pond of Wagaba for ever. As for Chisa, you know what she means to me. She is the reincarnation of my dead mother.'

'Yes, I often heard you call her "mother".'

'I call her "mother" not only because she is the reincarnation of my mother but also because of her surprisingly mature manners. You may not believe it, but she used to advise me on matters too deep for a girl of her age to understand.'

'I believe it, my lord.'

'And whenever I was ill she cared for me much better than any of my wives or other daughters did.'

'I know it, my lord.'

'And the things she used to say. When she was quite small she said to me one day: "Dede, you are a small child, I am older than you."'

'Children say funny things now and then.'

'No, this was not funny. The child knew what she was talking about. Indeed, her statement more than anything else confirmed Achichi's divination.'

'You are right, dede.'

'And do you know she prepared me a special dish just before she was kidnapped?'

'Really?'

'Yes, she did. She said: "Let me do it now for a time may come when I may not be able to cook properly for you."'

'"Why?" I asked, surprised.

'"Because so many people are being killed in battle that soon I may not have the mind to cook nor you the appetite to eat." She was right and I scarcely knew what to say. While I was searching for an answer she asked: "Do you think anything will happen to Ikechi?"

'"I think not," I replied. "Ikechi though young is strong and careful."

'"He is not stronger than some of those already killed," she observed.

'"That is true," I said, unable to look at her. She walked away, her eyes filled with tears.'

Ikechi felt a lump in his throat. He said good-bye to Eze Diali and left. He went straight to Olumba's compound. Olumba was sitting in his reception hall with his son in his arms. Ikechi came into the reception hall and coughed before Olumba was aware of him.

'My stalking has improved,' Ikechi said smiling.

'Yes, it has,' Olumba said languidly. Ikechi would have treasured this compliment but for the fact that he had done no stalking at all. He had walked up to Olumba quite noisily.

This incident weighed heavily on Ikechi's mind. He realized fully now that Olumba was wasting away in mind and body. The body was growing flabby and weak, the mind slow and indifferent to the world around him. Ikechi did not sit although there were many chairs in the hall. He stood gazing at his friend in wonder and pity. Olumba did not stare back at him. He seemed to lack the energy and concentration to look at a man fully in the eye. Ikechi felt his blood boiling. Whatever forces were responsible for this drastic change in this man were to be fought fiercely. He began to finger the handle of his matchet and a faint red hue spread over the whites of his eyes.

'Olumba, we are about to set out,' he said.

'Do your best,' Olumba replied shortly. It was clear he was in no mood to talk. Ikechi turned to go.

'Wait,' Olumba said and rose from his chair. He set Nchelem on his feet but the child cried, flexed his legs and refused to stand.

'Hold him for me a moment.'

Ikechi carried the child while Olumba entered his medicine-hut. Soon he came out with some talismans. 'Hang these round your neck, they will help you. I should give you my charm for invisibility if it were not designed for me only.'

'Thank you, Olumba.' Ikechi went to join his companions. Ikechi had never felt so keen on any venture before. His love for his fiancée and his devotion to Olumba provided twin forces that made his nerves tingle.

Long after Ikechi had left Olumba still sat in his reception hall rocking the child and mumbling to himself. Wogari had come twice to announce that lunch was ready. He had paid as much atten-tion to her as he paid to the vultures flying very high overhead. The woman was too frightened to come a third time. Nyoma decided to try.

'My lord, your food is ready.'

There was no reply.

'My lord, my lord.' Nyoma's voice was a little higher this time. Still there was no response. Her husband stared at the floor with fixed eyes and rigid features. Nchelem slept peacefully in his arms. Nyoma's heart began to beat wildly. She thought of going back to confer with her junior partner. She changed her mind, stepped forward and shook her husband. He came to consciousness with a jerk.

'Food is ready, my lord.'

'Bring it here.'

'Eat inside; there are too many flies here.'

'Bring it here.'

Nyoma brought the food. After a few balls of foofoo Olumba gave up. Nyoma felt very unhappy.

'Eat more, my lord,' she implored. 'You have been starving for the last few days.'

'I have no desire to eat and you know I can't force myself.'

'You can if you try, my lord.'

'I can't.'

'Just try.'

'I say I can't.'

'A few more balls will do.'

'Carry away the food, woman!'

'I won't until you have eaten some more. You can't go on like this. Chei! you can't!' Nyoma cried. Olumba swallowed the scold that was budding in his mouth. He looked at his wife and said mildly:

'All right I shall eat a little more, but not now.'

Nyoma removed the barely tasted meal. Wogari who had over-heard everything was already crying when Nyoma entered the house. Their daughters joined them and soon there was a din in the house. Olumba was roused to action at last. He walked into the house to quell the noise.

'Stop this. One would think there was a death in the family.

Nyoma you are too old to behave this way. You know very well that Wogari and the children look up to you for leadership.'

But the wailing continued unabated. Olumba was stunned. For the first time Nyoma was flouting his authority. He dumped Nchelem on a sleeping-mound and dashed outside in search of a cane. He came back brandishing a heavy one. Wogari and the children fled into the back-yard, but Nyoma stood her ground fearlessly.

'Yes, come and flog me,' she said. 'Beat me and let me die so that you can bury me decently before you kill yourself. Beat me I say, beat me. I prefer to die than to see you behave the way you are doing. In the midday of your life you are turning into a woman and you expect us to remain calm. Chei! Chei! What has come over you, my lord? Great warrior of Chiolu, Agadaga the terror of wrestling champions, where is your manhood? We are ready to die with you but not in this way. Let us wait bravely and cheerfully for Ogbunabali or whatever gods will kill us. Who else in this village can play the part you are playing? We are proud of you. Please give us more confidence.'

Olumba's upraised arm had fallen to his side long ago. He stood looking at his wife as she talked herself into hysterics. Then he turned and walked into his bedroom. When he left, Nyoma calmed down. Wogari and the other children joined her again.

'Wipe your tears all of you. I am sure nothing will happen to our lord.'

Nyoma was not a particularly firm woman. She was quite pliable especially in her husband's hands. She said 'yes' automatically to whatever orders her husband gave. Her mother had taught her that compliance was the best way to a husband's heart; argument the worst. What she had just said was dictated by hysteria, but when she grew calmer she realized it had done her husband some good. Far from feeling angry he relaxed somewhat, and though the number of wrinkles on his brow did not decrease they were not quite as deep as before.

This incident set the pattern for many days to come. Nyoma now believed that merely being passive would not do. Her husband needed someone to talk confidence into him. She knew his great respect for the gods. She knew that for all his manliness a great fear pervaded his mind. What was worse, she knew that this fear was growing at an alarming rate. That her husband could sleep in the reception hall with his eyes open was in her reckoning ample evidence for this.

Still Olumba could not shake off the pervading fear that gripped him. In the first two months of his oath he had found it possible to suppress his fears. He was surprised that now that victory was at hand, just less than two months away, he found it difficult to maintain his equanimity. He worshipped in his medicine-house more often than before, and kept as strictly as possible to the rules drawn up by Eze Diali and the elders. Yet his fears grew, defying all attempts to control them. He was like a man swimming against a strong current. By frantic efforts he could gain short distances, but invariably the current swept him back, draining energy and confidence out of him.

If Olumba was sure of an heir he might have controlled his fears better. But Nchelem was ailing because of his mother's absence. If he died, then as the parable put it, both the canoe and the paddles would be lost. Olumba could easily visualize his compound overrun with weeds and the houses in ruins. First the roofs would fall to pieces and then the rain-soaked mud walls would crumble. On sunny days lizards would bask on the walls and on bits of broken clay pots. Giant rats would make intricate tunnels all over the ruins and establish themselves as masters where once they were content to peep out only at night when cats tired of waiting indoors had gone outside to hunt. Children playing when older folks would have gone to the farm would by-pass his compound, frightened by his grave which would be in the middle of the compound. The very mention of 'Olumba's compound' would conjure up a perfect vision of desolation in the minds of the old and the young.

Olumba had gone through these mental pictures several times over. They were now a part of him, occupying well-worn tracks in his imagination. One day he dreamt that he was dead. By the queer laws of dreamland he watched himself being lowered into the grave.

He protested as the grave was being covered but no one listened. Even his wives who were standing by said nothing. When he was completely buried he made a frantic effort and woke up. In time this dream became recurrent.

Olumba's imagination was most uninhibited when he was imagining the worst things. His mind ran freely without distraction. On the few occasions when he tried to be optimistic he failed utterly. Powerful counter-arguments always invaded his mind, pointing out the futility of hoping. The voice, as Olumba called it, was always with him, guarding against optimism. That was why Olumba allowed Nyoma to talk confidence into him. She acted as a visible agent against this voice of doom within him. He sought more and more of her company, letting her talk as much as possible when they were together. Nyoma improved on her performances when she noticed her husband's growing dependence on her. But she was also sad over the change in him. No one cared much for a weak-willed husband whose morale was a plaything in his wife's hands. However, she hoped he would revert to normal when the present threat to his life was removed.

Wogari too was thoroughly frightened by the total change in her husband. Was this Olumba? Was this the man whose voice commanded attention in the whole village? She felt that Ogbunabali was already working. Her husband would die a slow but sure death. She said nothing, but at night she wept quietly on her sleeping-mound. How could she be a widow, young as she was? She thought of the widows in the village. They were all unhappy hardworking women. Some of them laughed at the least provocation and tried to be friendly with everybody, but Wogari knew they were terribly unhappy. The best Wogari could do was to co-operate with Nyoma in whatever schemes she had for keeping up their husband's morale. She had always been afraid of her husband. She was more so now that he had developed a strange personality.

Time was Olumba's enemy. Gradually, very gradually the fifth month dragged on. One day was as long as four days. The mornings were long, for Olumba sitting in his reception hall could journey mentally into all the corners of his world several times over before the lazy sun struck the top of the head. The evenings were equally long, for the children seemed to play in the moonlight much longer than usual. Olumba could hear them shouting and running about tirelessly as the brilliance of the moon-drenched arena spurred them on. In his own hearth Nyoma's fairy tales seemed as protracted as a village meeting, and often Olumba had to force everyone to go to bed. Sometimes he himself went so early to bed that he woke in the small hours of the night unable to sleep any longer. On such nights he sat on a chair in his bedroom waiting for daybreak. Those were fertile moments for forebodings. The voice was usually at its best then.

'It is only a month to go,' Olumba would muse.

'It is more than a month,' the voice would say.

'No matter, I shall survive it.'

'You will not survive it. You are dead already. It is only your shadow that is on this side, your soul is gone.' He always gave up all optimism at such points in his frequent wrangling with this built-in aggressor. He would then proceed to imagine the worst, if only to keep this voice quiet.

Olumba's fears were not unfounded. Ogbunabali was a god to be feared. There were so many instances that testified to its ability to deliver judgement without erring. All those who took chances with it died, most of them at night. There was no known pattern as far as timing was concerned. If a guilty man swore by it he could die in the first few days, on the last day, or somewhere in the middle. The only sure thing was that the victim would die within the period and most probably by night.

There was a belief that Ogbunabali was introduced into the Erekwi clan by strangers from Amazo, another clan to the north. Old Ochomma said that the god was unknown in Chiolu when she was a girl with undeveloped breasts. But that was a long long time ago, beyond the memory of even old men like Diali.

There was much to be said for having a god's shrine in a village. It made the god seem less remote. It's priest worked among the people expounding its mysteries, and letting people know the right time for the various sacrifices.

One could look towards the shrines of Amadioha and Ojukwu while offering a prayer or registering a curse. Not so with Ogbuna-bali whose shrine did not exist in Chiolu then. Ogbunabali was therefore non-directional, distant, menacing, ubiquitous. He was king of the night; darkness was his agent. In a way everyone wor-shipped him for who did not fear the dark with its unpredictable dangers? No priest to look up to, no shrine to worship at; nothing but the name – that awful name that planted solid fear into the minds of all who swore by it. It was the type of fear that could turn a very brave man into a whimpering child. It was a fear that was worse than death. Olumba was overwhelmed by it. Anyone would be, even the dibias. Fighting human foes no matter how numerous and implacable was a straightforward affair. One could fight or run away. One could sue for mercy and know when it had been granted. But gods were invisible, elusive, woven into the fabric of time and space, nay woven into the very bodies of their worshippers, for one was born only at their pleasure, one worshipped them as long as one lived, and died when one had committed an unpardonable offence against them. Only idiots were free from the fear of the gods; like the man who said that the gods ought to contribute towards his upkeep and refused to offer sacrifices. But such fellows led worthless lives that no one envied. Olumba's fears began to materialize as physical aches and pains. He suffered pains in his stomach and under his chest. All this was in addition to the nagging backache which plagued him.

To ease his tension he took to walking around the village again. As he had less than two months to go he was more than ever an object of curiosity everywhere. But he did not mind. He had to walk about or face something terrible. He did not come to this conclusion through any logical reasoning. It was just an instinct powerful enough to push him around.

He was emerging from Diali's compound one day when Ikechi and his party met him. One look at them and he knew their journey had been fruitless, for otherwise the whole village would have been wild with excitement and happiness. As it was, only a handful of people knew the search-party was back and these slipped back into their compounds as soon as Ikechi had waved his hand to them to signify failure.

The four men looked wretched. Ikechi's face wore an unmistakable air of tragedy.

'Are you back already?'

'Yes, Olumba, we are back,' Ikechi said.

'How was it?'

'Come over to Diali's and hear it.'

Olumba went back to Diali's reception hut.

'What happened?' Diali asked.

'We were unable to trace the women.'

'How far did you get?'

'First we arrived at Isiali and stayed a night. We interviewed as many people as possible to find out what had happened to the women.'

'Did you interview Elendu?' Olumba asked.

'Of course. He was the first man we spoke to. He said he sold the women to some men who appeared to have come from across the rivers. He could not tell us which way they went.'

'And so you came back,' Olumba said with a mixture of contempt and disappointment.

'If we had come back just then, you would have seen us here the next day. No, we went to a village by the riverside. The people were suspicious and refused to talk at first. We began to feel that perhaps the women were in this village. However, two days' search convinced us that our guess was wrong. Just before we left, a kind young woman informed us that she had indeed seen two men with two sad and unwilling women companions. She could not remember which way they had gone.'

Olumba sighed.

'We hired a boat, crossed the river, and landed secretly on the other side for we were not sure of the type of reception we would have. It was a strange place with crabs crawling all over the bank of the river. We made our way to the nearest village the ferryman had indicated and hid somewhere close to the village. As we could not understand the Rikwo language we realized it would be dangerous to stay in hiding for long. If we were discovered accidently we should be lost men. So we decided to go boldly to the chief's house and explain our mission. Fortunately one of us knew the word for chief in the Rikwo language. We marched into the village, stopped a woman and pronounced the word. Too frightened to shout she pointed to a house in the centre of the village and disappeared into the house probably to call her husband. We walked quickly to the chief's house. He was sitting outside and we picked him out as soon as we saw him. He was very well dressed and two men were fanning him.

'When we stopped near him to address him half a dozen strong men grabbed us and held us fast. They were all speaking at once and we felt lost. The chief appeared to take no notice of us and carried on his conversation with another important-looking man near him. Struggles were useless and I told my men to keep still. Our captors waited for orders from their chief. The chief said nothing. He merely indicated a certain direction with his left thumb and our captors proceeded to drag us that way. Then I shouted "Chiolu! Erekwi clan! Chiolu! Erekwi clan!" The chief burst out laughing. At his orders we were brought back to where he was. A little later an old woman was called and we were very surprised to hear her speak the Erekwi tongue perfectly.'

'Must be one of those carried away during the slave raid twenty years back' Eze Diali said thoughtfully. By now more people had arrived to listen to Ikechi's story.

'Through this woman we explained our mission. The chief received us well. He said: "My people have been trading with the Erekwi clan for generations. Apart from arguments over the prices of our fish and your yams we have never had any serious disagreements. We will not harm you, fear nothing." Thus reassured we went on to explain why these women were so important to us. The chief was sympathetic but he assured us that his village knew nothing about the women.'

'And then you turned back,' Olumba said.

'We had to. Our interpreter informed us that her village was at war with the next village which was two days away by boat. The war was over some fishing grounds.'

'Another war over fishing ponds,' Diali observed chuckling. Many people could not help grinning.

'I think you've done your best,' Diali said. 'As soon as Olumba is free from his oath we shall arrange another search-party.'

After people had dispersed Diali called Ikechi aside. 'I noticed you were chewing your words. Now tell me exactly what happened.'

'You are right, my lord.'

'What happened?'

'At the riverside village we were informed by a woman that two men and two women did arrive at the waterside. They had hired a boatman to take them across but the boat had turned over at midstream. We questioned our informant closely and she said she was sure the lost boat was the one in which the two women had travelled. Just to make sure we crossed the river. You know the rest of the story.'

By now Ikechi was barely controlling his tears. Diali was speechless, only his jaws moved as he gnashed his teeth.

'Keep this secret.'

'I will, but I must tell my mother that Chisa is gone.'

'Don't.'

'But she will guess it.'

'Yes, if you show your feelings.'

'How can I hide them, my lord.'

'Now, be a man. Getting a notch on your bow is not the only test of manhood. The pains of the mind are often harder to overcome than the toughest of human enemies. She was my daughter. If I can bear her loss, you can.'

Ikechi left but not before he had suppressed his tears. As he strolled home wearily he thought over the events of the last few months. The war had brought him recognition. He had smacked his lips as he sipped the Wine with the Eagle Feathers. He had re-enacted with relish his duel with the man of Aliakoro several times. But now he hated the war. He wished the Pond of Wagaba had never existed.

Chisa the rascal – he always thought of her that way. Chisa the sweet nuisance, witty but sensible. What a wife she would have made!

Suddenly Ikechi was mature, thoughtful, less impulsive. His world had acquired new dimensions – sorrow and uncertainty.

14

YAWS. This disease was so prevalent among children that it was thought that no child could be normal without it. It was a trial every baby had to face. Teething, crawling, toddling, then yaws. That was the usual order. Mothers were used to it. If a child remained too long without having yaws some mothers became uneasy or even angry. Why wouldn't it come so they would get through with it? However, if the disease came too early it was a very painful affair for the little child.

Nchelem was not three yet. All the other children in the family had had it. Now it was his turn. It developed from a burn he sustained while burning some broomsticks in the fire. His little body was covered with circular sores giving off yellowish matter which at night glued him to his mat. He moaned each time he changed his position. It was a trying time for Nyoma who took full responsibilities. During the day Nchelem was almost a permanent attachment to her body. At night she slept with him.

There was only one known way of dealing with yaws. The individual sores were scrubbed with a stiff coconut-fibre brush until their faces turned from a dull yellow to a bright blood-red. The scrubbing was an ordeal which no child ever forgot. Fever and stomach pains stepped in and weakened Nchelem so much that Nyoma discontinued the daily yaws scrubbing. She feared the child might collapse if she tried.

Nchelem lay wasting on his sick-bed and crying constantly for his mother whose image the illness seemed to have invoked in the child's mind. Olumba sat almost constantly by him giving him medicines and carrying him as often as he could.

'I have sent for Anwuanwu,' Eze Diali announced when he came to see Nchelem one morning.

'Thank you, Eze Diali,' Olumba said adjusting his son's head on his knees. 'When will he arrive?'

'Any time this evening.'

Anwuanwu arrived in the evening, examined his cowries and laughed. No one asked what he was laughing at. They were used to this divination chuckle. They waited for him to speak.

'What is the best way to catch a hen with young ones?' Anwuanwu asked Diali, smiling.

'Get hold of one of the young ones and the hen will follow,' Diali replied easily.

'Well, that is what is happening.'

'Do you mean our enemies are working on this child?'

'Yes, because I have made it impossible for them to bewitch Olumba.'

'But surely this is a case of yaws,' Diali said his brow wrinkled with doubts.

'Yes, to you who see with two eyes. But to me it is clear that this is not an ordinary case of yaws. Look at the cowries!'

'What can be done?' Olumba asked.

'I can clear your son's illness but I cannot erase his mother's image from his mind. Your enemies have invoked this image so strongly that only time or the return of your wife can stop your son from crying for his mother.'

Anwuanwu did his stuff as he promised and cleared Nchelem's fever and stomach pains. He gave Olumba a powerful potion for the yaws.

'Is there no powder you can give us to rub on the sores?' Nyoma asked.

The dibia said: 'The disease comes from within. The drug I have given you when swallowed will chase the disease out of the body and the sores will then disappear.'

Nyoma took the drug for Nchelem although she did not believe it would do any good.

As the dibia had predicted Nchelem continued to cry for his mother. Olumba became more and more attached to the child, afraid that he might die if he left him for a moment. One evening as Olumba nursed him on his knees the boy said suddenly:

'Doda is dead.'

Olumba was startled and all but trembled. He controlled himself and replied in an even voice.

'Doda is not dead, Lelem. She will be back soon.'

'Doda is dead, Doda is dead,' the child prattled laughing and caressing his father's beard.

'Doda is dead, Doda is dead, Doda is . . .'

'Hush, Nchelem. Say, Doda is not dead.'

'Doda is not dead,' the child repeated after his father.

When the child went to sleep Olumba stormed into Nyoma's kitchen.

'Now who has been saying that Oda is dead?' he demanded fiercely. Nyoma trembled. Wogari wished the walls were liquid so she could dive to the other side.

'Nobody, my lord,' Nyoma replied as best as she could.

'That is a big lie. Nchelem has been saying "Doda is dead, Doda is dead" and he must have heard that from you.'

'My lord, we were merely wondering . . .'

'Stop such stupid discussions, at least when Nchelem is with you. I know women never wish their rivals well, but you must keep your thoughts to yourselves.'

Nyoma was now crying. She cried as if broken-hearted and Olumba knew he had wounded her deeply by his remarks. He stopped berating her and went to bed. The next day, Nchelem's on-and-off illness started again in earnest. 'Doda, Doda-a-a, Doda is dead,' he cried. Anwuanwu's prescriptions were administered but he seemed no better.

What worried Olumba and his household was that they could not now pinpoint Nchelem's illness. The yaws were clearing. The back of Olumba's palm pressed against the child's cheek indicated that his temperature was normal. He no longer held his stomach when he cried. What was wrong with him? He was almost three years old and could indicate when and where he felt pain. But now he neither pointed to his stomach nor to any other part of his body when questioned. It was all 'Doda, Doda is dead'. Nyoma's efforts to make the child forget this sentence was in vain. When she tried to teach him to say something else she found no difficulty. But the child still said: 'Doda is dead' when he cried. At night Nchelem would wake up to cry when the whole village was slumbering. His high-pitched voice broke the silence of the night in a way that frightened Nyoma. Olumba, once a sound sleeper, began to despair of ever having a good night's sleep again. In between light dozes he ran this way and that fetching drugs, water and anything to make his son more comfortable. His wives pleaded in vain that he should go to sleep.

'We can look after him, my lord,' Nyoma said unconvincingly.

'No, only the gods can save this child,' Olumba said. 'Look at him; he is wasting away before our very eyes.'

'Let us get Anwuanwu again, my lord.'

'Anwuanwu has done his best. Who could have done more? Let the gods do what they will. Let them kill my son. Let them kill us all, and there would be nothing left to be killed. When a man is dead and buried the disease that killed him is forced to rest also. But Aliakoro! Aliakoro! I shall deal with them yet even if I have to defy the Erekwi people and their Ezes.' It was past midnight as Olumba raved and his wives watched him helplessly. Nchelem was laid out on his father's bed breathing at frighteningly long intervals.

Early in the morning Olumba knocked at Eze Diali's door.

'Come in Olumba,' the chief said recognizing his voice.

'I have a very important matter to discuss with you, my lord.'

'Not before we have had some kola and pepper,' the old man said, rummaging in a bag in a corner of his room. As the pepper and kola set their mouths tringling, Diali said: 'Now we can talk.'

'My son is much worse,' Olumba announced curtly.

'Why?'

'He wants his mother.'

Eze Diali seemed to be digesting the fact slowly for he did not speak for some time.

'I want to go and look for Oda,' Olumba said unable to wait any longer for Eze Diali to reply. He watched the old man as he made the announcement. If Diali was surprised he did not show it. He fixed his gaze on the floor as his old but strong jaws crushed the kola savagely.

'Suppose we send out another search-party to look for her?' the chief said at last.

'They will not know where to look. They will fail like their predecessors.'

'Do you know where to look?'

'I can find out.'

'So can they.'

'I doubt it.'

'We can at least let them try again.'

'No, my lord, I shall go this time.'

Eze Diali stared at his companion hard and long. Olumba was looking away, his dull eyes unwinking.

'Let me think this over,' Diali said. 'Come again after breakfast.'

Olumba rose to leave without a word. As he watched him Diali thought his gait was hardly that of a man about to embark upon a hazardous venture.

Olumba knew he was being difficult but he was so mentally tired that he did not bother to reason. He knew he had to do something about his lost wife or face the loss of his son. He knew also that the possibility of getting Oda back was remote. No matter, he would wander on and on in the forest, get lost, and die eventually. If he stayed at home he would die anyway. '*Of course you will die.*' That voice again. Olumba did not bother to argue with it. The voice was right; he would die, and Aliakoro would claim the Pond of Wagaba and fish as they had never done before. Suddenly he felt very tired. He sat on a log by the roadside and held his head in his two palms. A goat that had been resting on the log stood up in alarm, but seeing that the newcomer meant no harm it settled down again to chew the cud. Olumba gazed at the slowly moving jaws as they overlapped and coincided alternately.

'Olumba!'

He looked up.

'Eziho.'

'What are you doing here at this time of the morning?'

'Resting.'

'What have you been doing?'

'I have just been to see the chief.'

'That's no reason you should sit by the wayside like I know not what.'

Olumba got up and slowly made his way home. Eziho stared at the retreating figure with unconcealed surprise. He ran straight to Eze Diali.

'What is wrong with Olumba?' he asked urgently as soon as he saw the chief.

'The oath.'

'But the pond is ours.'

'That is true.'

'So he should not be sick.'

Eze Diali offered no reply. He laughed instead. It was a short mirthless laugh loaded with bitterness. Eziho stared at the old man wondering if everyone was going mad.

'It seems you are hiding something, my lord. Let me know what it is, perhaps I can help.'

'Go and tell the elders and warriors to come here after breakfast.'

Eziho left, the doubts on his face intensified rather than resolved.

The elders gathered fast enough, some leaving their walking-sticks behind in their hurry. A meeting summoned at such short notice was not to be taken lightly. When the elders were all seated Diali asked one of his younger sons to call Olumba.

'Let me do it,' Eziho said, getting up and running off. He was more worried than ever and wanted to have an idea of what it was all about beforehand if possible. But Olumba was silent as they walked towards the chief's house.

'Olumba wants his kidnapped wife back,' Eze Diali said as soon as Olumba was seated. 'His son cries for his mother night and day.'

A hush fell on the company. A spider let itself down from the roof by a thread. It remained suspended in the air at Diali's eye-level. Diali knocked it down with a movement of his right hand and lost the bit of kola he held in it.

'Does anyone know where Oda is now?' someone asked.

'Nobody knows,' Diali answered simply.

'She might have been sold to the more distant Rikwos across the river,' Chituru said. 'In that case recovery is impossible.'

'That is true,' Wezume said. 'Some of the Rikwos live in unapproachable villages near the Great Abaji.'

'Some even live in the water, they say,' someone added.

'That is impossible. They would not be able to cook,' Chituru said.

'They say it is dry inside there.'

'Who says?'

'So people say.'

'What people?'

'Those who have been there.'

'No one in this village has been there and back,' Chituru insisted. 'Ikechi and his men stopped at the first Rikwo village.'

'Well, you haven't been there yourself, so you can't be sure of anything either.'

Eze Diali called the two men to order.

'A man does not chase rats when his house is burning. We have a big problem on our hands. I want you to suggest ways of solving it.'

'It can't be solved,' Chituru said solemnly. 'Olumba has to resign himself to this loss. It is unfortunate that he who has staked his life for the village is also the one who has sustained this loss. But we know he is in every way a man and can bear it.'

'I can bear it, but my son can't,' Olumba said.

'He will forget her in time,' someone said.

'He may die before he forgets.'

'What do you want done?' Wezume asked.

'I want to travel out and look for her.'

'You?'

'Yes.'

'But you are under an oath.'

'I know.'

'Do you know where to look for her?'

'I shall find out.'

'And if it is across the river?'

'I shall go across to search for her.'

Chituru slumped back in his three-legged chair and stared at Olumba in utter disbelief. An uncomfortable spell of silence set in. Diali broke it.

'Olumba, we shall again pick four young men to look for your wife,' he said. 'You will stay at home until the six months are over. If by that time your wife has not been found we shall send out a larger search-party which you can lead if you like.'

The elders agreed that Diali's suggestion was the best way out although many thought the search would be fruitless. All eyes were now turned on Olumba.

Wezume said: 'What do you say to that, Olumba?'

'I shall go and look for her myself,' came the reply.

This was incredible. Was Olumba losing his head? The elders redoubled their efforts to make him accept their decision but in vain.

'I know what is happening,' Chituru said. 'Olumba is being bewitched again. He is not himself. It is up to us to take counter-action.'

There was a general murmur of agreement.

'I shall go to look for my wife whether I am being bewitched or not,' was the reply.

Eziho raised his voice in barely concealed anger. 'This is very strange. You have kept to our restriction for over four months, why can't you control yourself for less than two months? The forest is full of dangers. Our enemies are on the watch and can do anything to you. Don't you see the risks involved in what you intend to do? You are a brave man, you fought more than any man here in the last war. Why do you want to undo all this simply because your child is crying? What child would not cry if its mother were kidnapped?'

'Whatever you may say,' Olumba replied, 'I shall search for my wife. I shall not let that boy die. Few know what I suffered before he was born. My first two wives died without children. A dibia said there was a curse in the family. I struggled and married two more wives. They produced females. Nyoma's only son died. You know how. But I could not die without an heir; my compound had to stand, my family name had to be perpetuated. I married Oda hoping she would give me a son. I called one dibia after another and spent all I had in unheard-of sacrifices. When all attempts failed I was advised to consult the priest of Igwekala the great god of Umunoha. Although I had no idea of the place I had packed, ready to go, when Anwuanwu, whom I shall never forget, proposed an alternative step which I accepted. I was obliged to cut off half of the little finger of my left hand for a sacrifice involving a walk to the Evil Forest at midnight. What I saw in that forest that night will for ever be a secret between me and the gods. Look at my finger if you doubt my story. Ask Anwuanwu of Abii if you still don't believe. I tell you, I snatched that boy right from the gods; I shall die before he dies.' Towards the end of his speech Olumba was on his feet glowering at the elders, his sunken eyes aflame.

No one was in the mood to say anything after Olumba had done. At last Eze Diali rose. He looked round him and then said slowly but firmly: 'Olumba, go and look for your wife. Elders, the meeting is ended.'

Olumba got up and began to move away. Eziho leaped to his feet.

'Olumba, I go with you!' he shouted.

'And I,' Ikechi shouted.

'And I,' said another. Soon Olumba was surrounded by a score of eager young men. He said nothing but they followed him as he walked thoughtfully along the main village road towards his compound. Half-way he looked up. Far ahead loomed the forests of the Great Ponds. It was a clear morning and the mist that usually enveloped it was not there. Olumba stopped abruptly. His companions stopped and like him stood gazing at the far outline of the forests of the Great Ponds.

15

OLUMBA did not go to search for his wife as he had threatened for two reasons: his son would miss him badly and might grow worse; his son's foster-mother, Nyoma, was also ill.

Diali and a few other elders winked at one another when Olumba announced two days later that he had changed his mind. They had secretly employed Anwuanwu of Abii to work on Olumba's mind and were impressed at the quick results. The dibia had not even bothered to come to Chiolu.

Nyoma had complained of a cough two days before.

'The pain in my chest is increasing,' she said.

Olumba fingered her chest and ribs.

'Can it be the cough?'

'I don't know, my lord.'

'How long has this cough been on?'

'About three days.'

'I shall get Achichi to give you some cough medicine.'

Achichi came round the next day with a small calabash containing some cough medicine. It was a mixture consisting of the ashes of rare herbs, palm-kernel oil and honey.

The cough got worse. Nyoma grew weaker and stayed longer in bed. She was not just a broomstick; she was now an emaciated broomstick. Achichi prescribed some routine sacrifices and rubbed Nyoma's chest with some lotions. There was no improvement. The woman deteriorated steadily. A cloud descended on the already gloomy family. Was it 'lock-chest'? Achichi was convinced it was not, for his patient was breathing with ease, if noisily. The noise was much like the usual wheezing sound made by cough and catarrh sufferers.

'Achichi, you have to do something,' Olumba said. 'Nyoma is very sick.'

'I shall try a purgative,' the dibia said.

'Can she stand it?'

'Yes.'

'Please give her a small dose.'

'I shall do that. What is troubling her is in the stomach and I want her to void it.'

Nyoma drank the liquid which Achichi had extracted from three different roots but she grew much worse. Achichi was called. He gave an effective antidote but by this time Nyoma was so weakened that her illness took a really serious turn. Her coughing was deeper and more prolonged and could be heard a long way off. Her ribs, which could easily be counted now, fought to keep her chest in one piece as she coughed.

It was now clear that Achichi could do nothing. However, it must be said that he showed great concern. He ran this way and that trying out anything that came to his mind. Olumba appreciated his efforts and said so.

As Nyoma lay groaning neighbours turned up in great numbers to stay by Olumba. Diali had no words. He and some other elders stayed in Olumba's reception hall eating kola and occasionally sipping some stale palm wine.

Olumba was a shadow of his former self. Emaciated and haggard he shuffled about with hunched shoulders. His hollow eyesockets could hold a cup of water each. Looking at him people feared he would collapse any moment and die.

What hit Olumba hardest was the fact that his wife seemed utterly resigned to her fate. She seemed sure she was going to die and made no fuss over it. She took the medicines Achichi gave her merely to please her husband. When they were alone Olumba tried to instil confidence into her.

'Nyoma, you must have a stronger will than this. The gods give

160

up only when we give up. Look at me, look at little Nchelem and the other children. Must you leave us?'

A prolonged cough checked her reply for some time.

'I don't want to die, my lord,' she whispered.

'Then behave as if you don't want to die.'

The woman could not talk now. All her answers were in her tear-filled eyes. A heavy spasm shook her and the tears rolled down her cheeks.

When a man swore, his family was always involved. If the man was guilty it was not unusual for the god he swore by to kill several people in the family along with the man himself. Most people saw Nyoma's illness in this light. Ogbunabali the god of the night was at work. Nyoma herself knew this and it accounted for her resignation. She knew her death was inevitable.

As death drew near Nyoma felt no pain of separation. She was sure her husband would join her in the spirit world in a matter of days. She wondered if Wogari and the children would survive.

Those who came to sit by Olumba could do nothing. What was happening could not be arrested if Ogbunabali was behind it. And who could doubt that? Nyoma's illness had struck her suddenly. It did not respond to the usual treatment. Okwaranta, the cough that killed people, usually took several months or even years to do so. How could anyone die of a cough in a few days?

Strangely enough Olumba appeared more composed now that he was sure he was going to die. As Nyoma lay gasping in what seemed her death struggle Olumba called Eze Diali, Eziho, Ikechi and a few other friends together in his reception hall.

'You see how it is. My wife is about to die. I shall probably go next. If Wogari and any of the children are spared, pleased look after them. I owe no one anything.' Olumba ground his teeth when he had done. His sunken cheeks seemed to be adding emphasis to his last speech. Eze Diali could not help noticing the awful resentment in Olumba's voice. He could hear him accusing the whole village of leading him and his entire family to their death.

As Diali and the others sat speechless Olumba came out of the reception hall and stood outside with his arms stretched upwards.

'It is night. Ogbunabali I am sure you are listening. Spare my wife; she is someone else's child. I alone swore. I alone should die if you so desire. Let her not suffer because she has chosen to be my wife. It is no crime to marry.'

He strode up to the door of Nyoma's room and shouted: 'Nyoma, lift your hands upwards to the Creator and declare your innocence. Let Amadioha, Ojukwu, Ali, Mini Wekwu and Ogbunabali himself hear it. Let the earth hear it, let the heavens hear it, let men and spirits hear it.'

Diali feared Olumba was losing control of himself. But he was mistaken. Olumba was worked up but had control of himself.

To Wogari the situation was unlike anything she had ever seen in her twenty-five years of life. It looked like the end of the world. As her husband addressed the gods in his booming voice she shook with fear. The whole place must be full of spirits waiting perhaps to lead Nyoma and subsequently the rest of the family to the spirit world. Her husband was a truly brave man, if he was able to talk under such circumstances. She watched him through the open door. He was a changed man. His fears were gone. He was bold, desperate, defiant. The certainty of death brought back his manliness, his fighting spirit.

It was difficult to say whether Nyoma heard the shouts of her husband. She lay tossing on her bed surrounded by Wogari and other women. Outside more women hung around listening to Olumba and weeping. The darkness established itself eagerly. A new moon – the fifth since Olumba swore – struggled in vain to maintain the illusion of twilight.

Nyoma was not dead yet. Olumba was very much alive; yet a terrible sense of tragedy pervaded the village of Chiolu. Few men ate their supper that night. The imminent loss of the Pond of Wagaba was painful; watching a brave man and his family die was more so.

Eze Diali instructed Ikechi to bring word to him as soon as Nyoma breathed her last. Slowly, the Eze with some other elders walked away. Ogbunabali had a cruel sense of humour, Diali mused. The god was acting just when hope was replacing doubt and fear in their minds.

'What shall we do?' Eze Diali asked as soon they were all seated in his reception hall. No one offered any solution.

'Shall we let Olumba die?' the chief mused aloud.

'Olumba is not dying!' Chituru pointed out.

'But it is clear that Ogbunabali is at work,' Wezume said. 'There is little doubt that Olumba will not live much longer after Nyoma's death.' Many elders murmured their agreement.

'Are we absolutely sure that Ogbunabali is at work?' Chituru asked again. 'Let us consult a dibia and know exactly what the position is.'

'No dibia will offer to help if he knows Ogbunabali is involved,' Wezume observed.

'True, but at least let us find out the facts.'

'What good will it do if we know for certain that the god is at work?' an elder asked. Chituru had no immediate answer to that.

Diali said: 'I suggest we go to Aliakoro and persuade them to release Olumba from his oath.'

'But we can't do that without first finding out whether indeed Olumba's misfortunes are from the God of the Night,' Chituru insisted.

The elders agreed to consult Anwuanwu. Three elders, among them Eziho, were chosen to do the journey the next day. The elders dispersed to their compounds. They were to meet again in Olumba's compound to watch with him.

Nyoma did not die in the night. Some keen-eyed observers thought she had improved slightly in the morning. By the afternoon they were proved right. Nyoma asked for water, then for food. Wogari quickly warmed the pepper soup that was prepared the night before. The patient drank it and ate two slices of soft-boiled yam.

The next morning there was no doubt that Nyoma was on a slow path to recovery. Although her cough showed no improvement, she was able to sit up on her bed.

Eziho and his party came back with the report that Anwuanwu had travelled away. As Nyoma seemed to be recovering no further attempts were made to contact the dibia. Olumba refused to hope. He had conditioned himself for the worst. He did not want to go through the whole process again. People had been known to die just when everyone thought they were recovering.

But eventually Olumba was forced to hope as Nyoma lingered between life and death for several days. With hope came its triplet brothers doubt and fear. Olumba's mental battles started again as he hovered round his wife trying to encourage her.

'Remember the advice you gave me,' he said. 'You need that advice now.'

'I am doing my best, my lord,' the sick woman said.

'The important thing is to believe firmly that you will not die.'

'I believe so,' came the unconvincing reply.

'Since you didn't die two nights ago, you will surely live.'

Olumba sat on the bed and placed Nyoma's head on his knees. He said nothing now as he stared thoughtfully at the floor. When he looked at his wife again she was asleep. He rose and placed her head gently on the bed. Nyoma opened her eyes in the process. Olumba sat down again and put her to sleep as he would a child. A barely perceptible smile froze on the woman's face as she fell asleep.

'Have the children eaten?'

'Yes, my lord,' Wogari replied.

'Don't let them disturb Nyoma. Let them play outside, or in the other room.'

Olumba went into his medicine-hut to worship. When he came out he sat in his reception hall for a while but as his thoughts overwhelmed him he strolled into the village after telling Wogari where he could be found in the event of an emergency. Well-wishers ran to him to inquire after his wife's health. Others passed him on their way to see her.

A little later Olumba found himself near Ochomma's house. Ochomma's grandson, the thirteen-year-old who was entitled to the Wine with the Eagle Feathers, was gathering wood outside. Olumba watched him with unconcealed admiration.

'Okatu.'

'Olumba. How is your wife? I hear she is ill.'

'She is much better. How is your grandmother?'

'She is well.' Okatu ran into the house at his grandmother's call. The next moment he was out again.

'Chocho wants to speak to you,' Okatu said.

Olumba entered the house. The ancient woman was warming herself by the fire although it was nearly midday.

'How is Nyoma, that beautiful girl?'

'She is improving,' Olumba said.

'Well you know how it is,' Ochomma said in her tremulous voice, 'the head is getting too heavy for its owner to carry about.'

'I understand,' Olumba said softly.

'If I could, I should come. Nyoma is one of the best girls in this village. I remember how when she was small she used to run around with one of my granddaughters now married to Chioma.'

'You mean Wepere?'

'Yes, that's she.'

'I believe Nyoma will get well.'

'Of course she will. Amadioha will never shame himself.'

Olumba espied Ihunda, Ochomma's ten-year-old granddaughter lying in one corner of the room.

'Is she not well?'

'No, she has cough and chest pains.'

'Has she taken any medicines?'

'Yes.'

'Shall I fetch Achichi for you?'

Ochomma laughed in her shaky voice.

'I have medicines that Achichi will never dream of. My son, great dibias are no more. We now have laymen posing as dibias.'

'That is true, mother.'

Ihunda opened her eyes, woken by a fit of coughing. 'How are you my child?' asked Ochomma.

Ihunda squinted as she tried to open her eyelids swollen with sleep. She closed them again when her coughing ceased. Okatu adjusted her covering cloth that was displaced when she was coughing.

'How long has she been coughing?'

'Two days,' Okatu answered.

'And it is already so serious.'

'It is a male type of cough,' Ochomma said. 'Okatu, get this fire going.'

Okatu put more wood into the fire and went down on his knees to blow. Ochomma drew back a little as the flames leaped higher.

Ihunda coughed again. Olumba studied the young girl. It was surprising that such a deep rattling sound could come from a chest so small.

'This is how my wife coughs,' Olumba thought aloud. He reached over and touched the child. Her body was hot. Olumba said: 'The cough seems to be mixed up with fever.'

'Yes. I have sent for some anti-fever leaves and roots. I wonder why they have not been brought.'

'Ochomma, I want to go now.'

'When will you be released from your oath?'

'When the next new moon appears.'

'Amadioha will protect you, my good son.'

'He will, mother.'

Olumba left the old woman. As he walked away he could hear Ihunda coughing. On his way he popped into Diali's. The Eze was not in his reception hall. A child explained that he had a slight fever and was lying in bed. He returned home.

'You will eat now, won't you, my lord?' asked Wogari.

'I shall.'

Wogari set some food before her husband. He ate with some appetite. It was not surprising for he had not eaten since morning.

'How is Nyoma?'

'She is sleeping peacefully,' Wogari replied.

'Ever since I left?'

'Yes, my lord.'

'That is good. I think we can say she is safe now.'

'I think so too.'

'And you can now sweep my rooms. They are littered with odds and ends.'

'I shall, my lord.'

'And get your hair plaited.'

'Not while Nyoma is still sick.'

'All right you can go on looking like a wet vulture if you like.'

Wogari chuckled. Her laughter was checked by a cough. She stopped laughing and coughed once or twice.

'Have you a cough too?'

'No, my lord. I think some spittle went the wrong way.'

The next day Diali called to see Nyoma in spite of his own indisposition.

'She is definitely improving,' he said. 'Olumba you don't need to worry, I think it is an ordinary illness.'

'I think so too. Were you told I called yesterday?'

'Yes.'

'Are you well now?'

'Well, yes but for a slight sore throat. I feel pain when I swallow anything.'

'That should clear without any trouble.'

'It should although it is surprising how little things like this get people down these days. See how your wife nearly died of a few days' cough.'

'It is truly surprising.'

'Do you know that Ihunda, Ochomma's granddaughter is now seriously ill. Her illness is similar to your wife's – coughing and chest pains. When I was coming I saw quite a crowd near Ochomma's house. I am going there right away.'

'I am coming with you.'

The two men made for Ochomma's house. Inside, there were many people surrounding the sick child.

'Why this crowd?' Eze Diali asked.

'The child is dying,' a woman said.

'Dying?'

Diali and Olumba squeezed their way into the room. The child's mother was kneeling by her crying. Ihunda was tossing this way and that.

'Is this not the child I saw yesterday?' Olumba cried.

'The same,' Ochomma said with the awful equanimity of the aged.

'Has a dibia been consulted?' Diali wanted to know.

'Achichi has been here. He says there are no gods directly involved but we have performed some routine sacrifices.'

'Achichi is losing my confidence,' someone said. 'His eyes are as good as mine when it comes to seeing spirits.'

'Ochomma, I can send for Anwuanwu if you wish,' Diali said.

'Do so if you can. I can't afford to lose this child.'

'Call me Ikechi,' Diali ordered.

When Ikechi and another young man came up, they were dispatched to Abii.

By nightfall Ihunda's condition was hopeless. By midnight her breathing became irregular. Her father took her in his arms and tried to control her struggles.

'Don't hold her quite so tight,' someone said. 'Let her struggle and fight the evil spirits pestering her.' The man relaxed his hold and Ihunda nearly fell off.

'Put her on the mat,' Ochomma said.

On the mat, Ihunda rolled this way and that. Then her movements became less, and eventually she lay still. Only her irregular breathing with its fearful rattle broke the silence in Ochomma's house.

Ihunda's father shook his head hopelessly.

'I think I shall carry her home,' he said.

'Let her die here under my eyes,' Ochomma said. The anguish in her face combined with her many wrinkles to produce a nightmarish effect.

Ihunda gasped as she drew a long painful breath. It was a very difficult one. The next breath was even more difficult. The hollow rattling at the back of her throat set everyone's hairs on end. The next breath fell short and she died.

Ihunda's mother was inconsolable. So were her many neighbours who had been keeping the vigil with her.

In spite of the hair-raising contortions on Ochomma's face, her eyes were dry. Seeing her weep was an experience for many in the crowd. Although she went through all the motions of crying, there was no sound. But only those near her were aware of this for the din in the house was deafening.

In the morning the corpse was washed, oiled and dressed for burial. As it was about to be carried to the grave, Ochomma let out a heart-rending cry. The corpse bearers stood still, arrested by the almost unearthly sound.

'And so you are gone. So will I, soon, soon. I have lived long enough. Listen people of Chiolu: a great calamity is coming. The gods have run wild and we shall know nothing but tears. I saw it all plainly last night, and I see it now as my child is about to journey to the spirit world. Carry her away gently. I need not cry for I shall join her soon. Soon, while there are still people to bury me.'

'Poor woman, she is almost out of her mind,' Eze Diali murmured.

Ihunda's death shook the village probably because she was so attached to Ochomma the oldest person in the village. She was a very beautiful child. When she was five years old her parents had suspected that she was an *agwuru* child destined to die young. Achichi had performed all the usual ceremonies. What now was responsible for the child's death? If Anwuanwu had come round maybe he would have clarified matters. But the dibia had told Ikechi and his companion that they were too late, as indeed they themselves found out when they came back after midnight.

After Ihunda's burial, Ochomma told Wepere to prepare her a good meal. It was a surprising demand at such a time. But Ochomma's word was law. The meal was prepared and she ate heartily.

'I want a bath,' she said. Wepere washed her.

'Open my box and give me a new wrapper.'

Wepere complied like a dreamer. She helped her tie the wrapper. The old woman thanked her and sent her away. Towards evening she said:

'Okatu, you will sleep with your parents today.'

'Why?' the boy asked surprised.

'Do as I tell you.'

The boy obeyed.

The next morning Ochomma was dead.

16 OCHOMMA died very old. It was a matter of pride for any family to have anyone so old among them. Usually deaths, like Ochomma's, were occasions for celebrations in the Erekwi clan. Apart from a few sensitive women and children, no one wept. Mourners, if they could be so called, turned out in their best wrappers. If enough money was available it could be a truly great occasion.

Ihunda's death damped everybody's spirits. Although Ochomma was buried with all the rites and pomp appropriate to the occasion gaiety was impossible.

No one went for a divination when a very old person died. But Ihunda's death needed investigation and accordingly Achichi was consulted. Achichi said:

'The gods are angry with the whole of the Erekwi clan. No individual sacrifices will do. The whole clan must get together to avert further loss of life.'

No one could make any sense out of this pronouncement. It was a strange divination. How could a dibia divine the fate of the whole clan? Eze Diali received the news in his bedroom. The fever that had been on and off was having a good grip on him now. It was Chituru who brought the news to him.

'How can the gods be angry with the whole clan?' Chituru asked. 'Such a divination over the death of a mere child is surprising. What would he have said if an Eze had died.'

'Only the seer knows the full contents of his own mind,' Diali replied.

'Since the clan can't get together for action, his divination is worth nothing.'

'It is possible for the clan to meet. Some years back Chiolu and Omokachi performed a joint sacrifice to avert a disaster predicted by a very famous dibia from across the rivers.'

'But according to Achichi this is not a question of two villages coming together, the whole clan is involved. I think Achichi had a little palm wine before the divination,' Chituru chuckled.

'He drinks neither gin nor palm wine,' Diali said.

'Do you take this divination seriously?'

'I don't know what it means exactly but I am sure there is something in it. That man is not a bad dibia.'

Chituru left to seek the opinions of other elders. Most of them agreed that the divination was extraordinary. They were convinced more than ever that Achichi was a long way below great dibias like Anwuanwu of Abii. That was why in critical situations they by-passed him and sought Anwuanwu's expert advice.

Achichi was not unduly worried over his falling reputation. He was a sociable easy-going man. He closed his ears to derogatory remarks and laughed and played with everyone. He did not grumble any time Anwuanwu's advice was sought. He was always sure of earning a living. Even those who preferred Anwuanwu to him were from time to time forced to come to him merely because he was readily available.

'Our fingers are not all equal,' he would sometimes say to some who tried to vaunt Anwuanwu's superiority in his face. He never went beyond this observation and showed no resentments. This care-free attitude and his simplicity endeared him to many people particularly those who dreaded the threatening airs of omniscient eight-eyed dibias. Wezume was indifferent over Achichi's divination. 'Since we can't do anything about it, there is no point discussing it,' he told Chituru. 'If Ihunda's parents are not satisfied, let them consult other dibias.'

Chituru went on to see Olumba and his sick wife.

'Olumba.'

'Chituru.'

'How is your wife?'

'Recovering gradually.'

'Can I see her?'

'Yes, come in.'

Nyoma was sitting on the bed trying to eat some yams. She looked very weak and her cough was hardly better. But she was generally far better than three days before when she nearly died.

'I gather Ihunda died of a similar illness,' Chituru said.

'That is true. Before she died she was coughing exactly as my wife is doing now.'

Wogari came into the room bringing more pepper soup for Nyoma.

'What did you rub on your forehead?' Olumba asked his second wife.

'Something for headache, my lord.'

'When did this start?'

'This morning.'

'It must be a result of your catarrh. I heard you sneezing and coughing last night.'

'You are right, my lord.'

As Wogari turned to go back into the kitchen she swayed and nearly fell. She clutched the wall just in time.

'Are you learning to walk?' Olumba asked impatiently.

'I felt dizzy, my lord.'

'Are you going to fall ill too? Go ahead!'

Chituru laughed.

'Olumba you surely can't blame her,' the old man said.

'Anyone with some sense should not fall ill in this compound at this time,' Olumba said. Chituru laughed again.

'If illnesses could see and hear, they would be too afraid to venture near you from the way you talk.'

'They see and hear all right. Haven't they tormented me for the past five months? First it was I, then my son, then Nyoma and now Wogari.'

'But Wogari is not really ill?'

'That is the way these things begin. Nyoma started with a mere cough and nearly died. Wogari is dizzy now, maybe by tomorrow her head will be falling off.'

Chituru laughed again then stopped abruptly with a groan.

'What is it?'

'A pain in the head. You have made me laugh too much.'

'I am sorry, Chituru. I was merely stating my condition. All my misfortunes are on a large scale. However, I don't care now; let the worst happen. I am like a soldier-ant that has attacked a pot of oil. Retreat is impossible.'

Chituru rose to go.

'I must go now,' he said, 'and see to this headache.'

'Do you mean it is serious?'

'Yes, it is.'

'You must have had it for some time.'

'No it started right here.'

'This is surprising.'

'More than one can say. And you know Diali is down, too, with fever and a severe headache.'

'It must be the change of weather.'

'Could be.'

The old man left with one hand on his head.

Olumba went into the kitchen to have a look at Wogari. He found her sprawled on a mat spread on the kitchen floor. She placed her legs as close to the fire as she could.

'What is this?' Olumba exclaimed with some bitterness.

'Headache and fever, my lord. It will clear by tomorrow,' Wogari replied almost apologetically. The bitterness she detected in her husband's tone made her nervous and miserable. Nyoma tottered into the kitchen.

'Go and lie down, Nyoma, you should not be moving about.'

'You are right, my lord, but I wanted to have a look at Wogari.'

'Please, Nyoma, don't move about on my account. I shall soon get over this.'

Nyoma sat on a beautifully carved kitchen stool and placed her hand on Wogari's cheek.

'As hot as fire!' she exclaimed.

Olumba did the same and bit his lips. 'I think I shall fetch Achichi.' With that he moved off. Near his reception hall he met his first daughter coming back from play. Her fingers were dovetailed behind her neck and she was looking miserable. Olumba looked carefully at her and discovered that her eyes were filled with tears.

'What is it?'

'Headache, dede.'

Olumba touched her. She was hot.

'Go into the house and lie down.'

The child ambled into the house, her small legs almost refusing to move. Olumba watched her disappear into the room. Then he sat in his hall lost in thought. So that was it, he mused. There could be no doubt now that Ogbunabali the god of the night, was all set to deal with him. He would wipe out his entire family. How stupid of him to have started hoping.

Was there any point in seeing Achichi? The dibia might well consider it futile and dangerous to pit himself against a god. Olumba decided to see Diali first and inform him of the state of affairs. He was shocked when he saw Diali. The old man could hardly talk.

Olumba interviewed Diali's second wife, an elderly queenly woman.

'What is wrong with Diali?'

'Fever, headache and severe catarrh.'

The woman stretched and yawned expansively.

'Has he taken any medicines?'

'Several but they don't seem to have any effect at all.'

'Call in Achichi.'

'I shall do so, but I doubt if he can help us.'

'Why not?'

'He could not help your wife. Also the divination over Ihunda's death was beyond him. He could not see a thing.'

'He saw much more than usual.'

'Did he?'

'He said Ihunda's death was part of a calamity about to befall the whole clan.'

'How does it help us?'

'He gave details of sacrifices that will be offered.'

'By whom?'

'By the Ezes of the Erekwi Clan.'

'Do you think it will be easy to convince them to assemble because of a divination based on the death of a ten-year-old child?'

'That is for us men to work out.'

The woman stretched and yawned again for a longer time than before.

'I don't feel too well either,' she said, stretching once more.

'Chei!' she cried.

'What is that?'

'I think I am developing some headache.'

'Quite likely, from the way you have been yawning and stretching. I am going to get Achichi to attend to my wife and child. I shall tell him to call on you as soon as he is through with me.'

Olumba went off to see the dibia.

'Chituru has just sent for me,' said the dibia. 'I shall see you as soon as I am through with him.'

'Is he that ill?'

'I can't say until I see him.'

'He was chatting with me a short while ago. He laughed and then complained of a headache. I tried to convince him it was nothing to worry about.'

'It is not easy to convince a person who has a headache that he is well,' the dibia said. Olumba laughed.

'You will have a lot to do today.'

'Why?'

'Wogari and my first daughter are ill. So is Eze Diali.'

When Olumba went back, he took a closer look at his daughter. She was as hot as live coals. Her headache was a little more than she could bear and she wept freely. Olumba carried her to the kitchen and laid her beside Wogari. He put more wood into the fire and got it blazing.

'How is she?' Nyoma inquired as Olumba came out of the kitchen.

'Getting worse.'

'I mean my daughter, Adada.'

'I know.'

Adada coughed. Olumba looked at his wife.

'Can that be Adada?'

'I think so,' Nyoma said despondently.

Olumba went back into the kitchen. His daughter was lying as she had left her. She coughed again. It was a dry, painful and unproductive cough. Olumba's heart sank as he recalled Ochomma's granddaughter's illness. He could not hide the anxiety in his face when he joined Nyoma again.

'I don't like that cough, my lord,' the woman said and hobbled into the kitchen.

'Do nothing until Achichi comes,' he called after her.

'I am here now,' Achichi said coming in. The dibia had a careful look at the sick persons and consulted his medicine-bag. He gave Wogari something to drink, rubbed her head and chest with a lotion which left a grey paint when it dried. He gave Adada a similar treatment.

'Adada seems to have a cough as well,' Olumba said.

'I shall give her some cough medicine later in the evening.'

'Have you treated Eze Diali yet?'

'Not yet. I am going to him right away.'

'Please do so.'

When Achichi came back later in the evening, Olumba called him aside and had a quiet talk with him.

'What do you make of all this?' Olumba asked earnestly. 'Is the god at work?'

'You can try a divination if you like, but I don't think so.'

The divination was hardly worth it. Achichi merely confirmed his guess that Ogbunabali was not involved at all. He prescribed simple routine sacrifices which Olumba carried out before he went to bed that night.

All night long Olumba thought of his family. The more he thought about his misfortunes the more he doubted Achichi's divination. If only Anwuanwu were near. The journey to Abii and back was a long one and he did not want to be away from his sick family for long. He would have to rely on Achichi's divination.

The next morning his compound was unswept. The healthy children were too small to do it, the rest of the family too sick. Worse still, there was no one to cook. Olumba walked over to his cousin's compound.

'I am in a fix,' he said, 'all my people are ill and there is no one to do the cooking. I have come to borrow your eldest daughter to help us out.'

'We are in the same trouble,' the man said. 'My wife is sick and my daughter is doing all the housework.'

Olumba went into the house to have a look at the woman. She was shivering and coughing by the fireside.

'It is the same illness,' Olumba said.

He went back, cut some yams into pieces and set the pot on the fire. He did not bother to peel the yams, nor did he wash the pot.

'Ikechi, keep an eye on things. I am going to see Eze Diali. I shall be back soon.' Ikechi had come round to tap the palm-wine trees as usual.

'Will you be long?'

'No.'

'Do come quickly. My mother is not well and I want to go and attend to her.'

Olumba paused.

'What is wrong with her?'

'Fever, severe headache and a dry painful cough.'

Olumba hobbled towards Diali's compound.

He found the chief very sick. He was breathing noisily and was scarcely able to talk. The Eze's second wife was also ill and so were a number of children in the compound.

'I think there is something wrong with the whole village,' Olumba said.

'I agree,' Diali whispered.

'What shall we do?'

'Elders,' Diali managed to say.

'Should I summon them?'

The old man nodded assent.

'Through the ikoro?'

Another nod.

Olumba sped to the ikoro just outside Diali's reception hall. He was so excited that he forgot his aches as he belaboured the instrument. The village was being threatened and his fighting spirit was up. His private fears vanished in the face of the village-wide consternation.

The ikoro rang out in the clear morning air. It indicated that there was an emergency but that no arms were necessary. Olumba was a sight as he beat the ikoro. With his sunken eyes and wild beard he looked like a risen skeleton beating the ikoro for the last time to announce the end of the world. Very quickly the men assembled unarmed. Olumba went in to find out from Diali what he was to tell the people.

'Call me Chituru,' the Eze whispered.

Olumba was quickly jolted back to reality. In his eagerness he had forgotten the rigid traditions of the village. It would be many years before he would be in a position to give the opening address to an assembly summoned by the ikoro.

'Chituru is ill, he is not here,' someone replied to Olumba's inquiry.

Wezume was the next in rank. Olumba whispered something to him. The old man went to interview Diali. Presently he came out, his face cloudy.

'People of Chiolu, I greet you,' Wezume began. He was not used to heading the assembly, but the urgency of the matter in hand drowned his slight nervousness. 'As you know, the call of the ikoro is always reserved for emergencies. Now there is one.'

The puzzled expressions of members of the assembly showed they did not grasp the situation. Many stared around trying to find out what the emergency was all about.

'Critical situations demand straight talk. Eze Diali is sick, Chituru is sick, Diali's second wife is sick, and so are Olumba's two wives and his first daughter. A few days ago . . .'

There was a flood of interruptions:

'So is my wife.'

'So is my daughter.'

'My neighbour is dying.'

The din in the reception hall was deafening. Wezume called for the igele. As its clear metallic ring rose above the noise, order was restored.

'So you can see for yourselves that all is not well,' Wezume resumed. 'What action are we going to take?'

Njola, Ikechi's father, rose to speak. 'There is no doubt the gods have a hand in these illnesses. A child usually sleeps when he has

178

eaten the thing for which he has been keeping awake. Let us find out the will of the gods and do it.'

Another elder said: 'I suspect that the Great Ponds have a lot to do with our troubles. Let us . . .'

'Are you saying that the Pond of Wagaba does not belong to us?' someone asked angrily. Once again chaos broke out, and once again the igele came to the rescue.

'Let's hear him out,' Wezume said. But the old man who had made the controversial remark refused to speak.

'Go on, say what you have on your mind,' Wezume urged.

'Since wiser men will not let me speak,' the man said. 'I am content to sit and listen to them.'

Many old men knew that the speaker's resentment was feigned. He had realized he was taking a most unpopular point of view and had wisely decided to shut up.

'Has anyone else something to say?' Wezume asked.

A few people rose to speak but all said the same thing in spite of clever parables. All agreed that the first thing to do was to go for a thorough divination.

'And not Achichi's stuff,' a fat middle-aged man observed. He quickly realized his indiscretion for Achichi was in the assembly. All eyes were turned towards the dibia. Achichi said nothing. His face was blank but for a very faint smile.

'Achichi is not a bad dibia,' Wezume said quickly to relieve the tension. His attempt was not quite successful. Achichi looked round and sensed that, as if by a common consent, everyone was waiting for him to say something. He cleared his throat.

'All fingers are not equal,' he said slowly. 'I do not claim to know everything. In fact I was about to suggest that we see Anwuanwu of Abii. That man is a great dibia. He sees much farther than I do.'

Achichi's calmness and humility won him much sympathy and support and many blamed the fat man who had, perhaps unwittingly, launched the attack on the dibia. But the man· did not mean any harm. He was a humorous easy-going man who rarely picked a quarrel. He hastily rose to make amends.

179

'Achichi, you know I was joking,' he said. 'The fact that I know no other dibia but you should convince you.' The tension died.

'Are we all agreed on a divination?' Wezume asked.

'Yes,' came the chorus.

'Where shall we go?'

'To Anwuanwu,' Achichi said quickly.

'To Anwuanwu,' all agreed, some men grinning at Achichi's rather exaggerated enthusiasm.

'We need three men, any suggestions?'

'Ikechi should be one of them,' someone said.

'Must this young man never rest?' another countered.

'Let's leave him out of this.'

'There is some truth in that,' Wezume said.

'We are wasting time,' Njola said. 'Let three men volunteer and . . .'

A loud cry was heard somewhere in the village. Several voices joined the first one to swell the volume of the lamentations. There are very few people who cannot recognize that special way of crying reserved for the dead. Women do not learn it; it is inborn in them. They cry that way automatically when they are bereaved. So everyone knew someone was dead.

'Will someone find out what is happening?' Wezume said. He might have saved his breath for already three or four men from the assembly were racing in the direction of the lamentations. They were met near Diali's compound by two haggard women. One of the men ran back to the assembly and announced that someone's wife was dead. The meeting broke up without concluding its business.

Olumba ran to his compound. Wogari and his daughter, Adada, were getting worse. Nyoma was weeping. Olumba could not stop her. She had genuine reasons. Olumba ran to Achichi's house. He was told the dibia had gone to the bereaved family. He went on to look for him.

Nearly all the men who had assembled in Diali's reception hall had gone straight to the bereaved family. So the compound was full and Olumba found it hard to locate Achichi. Meanwhile the wailing women arrested his attention. They tore their hair and wriggled on the ground.

'Who is dead?' Olumba inquired softly from another sympathizer.

'The second wife,' the man said without turning round.

Olumba watched the other wives crying and saying pathetic things. Their sorrow was genuine and Olumba was touched. So women loved one another in spite of their quarrels? He recalled how the dead woman used to wrestle and fight with her mates. Now they were mourning her. Truly, death was an efficient if a belated settler of quarrels. Olumba was roused from his reverie by a hand on his shoulder.

'I knew you would be here; come on let's see how your people are getting on.'

It was Achichi the dibia who spoke. Together the men left the scene.

Achichi said nothing as he examined the sick people. He gave them the medicines he had brought and turned to go. Olumba searched the dibia's face. It was an unrevealing blank mask. Before Olumba could question him he was gone.

'Wogari, how do you feel exactly?' Olumba asked.

'Pain, pain in the chest,' she whispered.

'And you, Adada?'

For answer the girl rubbed her chest.

Olumba felt less afraid now that three people were ill in his household than when only Nyoma was ill. That was because he was now sure that the disease was village-wide and he ruled out the possibility of Ogbunabali's direct intervention. Still he could not by any means be described as happy. The death of the woman about to be buried gave him a clear hint of what the future might look like.

Running the household proved a problem almost as difficult as finding a cure for the sick. Yams and vegetables had to be brought from the farm and water fetched from the well. But these were trifles compared to the preparation of soup. How would he grind pepper and egusi, and cut okro and other vegetables the way they should be cut? How would he wash the oily pot and scrub the mortar and pestle clean? Olumba could not help laughing at the absurdity of the situation.

'What is it, my lord?' Nyoma asked alarmed to see her husband laughing alone and in such circumstances.

'I was thinking of washing the soup pot.'

'Never, my lord. I can at least do that.'

'You are still too weak.'

'You are not telling me.'

Nyoma drew herself up to her full height. A sharp pain in the chest reminded her she was still an invalid. She managed to stifle a groan and joined her husband in the kitchen. She washed the pot and scoured the dirty mortar.

Olumba let her. He knew these things were beyond him. Brought up by a warrior father who taught him that all feminine chores were unmanly, he simply did not know how to set about these things. The prospect of cooking scared him.

'Nyoma, you must not tire yourself. A child who cannot cry usually learns to do so by his mother's grave. I have to learn to cook.'

'You will cook only when I am dead,' Nyoma replied as firmly as she could. Her husband had no choice, happily. He assembled all the heavier things within arm's reach and left her to prepare the soup.

Sitting still was out of the question. Olumba's mind was racing in all directions. He decided to check on other sick neighbours and find out what they were doing to combat the malady. He was appalled at the prevalence of the disease. Only a handful of compounds had no sick persons. No one seemed to know the cure. People merely threw in all the medicines they had and hoped for the best.

In the evening a boy aged twenty died. He was the only child of his mother. The woman, people feared, was now bent on suicide. Her crying was spectacular and quite a few villagers watched her out of sheer curiosity. Human desire for diversion and entertainment is a formidable drive which is often underestimated.

'Amadioha, where were you? Ojukwu, where were you?' the

woman wailed. 'Why did you not kill me instead? Chei! Chei! What has snatched away my beloved child, my only child, my handsome child? Is it Ogbunabali? It must be Ogbunabali. Chei! It must be. Ogbunabali, bring back my child, bring back my child; he knows nothing of the Great Ponds. Ogbunabali, bring back my child.'

'It is enough,' neighbours said. 'Nothing can bring him back now.'

As if realizing this horrible truth for the first time the near-insane woman howled again. 'Ogbunabali, bring back my child, bring back my child.' She seemed to stick to this particular refrain. Each time she sang it people could not help discussing this possibility. Gods had been known to wreck whole families. If the Pond of Wagaba was Aliakoro's the god might declare war on the whole village in righteous anger. The man who had raised this point during the general meeting in Diali's hall could be right after all.

It was one woman whose husband was about to collapse who brought matters to a head. She said in her despair: 'We must tell Aliakoro to release Olumba from the oath or face real disaster. People of Chiolu, what are you waiting for? Do you want my husband to die before you make a move? I won't take it. Chei! I won't take it.'

Other desperate folks echoed the suggestion and by nightfall several people gathered in Diali's reception hall as if by pre-arrangement. They demanded that delegates be sent to Aliakoro forthwith to plead for the withdrawal of the oath. Aliakoro could have the pond if only the lives of their dear ones could be spared.

Wezume and two other elders interviewed the sick Eze on the matter. Diali could not find his voice although his lips moved. By careful lip reading Wezume knew that Eze Diali would rather have a divination first. When Wezume relayed this suggestion the frightened motley assembly wailed out a solid 'No'. In the background could be heard the faint cries of people by the sick beds of their loved ones.

'Men of Chiolu, listen to me.' It was Olumba's voice suddenly rising to prominence in the din. 'The image of the god was waved round my head three times, was it not? My two wives and Adada are ill, are they not? Yet I want to plead with you not to rush to Aliakoro. The moon should be out in at most twenty days; can't we hold out for so short a time? Remember that whoever gets the pond now holds it for ever.'

Having spoken, Olumba maintained his pose and people stared at him, wondering how such brave words could come from such a gaunt and miserable figure. Quite a few thought he was not quite sane. They felt this brave front was comparable to that of a chicken fluttering about after its head had been cut off. To many Olumba was half-dead. Anyone would be who had to contend with Ogbunabali.

For a time no one could reply. Olumba had struck at the villagers' sense of pride and the men looked down in confusion. At last one man cleared his throat and said:

'Olumba, no one can argue that you are wrong. However, this is not exactly a test of bravery. Someone, I have forgotten who, once said he would rather fight a whole village than face a god.'

'That's Olumba's saying,' a voice said.

'Aha,' the man went on. 'We have all shown admirable courage in battle. Now we are fighting against a spirit whose ways no one understands, a god powerful enough to clear whole families. Trying to be brave is unwise for in the end there may be no one left in the village to claim the pond. He who cannot recognize a superior when he sees one is a fool.'

The murmurings and broken sentences from the crowd showed it was in support of the man. Olumba felt powerless. The crowd grew bigger.

Wezume said: 'It is difficult to arrive at any decision standing, and with everyone talking at once. I think the elders should get together now and . . .'

Fresh lamentations broke the air with an intensity that could only mean that another victim had been claimed by the scourge. Every member of the crowd trembled. Many rushed towards the source of the sound. Others stood their grounds and renewed their demand for a delegation to Aliakoro.

'Eze Diali, do something,' they shouted. 'Do something or the village will be lost.'

When Olumba went back to his compound that night Wogari's condition scared him. The woman was barely able to breathe. She was unable to talk. Nyoma stood by her weeping noiselessly. Olumba moved over to his daughter. Her condition was as bad as Wogari's.

'Amadioha, this is where you come in,' Olumba muttered as he left the sick-room. He suppressed the impulse to call Achichi, the dibia. They were all going to die anyway. It was just a matter of time. He sat in his room clutching his son in his arms.

In the small hours of the night, an outburst of cries announced the death of yet another villager.

17 EVEN the children knew the facts by now. Their parents whispered their fears to one another in the hushed gloomy sick-rooms of those about to journey to the spirit world. While the older children shared their parents' fears, the younger ones made a joke of it all, frightening one another with the dread name. 'Look! Ogbunabali is behind you!' a child would say to another in the night. Their parents would hush them sternly. The god was on the warpath. Calling his name was a way to invite him to strike.

Eze Diali reviewed the situation on his sick-bed. Yes, it was glaringly true. Ogbunabali was executing judgement and in a way that four hundred future generations would talk about. For the first time Diali blamed himself for dragging his village into the war of the Great Ponds. He recalled the day he despatched Olumba and six others to capture poachers from the Pond of Wagaba. It was a brave move worthy of a brave Eze. But now . . .

Under mounting pressure he gave the elders permission to choose six men to go to Aliakoro and ask for a withdrawal of the oath. As the delegates set off that morning, the villagers could not fight off the strong feeling of humiliation that assailed them. Even those who had been clamouring for the delegation bit their lips in disappointment.

As Chituru the next Eze to Diali was too sick to lead the delegation, Wezume assumed the responsibility. Omenka, Ikechi and three others made up the rest of the team.

They did not meet anyone on their way to Aliakoro. The forest track was lonely. The farm sections of the track appeared deserted. It was not surprising for it was a Great Eke, a day of rest.

'Eze Okehi and his people will be happy today,' Wezume said as they sighted the first house at Aliakoro.

'Anyone in their position would,' Omenka said.

'If only our people could be a little more patient.'

'I don't blame them much. I don't like the way people are dying. Even smallpox does not claim victims so rapidly.'

'Perhaps you are right.'

'I am sure I am right.'

They walked slowly through the village.

'Someone is dead here,' Omenka observed pointing to a recent grave in a compound.

'That is true,' Wezume said.

They walked on abreast.

'And here is another new grave,' Wezume said nodding towards a compound on his side of the village road. Before they came to Okehi's compound they saw four new graves.

'Wezume.'

'Yes, Omenka.'

'What do you think of these graves?'

'That is what is puzzling me.'

When they entered Eze Okehi's compound they found many people gathered. It was easy to guess that all was not well. Those sitting in the reception hall carried their chins in their hands. Others standing folded their hands across their chests as if they felt cold.

186

The visitors approached cautiously. No one took any particular notice of them except a few men.

'You are from Chiolu?' a man asked. 'I think I recognize you.'

'Yes,' Ikechi said.

'How is Olumba?' The man could not suppress a grin. He seemed a funny happy–go–lucky fellow.

'Olumba is well. Tell me, what is happening here?'

'One of Okehi's children is seriously ill, about to die I should say.'

'What is the illness?'

'They call it wonjo.'

'Wonjo?'

'Yes. Five people have already died of it.'

Ikechi and the others exchanged glances.

'What are you doing about it?' Omenka asked.

'Nothing.'

'Have you tried a divination?'

'Yes.'

'What did the dibia say?'

'He said a great calamity was about to strike the village. He listed a very costly sacrifice to be performed but hinted that even these might not avert the calamity entirely.'

'Has the village offended the gods in any way?' Omenka asked.

'The dibia did not say.'

The man was lying and Wezume knew it.

'Are you saying that the dibia listed sacrifices without saying what they were for?' Wezume asked.

'Of course he explained what they were for.'

'Which means he divined the cause of . . . what do you call it?'

'Wonjo.'

'Yes, wonjo.'

'Well he did.'

'What was it?'

The man did not answer.

'The Great Ponds?'

'Oh no, certainly not the Great Ponds,' he said unconvincingly.

Wezume paused to think.

'Can we see Eze Okehi?'

'Yes. He is in that room over there surrounded by sympathizers.'

Wezume called his men aside for a quick discussion. People began to take more notice of them.

'I think it is the same disease,' Omenka said.

'Obviously,' Ikechi said. He was the youngest man in the delegation.

'What then do we do?' Wezume asked.

There was a pause.

'Let's point out to Okehi that their bid to claim the Pond of Wagaba is the cause of their present suffering,' Ikechi replied. 'Maybe we can persuade him to give up the pond.'

'Not when his child is so sick,' Omenka replied with a faint smile.

'If we say that, our safety may be in doubt,' Wezume added.

They decided to call on Okehi, sympathize with him, and go back home to seek advice.

Eze Okehi was a very changed man. Few could look on him without pitying him. He was not sick really, but he seemed far worse than a sick man.

'Thanks for your sympathies,' the old man murmured.

'And now we shall leave,' Wezume said.

'No. You must have some kola first.'

'Don't bother. No one is in any mood to eat kola now,' Omenka pointed out.

'Tradition must have its way. I have lost many children in this life. I can't kill myself because of this one. No, my Chiolu friend, my thoughts are for the village as a whole.'

'Anything wrong with the village?'

Eze Okehi would willingly have poured out his soul to the visitors. But they were his enemies and he pulled himself together, annoyed at the little he had revealed.

'As the Eze of Aliakoro it is my duty to look after the village, is it not?'

'That is true.'

'Well, that is what I mean.'

Omenka pinched Wezume unobserved.

'Eze Okehi we shall go now,' Wezume said. 'Thanks for the kola.'

'Tell me what you have come for. I can discuss anything, my child's illness notwithstanding.'

Another Aliakoro elder supported Okehi's demand: 'You can't say you have come all the way merely to greet us.'

'We have a message for the whole village,' Wezume said.

'If you want to hear it, summon the elders.'

'Is it that important?'

'It is.'

A number of elders assembled within a short time. Wago the leopard-killer was among them. Younger men and women in the reception hall were cleared to make room for the elders and their guests.

'What is it?' Okehi asked as soon as they were seated.

'Are your elders all here?' Wezume asked, stalling for time. He was trying to work out the best approach.

'They are not all here but these are enough.'

There was a pause.

'What is it?' It was Wago who spoke this time. His sharp deep-set eyes were studying the visitors with a concentration that made Wezume and his train a little uncomfortable. Wago stared at them aggressively, making no attempts whatsoever to hide the fact.

'I thought we were waiting for kola and pepper,' Wezume stalled again.

'Yes, of course,' Okehi said and sent for kola. Meanwhile Wezume and his men went out for a brief discussion.

'We have come with a message from Chiolu,' Wezume said when they reassembled. He drew in air sharply to counter the effect of the pepper in his mouth.

'Say it,' Wago put in.

'It is this. We are aware of your sufferings in this village. We all know the cause; even without divination. The people of Chiolu have permitted you to withdraw the oath on Olumba before time,

189

if you like, to avert further loss of lives in your village. For our part, we have nothing to lose. The moon should be out in about twelve days and Olumba will surely live through this short time. We merely want to help you. We are all members of the Erekwi clan. Your loss is our loss.'

Wezume took a deep breath when he had done. It was the hardest speech he had ever made. At no point was he sure of the next word.

Okehi stared at the visitors, his face troubled. Presently he shifted his gaze to his own men. The Chiolu delegates sat rigidly on their three-legged chairs hardly daring to move.

Suddenly, as a clash of thunder, Wago's voice broke the silence in a loud peal of laughter. His shoulders shook and his head rolled from side to side as he laughed. The Aliakoro elders watched him with surprise mingled with some embarrassment. The Chiolu delegates felt very uncomfortable.

Wago stopped laughing as suddenly as he had started and faced the visitors. Without asking Okehi's permission he rose to speak. No one stopped him.

'Do you think you are clever?' he roared his eyes flashing.

'What do you mean?' Wezume asked in thinly veiled consternation.

'Do you think you are clever?' Wago asked again and laughed, this time mirthlessly.

'Say what you want to say?' Omenka said with some irritation. 'We are not children to be questioned this way.'

'You have behaved like children.'

'Eze Okehi, we can't have this insult,' Wezume flared out. 'If Wago can't talk like an elder – and he is not one – he should get out and let sensible men talk.'

Okehi intervened. He realized Wago was being rude.

'Wago, chew your words before you say them. Now what is it you want to say?'

'Listen, men of Aliakoro. For the past sixteen days I have been observing events in Chiolu. Like us they are plagued with wonjo. At least six people have died. Almost everyone in Olumba's family is ill with the disease. It is likely that Olumba will catch the disease. Chiolu is afraid, hence this delegation.'

'How do you know?' Ikechi asked. Wezume winced at Ikechi's youthful impulsiveness.

'Ha, ha, ha,' Wago laughed again. If only he would say all he had to say without this weird laughter, Omenka thought.

'There are few nights that don't find me in Chiolu. Diali is sick and may now be dead. Deny that.' Wago scored a complete victory.

Wezume and his embarrassed team went out to confer again.

'Wago is obviously well informed,' Omenka said.

'Yes,' Wezume replied. 'Let us have a straight talk with them and beg them to release Olumba from his oath.'

'And claim the pond?' Ikechi asked.

'Yes.'

'Why should we do that? They are harassed by the disease as we are. It means that Ogbunabali is angry with our two villages. I think we should tell them to withdraw the oath on the grounds that a widespread disease exists. If Olumba dies now, it may not be because of the oath.' When they went back, Wezume made the point.

'The gods always protect the innocent,' Wago declared.

'If Olumba dies the pond is ours.'

'And if *you* die?' Ikechi asked angrily.

'The living will enjoy the Pond of Wagaba.'

'Wago, you are a devil,' Omenka shouted.

For answer Wago laughed again, his deep voice sounding like an ikoro announcing an invasion.

Chiolu delegates conferred again. This time they came back determined to take a firm stand. But Aliakoro was unyielding under Wago's influence.

Wezume and his men reached home by cockcrow the next morning. The ikoro rang and as many elders as were strong enough to walk assembled. The delegates recounted their experiences. Wezume was praised for his change of tactics during the negotiations. A few men, however, felt he had no right to alter the original message from the elders, that he ought to have come back home for advice if he found circumstances different. But the few dissenting voices were drowned in the general approbation.

It was a surprise and a relief to the village as a whole to hear that Aliakoro was having its share of the disease, but individual sufferers were as worried as ever. It was still important to nullify the oath, and appease Ogbunabali the god of the night who was behind all their sufferings. A large delegation was sent to Aliakoro the next day. It failed. This time a fight nearly broke out under Wago's instigation. Meanwhile three more people had died in Chiolu, two in Aliakoro.

While Eze Diali lay unconscious on his sick-bed, he did not realize the extent of the plight of his village. As he recovered gradually and gained strength the nature of the unfolding tragedy seeped into his dizzy head. He reckoned that since the last delegates came back from Aliakoro three days before, six more people had died, two per day. Never had a god harassed a village so drastically and systematically.

What made the situation more frightening was that Achichi the dibia could not help in any way. Few people bothered to consult him. Only a few faithful clients still clung to him as their relations gasped to the spirit world.

Fewer and fewer elders turned up for meetings. They were either too sick or too pessimistic to attend. They knew nothing could be done to arrest Ogbunabali's onslaught. They stayed in their compounds waiting to die.

There was just one way out – a direct appeal to Ogbunabali. This called for a joint action between the two warring villages. Aliakoro's refusal to take any action blocked this avenue to salvation.

Nearly driven mad by the continual cries of mourners Diali decided to dispatch three men to Isiali. Their mission was to explain the situation to the priest of Ogbunabali and to bring back his advice. It was not easy to find three healthy men willing to go. Of those who volunteered one complained of a mild indisposition he could not locate. He feared wonjo had got him. His fears were dismissed by the elders.

The delegation which set out early one morning never returned.

18

NIGHT in Chiolu was a shroud cutting off not only light but all the pleasant sounds. No children played, no songsters sang, no irate husbands beat their wives. Villagers had the feeling of living in a vast communal grave where the processes of dying and being buried were compounded into just one quick simple motion of lying down.

'Olumba, my lord.'

'Is that Nyoma?'

'Yes, my lord.'

'What is it?'

'Adada is in a bad shape.'

Olumba leaped out of bed and opened the door. His wife stood by the door trembling. Beyond lay the shroud of a charcoal-black night. Together the couple walked back to Nyoma's room.

Adada lay limp. Olumba took her in his arms. Her body was clammy and cold. Olumba stared at Nyoma. The woman understood.

'Chei!' Nyoma shouted. It was loud and sharp. Her husband held her.

'What good does it do? It is happening everywhere. Crying is out of fashion these days.'

It was a useless argument. Nyoma cried, waking up Wogari and the children.

'I am going to inform Eze Diali.'

'Wait till morning, my lord, the nights are foul,' Wogari managed to say. She was too sick to cry aloud.

It was true. These days even dibias dared not walk about in the night.

'There is no need to fear now. It is a matter of time for everyone.' With that Olumba disappeared into the night. He arrived at Diali's compound to meet Chituru's eldest son.

'What is it?' Olumba asked.

'My father is dead,' the young man announced fighting back his tears. Olumba was not surprised; for two days Chituru had hung between life and death.

'And you?'

'My daughter Adada is dead.'

'Hmm,' the young man sighed.

They woke up Diali. The old man stared at them tongue-tied. Without being told he knew their horrible messages.

'Who is it this time?' he asked simply.

'Adada my daughter.'

'And Chituru my father.'

A sudden wave of loneliness swept over the old man. Chituru his second-in-command was dead. Not only would the boat sink, the paddles would be lost also.

'Wash and dress them,' Diali said. 'I shall send grave-diggers around in the morning.'

That was all the visitors had come to ask. They had not come to invoke tears and sympathies. People were running out of those. They came to ask for grave-diggers, for it was not usual for a man to dig the grave of his near relatives. Grave-diggers were getting scarce. Many volunteers fell ill soon after burials and it was not long before grave-digging was regarded as a sure way of catching the disease. Even without this fear, the numerical strength of potential grave-diggers diminished daily as Ogbunabali the god of the night continued its onslaught.

In the morning three people came and scratched out a shallow grave for Olumba's daughter. A few sympathizers came round. They looked on unable to cry. Even Olumba's family had long shut up. The widely spread tragedy had a numbing effect.

Olumba hurried to Chituru's compound as soon as his daughter was laid to rest by midday. Chituru's body was being washed by his wives. Eze Diali was there. By a supreme effort, and supported by his sons, he had walked to Chituru's compound to pay his last respects. Villagers tried to persuade him to go back.

'You are too ill to move about,' they told him. 'Go back and rest.'

'Why?' he asked. 'Have I not lived long enough? A moment ago Olumba buried his daughter. It is a shame that I am still living and looking on.'

By the evening Chituru was buried. He was entitled to lie in state for three days but these days things were different. As people remarked, everything was working upside-down. Strong traditions were bowing one by one to wonjo, Ogbunabali's agent of death. Perhaps the most notable departure in tradition was the very poor response to the call of the ikoro. It was very difficult these days to get many people when the ikoro howled in the cold morning air. Those who failed to turn up were either too ill or else too steeped in sorrow to do so. Yet these reasons did not stand alone, the morale of the village was disappearing.

Back in his compound, Olumba took another look at his daughter's little grave. He went into his medicine-hut and worshipped. He came out and examined Wogari. She seemed to have survived the critical period of the disease. Her eyes were clearer and her voice firmer.

'Wogari, how do you feel?' Olumba asked.

'I don't know, my lord.'

'You look better.'

She said nothing.

Olumba walked over to Nyoma in the kitchen. The woman was trying to prepare a meal for the children. She was still very thin and Olumba thought she was trembling as she busied herself over the meal.

'Nyoma, what is wrong? You are shivering.'

'Nothing, my lord,' she said turning round. Olumba had a feeling she was trying to avert her face and went nearer. Before he got to her, she slumped into a seat and covered her face with her hands.

'Adada is gone,' Olumba said. 'Weeping can't bring her back.'

Nyoma paid no attention to her husband but her weeping increased. Heavy sobs shook her hunched shoulders.

Motionless, speechless, Olumba watched her. He rose to leave the kitchen. Then for the first time, he saw a figure bundled up in wrappers lying behind Nyoma. Olumba stared at it. It was Nchelem. In a flash he realized why Nyoma was crying. Nchelem had the disease.

'Is Nchelem ill?'

'Yes, my lord,' Nyoma murmured.

'Is that why you are crying?'

She nodded.

Olumba touched his son. He was very hot. He covered him up again and went into his room.

The wide spread of the scourge of the angry god did much to lift Olumba's private fears. The realization that the anger of the god was not concentrated on him and his family alone made him relax.

But now with Nchelem ill his attitude changed again. He knew that in spite of the general calamity he was still marked out as a special target. The god was merely being systematic.

That night he did not sleep. Before dawn he came out and looked at the moon. It was waning fast and should disappear in a few days. The new moon would then hide for a day or two – shy like a new bride – before appearing.

'I know I will not die before the moon is out,' he muttered encouragingly to himself.

'Yes, you will.'

It was that voice, back again after a long time.

'I don't care,' Olumba heard himself saying again.

'Your son will die too,' said the voice.

'Many have lost their sons.'

'But you have only one,' the voice replied.

Olumba bit his lips and went back to bed. The room was uncomfortable. He felt he was not alone. His hairs stood on end and his head felt very large. He rushed out and woke his wives.

'I want to see Nchelem,' he said urgently.

'Here he is,' Nyoma said.

Olumba touched him all over. 'Did he sleep well?'

'He did, although his body was hot all through the night, my lord.'

Olumba stayed with his son till daylight. The next day he did not leave his side until towards evening when he went to see Eze Diali. The chief had been recovering steadily. He still coughed but he was far from the critical stage in which he was once.

'My son is ill,' Olumba announced.

For answer Diali looked straight at him.

'My son is sick,' Olumba said again.

Diali got up and beckoned to him to follow. They entered a room with four children in it. They were all sick and their groans filled the room. Quietly Diali shut the door and they went back to the reception hall.

'You have so many, my lord,' Olumba muttered at last. 'I have one, just one.'

'I have nothing to say, Olumba.'

'What type of a world is this anyway?' Olumba mused bitterly.

'It is a world of the dead and the dying,' Diali replied grinding his teeth.

Suddenly a haggard-looking woman rushed into the reception hall and flung herself on the floor.

'It has happened, my lord, it has happened!' She wailed. 'I knew it would happen. I am now alone in the compound. Chei! Ogbunabali why don't you kill me! I begged you to kill me first, but you refused!'

The two men stared at the woman. As she cried a few people gathered to watch her. When she threatened to do herself some damage Olumba held her. Meanwhile Diali called his son and sent him off to fetch two men to bury the woman's son, her last companion in the compound. Her first son was one of the delegates dispatched to Isiali to see the priest of Ogbunabali. Like the others he was not back yet. Diali was very worried. He did not know how to comfort the hysterical woman. He wanted to tell her she still had one son left, but that sounded so much like a mockery that he swallowed the words.

Olumba walked home like a dream-walker.

'Wichegbo is now left alone in the compound,' he told his wives quietly. They shuddered but said nothing. Olumba examined his son. He was getting worse. He reckoned he would be dead in a day or two. At the back of his mind Olumba had a strong feeling that the old curse in his family was working again, this time through wonjo. He would be without a son once more in spite of his struggles to marry three wives. He thought of a neighbour of his who had six sons from his one wife. Wonjo had claimed two and four were left.

'Olumba.'

Olumba turned round and saw Ikechi at the doorway.

'Ikechi.'

'How are you?'

Olumba laughed a hollow laugh.

'You can see I am all right,' he said.

'That was terrible about Adada, but there is nothing anyone can do.'

'Don't bother yourself, my son.'

'My father is sick.'

'Since when?'

'This morning.'

'Wonjo?'

'What else?'

Those delegates sent to Aliakoro had brought back the name. Chiolu quickly adopted it, for wonjo was shorter and seemed more apt than 'Ogbunabali's disease'. No one knew the meaning of the word. It was just as well: Ogbunabali's action, killing off both parties to a dispute, was equally meaningless.

'I shall come and see him,' Olumba said.

'Please do, it may give him some comfort. He is so sure he will die. Not that he is afraid. No it isn't that. He just thinks he can't survive. He has shared out his property already.'

Ikechi went back, strolling slowly through the quiet village. He wondered how soon he would get the disease. He would probably die after his father. If the current trend continued no one would weep for him, for a belief had just been established that crying attracted the disease. Many compounds were banning crying of any sort.

There were other changes in the people's attitude and way of life. Most people now dressed in black not merely as a sign of mourning but in deference to Ogbunabali, the god of the night, whose colour was black. Shrines were set up at strategic points in the village for the god. In the morning and evening scared worshippers trooped to the brand-new shrines with chickens and yams. There were smaller shrines in many compounds. The worship of Ogbunabali was now a vital process.

Olumba had felt it coming all along but he had not told anyone for fear of causing panic in the village. He moved about as much as he could hoping to 'scare' it away, but it persisted. He decided to tell his wife only.

'I believe I have got it,' he announced one morning.

'Wonjo?' Nyoma gasped.

'Yes.'

'I should go first then,' the woman said softly.

'Hush! we shall all recover.'

By bedtime Nyoma developed a very high temperature, the relapse which her daughter's death had sparked off suddenly took a critical turn.

'My lord, I have wonjo again.'

'Amadioha will save you as he did last time,' Olumba said.

He staggered over to where his wife was lying and touched her all over. It was difficult to tell who was more ill, she or Nchelem.

By midnight Wogari woke her husband.

'Nyoma is behaving queerly,' she said.

In spite of his weak condition Olumba went over to the sick woman in a flash. Wogari wondered where his sudden energy came from.

'How is it?'

For answer Nyoma smiled. It was a surprisingly calm and sweet smile but its effect on Olumba was terrible. He hugged his wife and placed her head on his knees.

'Nyoma, don't do it!'

'I, I . . .' She smiled again but this time the smile froze on her lips. She was dead.

Olumba lost all sense of reality. It was a mad unforgiving world. He shouted and bellowed hardly knowing what he did. The echo of his voice died quickly in the cold dewy night air. No one came to his aid. He looked at Nyoma's corpse, at the sick children, at Wogari who was watching speechless by him. He rubbed his eyes to end the nightmare. It persisted.

'I must be dead,' he muttered. 'This is all happening in the spirit world.'

With that Olumba relaxed and to Wogari's intense astonishment he fell fast asleep. Wogari thought of waking him but could not bring herself to do it. In a short while she too fell asleep leaving the door ajar.

Diali was the first to call in the morning. It took him some time to sort out the dead from the living.

 19 NYOMA was buried towards evening. Olumba's senses were buried with her. He raved and talked nonsense. Eze Diali, Eziho and a few others came to watch by him, as dusk merged with night, Ogbuna-bali's busy time.

'Five people have died in my compound,' Diali said trying to comfort Olumba and make him get a grip on himself, but conversation with him was impossible.

Ikechi came in. Diali looked hard at him.

'Is it your father?'

'No,' Ikechi replied. His eyes were studded with tears.

'What is wrong?'

'I am just from your compound.'

'Yes?'

'One of your sons has just died.'

'Which?'

'Onwukwe.'

'Poor boy,' Diali said rising.

'Who is dead?' Olumba asked, talking sense for the first time.

'My son Onwukwe,' Diali said calmly.

Olumba bit his lips and stared at the chief.

'What can I say?' he murmured.

'Nothing,' Diali said and rose to go.

Ikechi went with him. He was very surprised at the old man's calmness.

'Accept my sympathies, dede.'

'Don't cry, my son.'

'He was such a good boy.'

'Yes, he was.'

'So much like Chisa.'

'Indeed.'

'I wonder who will be left in this village.'

'Don't worry. The village will survive. Worse things have happened. Villages have been all but wiped out in wars.'

'But this is no war.'

'Yes it is.'

'Because the war brought wonjo?'

'Yes, my son.'

They parted at the entrance to Olumba's compound; Eze Diali to bury his son, Ikechi to watch by his sick father. Ikechi stood for some time weighing Diali's words. He realized how little he knew the man.

As Ikechi was about to move on he noticed two figures moving towards him in the semi-darkness. These days when Ogbunabali walked the night in all sorts of shape few dared to accost anyone at night. But Ikechi stood his ground as the figures approached. When they came closer he observed they were women. He thought they were bereaved women going to implore Diali to provide grave-diggers.

'Who are you and who is dead?' Ikechi asked in a level voice.

'That sounds like Ikechi,' one of the women said.

'Yes, I am Ikechi. Where are you going at this time of the night?'

'Home,' the second woman said.

'Where?'

'Come and take us home instead of asking questions.'

Ikechi's heart took a wild painful leap.

'Who . . . are . . . you?' he asked again in a shaky voice.

'Ikechi, take us home. We have travelled far enough without a man by us.'

Propelled by an instinct he could not control he went very close to the women.

'Whose voice do I hear?'

'Take us home, my dede.'

'No, but it can't be, it can't be,' Ikechi almost groaned.

'Why not? The gods are not dead.'

'Please, who are you?'

'Chisa and Oda,' the other woman said.

Unbelieving, Ikechi peered into the women's faces, then suddenly two people coalesced in a long, fierce, painful embrace.

When Ikechi recovered at last he shouted. No one paid any attention. The agonizing cries of bereaved persons were as common as the crowing of cocks in the village. Ikechi ran excitedly towards Diali's compound trying to drag the women with him. When Oda stumbled and nearly fell he realized how tired they were. He led them on more slowly.

A little later he was leading Oda home while Chisa was being smothered with embraces from members of her family. Meanwhile the ikoro boomed forth a joyful message, the first of such in many months.

'Tell me that I am not dreaming,' Ikechi said for the third time as he led Oda home.

'You are not dreaming,' Oda said wearily.

'Where are you from?'

'I hardly know.'

'How did you travel?'

'It is a long story, a very long story.'

'Were you not afraid?'

'We were.'

'How? What? How? Chineke! This is amazing.'

Ikechi knocked frantically at Olumba's door.

'Olumba! Wogari! Wake up! Oda is back!'

There was no response. The compound was still save for the coughing and faint groans of the sick. Ikechi's enthusiasm lost its edge. What if Olumba was dead.

He knocked again, this time more gently. It was Wogari who opened the door. When she saw Oda she retreated several steps trembling.

'Oda!' she cried hoarsely. 'Oda!'

'Wogari!'

They hugged each other, both marshalling their flagging strength to maintain balance.

It took some time to make Olumba realize what had happened; he was so sick. When at last he opened his eyes and recognized Oda a sudden transformation came over him. Oda embraced him and wept. Ikechi left them.

'Where is my son?' Oda asked.

There was a trace of hysteria in her voice.

'He is lying here by me,' Olumba said.

'Let me carry him.'

'He is sick, let him sleep.'

'Please, my lord.' The plea in her voice was awful and Olumba let her hug the ailing child.

'How did you come back?'

'It is a long story, my lord.'

'Yes, you are tired. I shall hear your story in the morning if the whole thing is not a dream.'

'It is not,' Oda said.

'Some dreams are very vivid.'

'True, my lord.'

'You know the type of dream in which you realize you are dreaming but yet continue to dream.'

'Yes, my lord,' Oda replied with a smile, 'but this is no dream.'

'If it is a dream I still thank the gods. I have never had such a wonderful dream since you left.'

'Where is Nyoma?'

'Let's leave that till morning.'

'And Adada.'

'We'll talk about them later. Meanwhile it is enough that you are back.'

Oda's features saddened with grave forebodings.

Early in the morning when the cock crew the second time Olumba woke from a very deep sleep with a start. He stretched an arm eagerly and touched Oda. He caressed her hair and face and called her by name.

'Yes, my lord,' she replied.

'So this dream is persisting.'

Oda smiled.

'Oda, are you really with me?'

'Yes.'

'What a dream!'

Oda smiled again. Her mouth was too stale to permit a laugh.

Olumba rubbed his eyes vigorously and stared at his wife. He drew her to him and held her fast.

'Don't vanish, please don't.'

'I won't.'

The faint daylight coming from chinks in the roof revealed Oda's features. They were the same but modified by much suffering. Oda related her story piecemeal. She was reluctant to talk and wept at several points in her narrative.

'Why did your masters let you go?' Olumba asked.

'They did not let us go.'

'You ran away?'

'No, my lord.'

Olumba waited for her to explain.

'When we found ourselves alone, we walked home.'

'Alone?'

'Yes.'

'Why?'

'Our masters died. Those who were left were too sick and frightened to care about us. Chisa and I walked to the riverside and found many deserted boats. We boarded one and paddled across, you see we had learnt to paddle. We travelled early in the morning and late in the evening to avoid people but we soon found out that no one was interested in us.'

'How did you find the way?'

'From kind women we met on our way.'

'So Ogbunabali is working everywhere?'

There was a pause.

'What a god! Never before has a god harassed the whole clan and beyond. What were they doing over there to combat the disease?'

'At first they offered sacrifices in the river and drank the medicines the dibias gave them. When they found they were no better they gave up and people died one by one.'

'How did they explain it?'

'They know Ogbunabali is responsible. They have heard about the wars of the Great Ponds, the swearing and so on. When the disease started at first they cursed Chiolu and Aliakoro and threatened to offer us as sacrifices to Ogbunabali. But luckily their dibias did not think this would help and we were left alone. Our masters also helped to shield us from bereaved families who wanted to mob us.'

Here Oda broke down. She shuddered and wept. Olumba held her close.

'What of . . . of . . .?' Olumba stammered gazing at his wife's belly.

'Dead.'

'Male or female?'

'Male.'

The woman wept again. Olumba stopped questioning her.

'It is enough that you are here,' he said. 'Look after him if I go,' he concluded pointing at Nchelem.

The dramatic return of the two women brought some joy and a little diversion to Chiolu. For a while people conversed on topics outside deaths and burials.

In the morning as soon as Ikechi had washed his face, he went over to Diali's to see Chisa. He could not be with her alone because of the many visitors who came to greet her. In the evening they had a better opportunity. They conversed for long in low tones. What shocked Ikechi most was that Chisa had lost her buoyant spirits. Gone were the smiles and the bantering. Ikechi wondered if she would ever be her old self again. He tried to cheer her.

'You were just in time,' he said. 'I was thinking about selecting another fiancée.'

Chisa neither smiled nor laughed. Ikechi grew uneasy fearing that she had taken him seriously.

'I am not serious of course,' he said at last as Chisa maintained her embarrassing silence.

'Chisa.'

'Yes.'

'What is wrong?'

'Nothing.'

'But you are crying.'

'Please leave me.'

'I shall not. Of course I shall marry you. Chisa, you know that I was only joking.'

Still she cried. Ikechi held her and wiped her eyes.

'I am sorry,' he said.

'You don't need to be.'

'But my joke has hurt you.'

'No.'

'Then what makes you cry, the death of your mother?'

'Not exactly.'

'What is it? Won't you tell?'

'I can't marry you, Ikechi.'

'Why not?'

'I . . . I . . . I am not a . . .'

'Say it.'

'Chei! Chei!' and she wept violently.

Chisa cried as if she would never stop. Ikechi wondered how two ordinary eyes could exude so much fluid.

'I did my best,' she whispered in agony, 'believe me I did my best. I slapped him, I bit him, I threatened to commit suicide. I even told him I was a leper. But he forsook his three wives and came after me time and again. He was a huge strong man. What could I do?'

Ikechi ground his teeth, a habit he acquired at the beginning of the war. Chisa watched him crestfallen.

'Is that all?'

'Yes.'

'I thank the gods.'

'Ikechi, you will have to look for another girl.'

Ikechi smiled.

'Chisa in spite of your wisdom, you are still a child.'

'I am not.'

'Tell me, did you ever dream of coming back home alive?'

'No.'

'Did you ever dream of seeing me again?'

She shook her head.

'Come.'

She went to him and he embraced her again and again.

 DIALI was at his wits ends. The old well near the arena which was being used as a common grave was now full. The joy which the unexpected return of his daughter had given him the day before was now replaced by a feeling of helplessness and despair. Ikechi stood before him, hoe in hand.

'I know there are no grave-diggers, but my father will not be buried in a well.'

'Of course Njola must be buried decently,' Diali replied, his weary eyes belying the enforced determination in his voice.

Ikechi went back to scratch out a grave for his father. Diali promised to send him some help but he knew it was a promise difficult to fulfil.

Suddenly a feeling of loneliness swept over him. Many of his friends were gone. Why was he still alive? It was cruel for Ogbunabali to reserve him for the finale.

He went into the back-yard picked up a hoe and began to walk wearily towards Njola's compound. Before he got there he noticed three men following him.

'Who is it?' One of the men asked.

'Njola,' Diali replied.

'We shall bury him, give us the hoe.'

Diali handed over his hoe and followed the men into Njola's compound.

Njola was properly buried but only because there were still willing and healthy people. Diali knew future corpses would not be as lucky.

There was another old well somewhere along the farm path. It was rather far, but carrying a corpse all the way was easier than digging a grave. As Diali passed by Wezume's compound, the old man hailed him.

'Eze Diali.'

'Wezume.'

'I am still holding out.'

'That's the work of the gods.'

'Njola is gone?'

'Yes.'

'It should be my turn next. I have stayed too long.'

Diali did not reply. He resumed his walk back to his house.

'Wait!'

Wezume hobbled to him.

'I don't know which of us will go first.'

'Well?'

'Promise you will be at my burial even if I end up in a well.'

'If I am alive I will be there.'

Wezume walked back coughing and tottering.

And so wonjo, Ogbunabali's messenger, took its daily toll. Already one or two compounds had no survivors in them. Many more had a few wretched inmates whom fright had made subhuman.

They crouched with fear in their houses listening to the rattling in rooms filled with the ghosts of the departed.

At night strange noises filled the air. The living heard distinctly the song and lamentations of the unhappy spirits of the dead as they marched through the village. Some who had keen ears made out some of the words of their song. It was only in later years that people had the courage to sing some of these songs. Today, old men in the Erekwi clan still stiffen and gnash their teeth when these melancholy songs are rendered:

> *Children are motherless,*
> *That is what wonjo has done;*
> *Maidens are now widows,*
> *That is what wonjo has done;*
> *Wonjo the curse of the gods,*
> *Wonjo will end the world.*

'I may not be able to pay you another visit,' Ikechi said.

'I know. I shall probably die in a day or two.' Olumba murmured.

'No, no, that is not what I mean.'

'What else can you mean?'

'After my father's burial yesterday I started feeling queer. I think I have wonjo.'

Olumba said nothing.

'How does it feel when one has it?'

'Difficult to describe,' Olumba replied coughing violently.

'I am sorry to upset you.'

Olumba coughed for a long time and lapsed into silence.

Ikechi rose to go. At the entrance to Olumba's compound he met Wago the leopard-killer. The Aliakoro warrior laughed as he observed Ikechi's uncontrolled surprise.

'Wago!'

'Yes.'

'Wago!'

'The same.'

'What do you want here?'

'I am here to greet my friends. How is Olumba? I gather he is very sick.'

Ikechi said nothing. He ran back to Olumba.

'Wago the leopard-killer is here!' he announced. Olumba's features immediately became rigid with anger he could not give vent to in his weak condition.

'Is he in this compound?'

'He is near the entrance.'

'He wants to know whether I am dead?'

'I wonder.'

'Then I won't die. I won't die before the moon is out.'

Ikechi left Olumba raving and went to Diali with his discovery. The chief showed little surprise.

'I know he has been around.'

'He is still thinking of the Pond of Wagaba.'

'Yes, my son.'

'And yet wonjo is raging in Aliakoro.'

'That is true.'

'He is a strange man.'

'He is.'

'We will show him that we are equally strange.'

'Do nothing rash, Ikechi.'

But Ikechi was out of earshot. He ran home, collected his matchet and consulted two other young men. Together they strolled out to confront Wago, but their quarry was gone.

All through that day Wago was the talk of the village. His strange visit generated so much indignation that for a moment the village showed signs of life. The angriest men were those who had fought at the Great Ponds.

'We shall not let go,' they cried. 'The Pond of Wagaba is ours.'

Suddenly Olumba's compound was flooded with visitors, some coughing, others limping with walking-sticks. They all did their best to encourage him.

In spite of his severe illness Olumba sat up to chat with his visitors.

'Men of Chiolu, the pond is ours. I shall not die,' he said.

'You will not die!' the villagers echoed.

These exertions and show of anger made Olumba very weak. The next day his illness took a critical turn for the worse.

'I shall not die,' he kept murmuring to himself.

'You will die.' That voice within him suddenly came to life.

'I shall not die!'

'You will die!'

Olumba was determined not to give up; not with Wago the leopard-killer laughing at him right in his compound. But slowly he deteriorated. Towards evening the enthusiasm of his visitors went down considerably when they saw his condition. Olumba's fears grew in spite of all his determination. Oda, Wogari and Nchelem watched him rave and toss on his bed. Nchelem whose condition greatly improved after his mother's return echoed whatever his delirious father said in a way which might have been very amusing under happier circumstances. The night closed in. Sensitive people heard the footsteps of ghosts marching round the village.

Wago stalked round Olumba's compound listening. At one stage he bumped into a man and fled. The man was so frightened that he fell sick there and then and had to be carried home. Ikechi and his two friends guessed that Wago was still around.

'I shall kill him,' Eziho swore.

'What really does he want to do?' Ikechi asked.

'Who knows?'

'Why won't he go home?'

'I wonder.'

The trio decided to keep watch in Olumba's compound till late. They told Olumba of their decision to encourage him.

Around midnight Olumba grew restless.

'Poke the fire,' he whispered to Oda.

'Yes, my lord.'

'And get me some water too.'

Outside, strange noises filled the air. Olumba found it difficult to distinguish between the songs of the marching ghosts and the muffled groans of the bereaved.

From feeling very cold, Olumba broke into a sweat. His hair stood on end and his head felt very heavy. What was that? Something seemed to be walking on the roof directly over where he slept. Could it be a vulture? Not at that time of the night.

'I shall not die,' he whispered to himself.

'You will die,' said the voice now disembodied. Olumba could see a misty shape by his bed.

'No, no, I shall not die,' he cried.

'Of course you will die, perhaps tonight,' the misty shape replied.

'Not tonight! Not tonight!' Olumba shouted. He grabbed his walking-stick and struck out in the air. Then he undid the door and walked out shouting: 'I shall not die, I shall not die.'

His wives could not stop him. They were frozen with fear. Where did he get all the energy from? Meanwhile Olumba reached the entrance to his compound. As he shouted, he worked his stick to the right and to the left. His voice grew louder and louder.

'I shall not die! I shall not die!'

'Let's hold him,' Ikechi whispered.

'Leave him,' Eziho said.

'Let's follow him then.'

Unobtrusively the three men followed Olumba as he walked through the village shouting:

'I shall not die! I shall not die! Not till the moon is out!'

When he reached the arena he sat down exhausted. Ikechi and his friends carried him back.

The next day Olumba's queer behaviour was the talk of the village. Ikechi related the incident to Diali.

'It was so frightening.'

'It must have been, my son.'

'I hope he won't do it again tonight.'

'If he tries to, don't stop him.'

'With Wago prowling around it is unwise to let him continue this.'

'Let him if he wants to,' Diali said again, 'but dog him as you did last night.'

For most of the day Olumba slept peacefully. Occasionally he would sit up and lunge at the air with his walking-stick.

When night came the misty shape was with him again. It was clearer and more solid than before. Olumba dropped his walking-stick and tried to grab the apparition. He caught the empty air. His wives watched his antics and sobbed profusely.

'I shall not die,' Olumba cried.

'You will die,' said the misty shapes. There were now several of them trying to close in on the sick man. The warrior grabbed his walking-stick again and jabbed at the air. Then he got up and walked out as he had done the previous night. He headed for the arena. People who were not too sick came out of their houses to watch him go by.

'I shall not die!'

'You will not die!' a few villagers echoed.

'You are already dead,' the misty shapes said.

Shouting and lashing out with his stick Olumba came to Diali's compound.

'Eze Diali,' he roared.

'Olumba.'

'Do you hear me?'

'I hear you.'

'I say I will not die!'

'You will not die!' Diali replied.

'Wago will not fish in the Pond of Wagaba.'

'No, he will not,' Diali said as calmly as he could.

Several people gathered in Diali's reception hall to watch Olumba.

'Look at them, look at them. They want to take me away with them. They will not succeed. They will not . . .' He struck the air fiercely. The stick flew out of his hand and struck a man on the back. The man went home screaming.

'Where is my stick? Where is my stick? Chei! They are coming! They are closing in!'

'Give him his stick,' Diali said quietly.

They gave Olumba his walking-stick and he resumed his battles with his invisible tormentors.

'I am Olumba! I am Agadaga the unbeaten wrestling champion, son of an eight-headed warrior! Come Wago and I shall beat eight like you.'

He rose suddenly and made for the arena. Ikechi and his two friends kept a few paces behind him. A few other villagers were farther behind. Their curiosity temporarily overcame their dread for the dark.

Olumba walked on like a drunken man. Now and then his steps faltered, but he always straightened up again.

'This man is strong,' Eziho said.

'Very strong,' Ikechi replied.

'I have never seen anyone with wonjo make such an effort.'

'It will not last.'

'But it is remarkable while it lasts.'

Suddenly a huge grey shape leaped out of the bush and made straight for Olumba. The man groaned as his assailant bore him to the ground. A few bounds brought Ikechi and the others to the scene. They found Olumba in a desperate struggle with a huge spotted animal. 'A leopard!' Ikechi panted. He was afraid to use his matchet for fear of hurting Olumba whose body was entwined with that of the beast. With a terrible burst of energy and mad fury Ikechi fell on the confused heap on the ground and held the neck of the animal in a vice-like grip. Meanwhile Eziho and the other man sorted out the hind legs of the animal. There was a shriek as Eziho's matchet found its mark. The animal relaxed its hold on Olumba and began to struggle free. Eziho's matchet sank home for the second time. Mad with pain the beast wrenched itself free and disappeared with two bounds leaving its skin behind. Ikechi stared at the magnificent leopard skin in his hand.

Chiolu was wild with surprise. All but the dying turned up in the morning to see the leopard skin which Ikechi and his friends had deposited in Diali's reception hall.

'There is only one man who could have done this,' Diali said.

'Wago the leopard-killer,' three people said simultaneously.

Diali examined the dried skin again. There were two knife cuts on it.

'Were these cuts deep?' Diali asked.

'It will be a miracle if he survives,' Eziho replied.

'Let's organize a search,' Ikechi suggested.

Diali was surprised at the enthusiasm the villagers showed. Half a dozen men, some of them convalescing from wonjo, volunteered to do the search.

'Ikechi, you can't go,' Diali said. 'You need a rest.'

'I shall go. Wonjo will have to wait till I am back,' Ikechi said grimly. Several people stared at him curiously.

That morning a search-party of four set out. Ikechi and Eziho were included. First the men went to the scene of the fierce struggle of the night before. From there they were guided by the track of blood of the wounded creature.

Meanwhile, Diali tried to instil more enthusiasm into the villagers.

'We are dying one by one,' he said. 'If we are counted tomorrow morning some of us might be missing. But we are alive today. Let us continue the struggle. You all know Olumba's condition. Let us watch with him.'

Some villagers followed Eze Diali to Olumba's compound. They found Wogari busy treating a gash in Olumba's shoulders and deep scratches on his face.

'Olumba.'

'Diali.'

'How do you feel?'

'I feel well. I feel very well. The Pond of Wagaba will be ours!' The onlookers applauded.

'Olumba, I greet you,' Diali said softly as he felt a lump in his throat.

'Truly the eye is an elusive organ,' someone said. 'Look at these deep scratches on his face.'

'Yes,' Wogari said. 'He was lucky to have come off with his two eyes intact.'

'This gash on his shoulder must have been made with a knife,' Diali said examining the wound.

He wanted to kill me,' Olumba murmured.

'He has killed himself,' Oda replied.

All through the day the villagers kept Olumba company. He behaved normally. His narrow escape seemed to have instilled a sense of reality into him once more.

Towards evening the search-party returned. Ikechi was riding on Eziho's back. Diali's heart took a leap.

'What has happened?' he asked.

'Ikechi fainted on the way back,' Eziho said as people helped him put the sick man gently on the ground. Diali examined him. It was wonjo all right, but he did not bother to say anything. It was clear to everybody.

'Did you see anything?' Diali asked.

'Yes, we saw Wago the leopard-killer,' Eziho replied.

The crowd hissed excitedly.

'Where?'

'By the Pond of Wagaba.'

A hush fell on the company.

'What was he doing?'

'Nothing.'

'You mean he just sat there?'

'He was dead.'

There was a long silence.

'You killed him?'

'He was already dead before we saw him.'

'From those matchet wounds?'

'It is difficult to say. We found him in the water.'

'Was he drowned?'

'He looked so; but he would have died of the wounds anyway.'

'Tell him of the terrible smile on his face,' Eziho's companion said.

'Yes, indeed. My lord, what frightened us most was the ghastly smile on the dead man's face.'

'But you say he is dead.'

'Yes, but there was an unmistakable smile on the face of the corpse.'

The crowd gasped.

'He committed suicide,' Diali said gnashing his teeth.

'That is his business.' Eziho said.

'And ours,' Diali said, his face heavily lined with care.

'What do you mean?'

'This is terrible! Terrible!' Diali cried in anguish. For the first time since the war of the Great Ponds began, the chief lost control of himself. People watched him amazed.

'What is it?' Eziho asked in consternation.

'Terrible! Very terrible!'

'Won't you tell us?'

'We have lost the Pond of Wagaba,' Diali moaned.

'Is Olumba dead?'

'No.'

'What then?'

'It would be an abomination to fish in a pond in which someone committed suicide.'

Eziho sat down on the ground wearily.

'Perhaps he was drowned accidentally,' he suggested weakly.

During a divination that evening Achichi confirmed that Wago the leopard-killer had committed suicide.

As Diali, Eziho and others came out of the dibia's house they espied the new moon, slim and clear, but too weak to make its presence felt.

They hastened homewards as muffled wails announced the death of yet another wonjo victim.

'The second well will soon be full,' Diali murmured.

'Do you know of any other old wells?'

'No,' Eziho replied hoarsely.

But it was only the beginning. Wonjo, as the villagers called the Great Influenza of 1918, was to claim a grand total of some twenty million lives all over the world.